Castle Drum Publishing

Printed in the United States of America
First Printing, 08/2023
ISBN 979-8-9872153-3-3
Castle Drum Publishing
www.castledrumpublishing.org
This novel's story and characters are fictitious. Certain long-standing institutions, agencies, and public offices are mentioned, but the characters involved are wholly imaginary.

To my wife Toni;

Who deserves a medal for her patience and support.

A House of Wolves

Chapter 1

Sibylla circled her opponent warily, just like she practiced, keeping light on her toes and her hands in a loose guard in front of her face. A tall, lanky boy named Chad circled with her, matching her step for step.

On the high school football team, Chad was normally the kind of kid who excelled at making friends, someone with an easygoing personality that people seemed to gravitate toward. On any given day Chad could be found hanging out with the nerds or the jocks or the cheerleaders or the goths, and always in a way that seemed natural.

However, at that moment, as they shifted fighting positions, he was anything but friendly. Oddly, he struck Sibylla as more of a barely controlled animal, like a feral dog. His eyes were wide and focused unblinkingly on hers as he let out explosive breaths through his nose, keeping his mouth closed in a thin line that pulled up in a sneer. He was rigid and tense, like a coiled spring about to tear loose. Keeping her eyes focused on his movements, Sibylla looked for anything like shifts in his weight or twitches in his face or limbs that could telegraph his first move.

One thing was certain: they couldn't keep dancing around each other. One of them was going to have to strike first. Waiting was an ineffective and inefficient use of time and energy. Few things in the world frustrated Sibylla more than wasted time and energy, and she certainly didn't have all night to wait. Adding to her frustration was her hesitation to make the first move. A part of her was scared of the Chad that stood in front of her. The unpredictability of his mood and actions made her nervous, even unsure of what was going to happen next. A sudden drop in his shoulder was all the warning she had of what was coming next.

Sibylla immediately adjusted her footing and was ready to block his wild haymaker before it had traveled the distance between them. To her surprise the strike hit harder than it had when they had sparred before, slamming her hands into her face and knocking her head back. Nose smarting from the impact and eyes watering, she was too distracted to see his kick coming in for her lower ribs, where it landed like a sledgehammer.

Heart racing and ribs aching, she danced back a few paces, trying to create distance. Chad was not giving her the space she needed to recover from the shock of his ferocity. A roar like a rushing wind filled her ears, the world teetering out of focus around her as tunnel vision took over. Where was this coming from? What had she done to earn his anger? Why wasn't he holding back even a little? It seemed like he was hitting her harder on purpose. The realization brought focus back in sharp relief, and the roar was replaced by a burning desire to hit him back.

Instinctively she glided forward, throwing a knee toward his groin. It went wide and missed, but it was close enough to put him on the defense.

Trying to ignore the aching pain in her ribs she threw a jab toward his face. It was another strike that would force him to duck or lean away to give her a chance to throw another knee or a kick to open the distance further. To her surprise he decided to take the jab, ducking to absorb it with his forehead, sending a shock of pain jolting up her forearm. Not even blinking from the impact, Sibylla wasn't sure he had actually felt it.

Instead, he launched another attack, throwing punches at her face and body, a feral barrage of strikes that didn't seem aimed at anything in particular. Doing her best to protect her head, Sibylla absorbed the strikes to her body, grunting with each impact. They wore gloves and padding, which thankfully helped take the edge off the strikes, though not by much. It was all she could do to keep on her feet and moving. The speed and ferocity of the strikes never changed as he kept pace with her movements.

Fear rushed in then. If she didn't know him any better, she would have thought that he wanted to hurt her. Chad had firmly left the realm of practicing in a controlled environment and had entered a headspace she had never seen before. Even the whistle, something Sibylla only registered on the edge of her perception, didn't compel him to stop. His strikes grew more and more powerful, sending waves of pain crashing against her brain, making it even more difficult for her to think. It was scary to see him so completely out of control.

Then it wasn't scary. It was infuriating. A fire sprang to life in her chest that only grew hotter with each impact. Sibylla did not like feeling weak or out of control. It wasn't in her nature. Since she wasn't convinced he would stop for anything, even the whistle, Sibylla knew she needed to take the momentum away from Chad. If he wanted to go hard, then she would go hard. Stronger than most girls her age, Sibylla knew that she had what it took to end the fight. All she needed was the right move.

Every strike had gotten harder and more savage, to the point that hitting Sibylla was the only thing keeping him on balance. Like leaning against a wall. So when she ducked, his strike swished over her head, his momentum nearly taking him off his feet. Her uppercut, fueled by anger, caught him square in his floating ribs, eliciting a grunt that Sibylla couldn't deny made her more than a little satisfied. When he looked over his shoulder he caught her jab, whipping his head back and cracking his nose. Hooking her leg behind his ankle she yanked him back, using his height against him to throw him into a heap on the thin mat that covered the floor of the high school gym.

He was on his feet in a flash, ready to attack again, his eyes savage and fixed on her when a piercing whistle cut through the air, this time seeming to gain his attention.

Body aching and the inner fire extinguished by the sound, Sibylla stifled a gasp of relief when Chad's eyes twitched to the side of the court they were sparring on. The jab had brought him back to the present enough that he could remember where they were. Not wanting to be caught off guard on the off chance he didn't care, she kept her own eyes locked on Chad and her arms in a low-ready position.

It was unsettling how wild and angry he looked, almost like he didn't recognize her, despite knowing each other for years. Those eyes were like looking into the eyes of a stranger. Blood trickled from his nose, but he didn't seem to notice as it dripped onto his shirt, staining the sweaty white with blotches of vibrant red.

"Hey!" Mr. Darrow, the instructor, shouted wheeling up from the sidelines, irritation at being ignored evident in his voice. "That's enough you two! Chad, pop smoke, you're done."

Chad didn't move at first, a fierce desire to keep fighting clear in his eyes. It was obvious he had plenty of fight left in him, eager to come out. Sibylla brought her arms a little higher, prepared for what she was sure to be another vicious attack.

"Chad," Mr. Darrow said, a tone of warning in his voice that did not leave room for disobedience.

Chad sneered and spat blood on the mat before heading off to the locker rooms, tearing off his padding and throwing it carelessly to the side, his final protest. He kicked the locker room door open with a reverberating bang and disappeared inside. It wasn't until the door had closed that Mr. Darrow motioned Sibylla over.

Mr. Darrow had the physicality of a bear, the kind of presence that made it possible for him to run a self-defense class despite being confined to a wheelchair. Years before he had been in the army, and had been severely injured in an explosion. When all was said and done one of his legs had been amputated and the other had been rendered useless. Despite that, he had worked hard to become one of the most impressive teachers in Wyoming, not just on the mat but in the classroom as well. At Loup-Garou High he had won Teacher of the Year more than once. That drive was one of the many things she absolutely admired about him: the man didn't know the meaning of the word quit.

"Red," he said, gentle but firm. "You know better."

"I'm sorry," she said sheepishly, keeping her eyes on her feet.

Of all the people in the world Sibylla wanted to disappoint, Mr. Darrow was last on the list. Over the years since her mom had died, Mr. Darrow had become something of a surrogate parent. Critical skills like hunting and fishing she had learned from him, and he even allowed her to join the weekend self-defense class that he called the "Fight Club" as a Freshman, even though it was normally reserved for upperclassmen and adults. Even her brothers, the ginger twins, had been allowed to join when they came in as Freshmen.

"It's been four years now," he said, leaning back and crossing his massive arms over his chest.

"I'm sorry," she said again. The expectations for her were higher than they were for Chad, who had only been attending Fight Club for a little over a year. Being one of his oldest students, he expected more of her. "I just lost my temper."

"You lost control," he said. "Why?"

The words stung, but Sibylla knew that he was right. While there was no doubt that Chad had been completely out of line, she had lost her temper and had broken one of Mr. Darrow's few rules for the class: don't fight angry. Anger had always been a big part of her life, and it was difficult to control it. Though there were times, not that she would ever admit it to Mr. Darrow or anyone else, that she didn't want to control it. It felt good to be angry and to just let it go.

Yet she had done a good job so far controlling it, determined to prove to him that he hadn't made a mistake in taking her in.

"He was just being… weird," she answered, risking sounding like she was justifying her mistake. "It was different today, I didn't think he would stop unless I did something to make him stop. It's almost like he's someone else since he got sick."

Sibylla looked away from her shoes to look at the battered locker room door and temporarily forgot that she was in trouble.

"Who is that?" she asked, pointing at a girl who was picking up Chad's discarded padding.

The girl couldn't have been older than Sibylla. Black and purple hair, like raven's feathers with silver streaks, contrasted strikingly with her tanned skin. It was shaved on the sides and braided down the middle like a Viking. Tattooed lines swirled around her eyes in beautiful patterns, looking like tiny birds in flight. Shorter than Sibylla, she was lean and moved with a gracefulness that captivated Sibylla's attention, even under the baggy clothes that were obviously too big for her.

Mr. Darrow followed her gaze.

"Aubri, an out-of-towner," he said. "Way out of town, to be honest."

"How'd she end up here?" Sibylla asked, curious.

"Well, the short answer is that she responded to an ad I put out for more instructors. Since I've been getting more interest I decided to expand the class," Mr. Darrow replied, his answer sounding mechanical and rehearsed.

"She has fight experience?" doubtful, Sibylla glanced back at the girl. "She can't be older than me."

"She's not," Mr. Darrow confirmed, then reconsidered. "Well, ish. She might be a year older if that. Regardless, she has a lot to bring to the table."

"And she decided to bring her talents here, to the middle-of-nowhere Wyoming?" Sibylla pressed. "Is she even out of high school?"

"You'd be surprised," Mr. Darrow said, "though you know more than most that there's more to our little town of Red Falls than meets the eye."

Red Falls was undoubtedly an interesting place, with plenty to see and do, but it was hardly the kind of place someone traveled to to start a new life. Especially for someone who was coming from a place where a seventeen-year-old could be out of school and traveling alone.

"Want me to introduce you?" Mr. Darrow asked, noticing how she was staring across the court at the stranger.

Another reason Sibylla appreciated Mr. Darrow was his continued support of her when she came out to him as bi the previous year. It wasn't common knowledge yet, since she had only chosen to tell Mr. Darrow and her brothers. She wanted to tell her best friend Kayla about it at some point, but even though she had known her for years, Sibylla wasn't sure how she would take it. She wasn't sure how anyone would take it.

For years she had struggled with the idea of being bisexual, not sure what it meant and how it affected her life. It wasn't like she had a lot of people to ask. Small Town, USA was not known for being open-minded about much, and the LGBTQ+ community was nonexistent in Red Falls to prove it. Thankfully she had found a community online who had been open to sharing their perspectives and stories.

Fortunately, Mr. Darrow had taken it well. He had even hugged her and thanked her for telling him. Her brothers had also been very supportive, agreeing not to tell their dad until she was ready. As much as she wanted to hope that others would have the same reaction, she just couldn't be sure.

A cheerful chirping noise from her bag, and the sound of a phone alarm going off, saved the day.

"Not right now," she said, sweeping up her bag to turn off the alarm. "I gotta meet Kayla over at the gate."

"The tradition continues, eh?" Mr. Darrow asked. "I'm surprised y'all are still believing in that haunted nonsense."

"It's more about the experience," Sibylla answered. "Nothing spookier than a haunted sleepover in the gate tower on Halloween."

"Still swiping the keys from Mr. Eric?" Mr. Darrow asked, feigning a disappointed tone.

"First of all," Sibylla said with mock defensiveness. "Those keys were never officially missing."

Technically true, since she had gotten the keys back to Mr. Eric before he had ever known they were missing. And it had only happened in the first year that Sibylla and Kayla had started the tradition. Since then Mr. Eric, the caretaker of the ancient structure, had merely been excited that anyone was showing interest in the old heap of stones at all.

"Second of all, you know we're the only ones who ever go into that old building anymore anyway. Our patronage is keeping the old girl standing."

"I'm almost positive Mr. Eric and the town of Red Falls would prefer money to two teenagers spending the night there, but I'm sure it's all the same," Mr. Darrow said.

"Exactly!" Sibylla said with mock enthusiasm while she slung her bag over her shoulder.

"All your homework done?" he asked before she turned to leave. "I'd hate for you to be stressed over your papers while searching for monsters and ghosts."

Sibylla patted her bag, "of course! What kind of irresponsible teenager do you think I am?"

"Whatever," Mr. Darrow said dramatically, "Go pretend to be irresponsible with that hooligan friend of yours."

"Will do, sir!" Sibylla gave a loose salute. "You know how we party!"

"Before you go," he interrupted her exit again. "You're going to apologize to Chad tomorrow." It was not phrased as a suggestion, and she knew he would follow up to make sure that she had.

"Okay," she said, edging away from him, exaggeratingly eying the girl's locker room door.

"Yeah, yeah," he waved her off, "Drop your pads off with Aubri on your way out."

Sibylla nodded and continued on her way to the girl's locker room. Aubri hadn't moved since she had picked up Chad's pads and appeared to be waiting for Sibylla. The closer Sibylla got the more nervous and excited she became. Since embracing the fact that she was bisexual, she had been trying to figure out what it was that attracted her to girls. Looking at Aubri, she was sure she now had an idea of what that was.

"I will take those for you," Aubri said, holding out her hand for the pads.

Her voice was light and confident, playful, like there was a joke between them that Sibylla didn't know yet. An accent played on the edges of her words, something that Sibylla had never heard before, at least not in Wyoming. It sounded absolutely musical.

To hide the sudden flushing in her face that came at the realization that she was making very intense eye contact, Sibylla quickly handed the pads to Aubri, mumbling 'thanks' before brushing past her. Sibylla didn't look back as she passed through the door, too nervous about whether or not she would see Aubri watching her leave. Though that particular idea didn't trouble her too much.

"Good grief," she muttered, sliding into the locker room with only a glance over her shoulder that confirmed Aubri's eyes were still on her. Just before the door closed Sibylla swore that Aubri's smile broadened at her glance.

ψ

Back in the gym Aubri's smile lingered. There was something about Sibylla that resonated with her, something like a connection between them. Ignoring the glances and stares from the people sparring in the gym, she made her way back to Mr. Darrow. She hadn't been in town long, but she had quickly grown accustomed to people staring at her.

"So that is Sibylla?" she asked, shoving the pads in a white mesh bag.

"That's Sibylla, yeah," Mr. Darrow replied. He blew his whistle and shouted "Times up! We're ending early tonight, go enjoy the Halloween festivities!!"

There was a brief cheer and a collective sigh of relief. Mr. Darrow ran a tough program, and rarely let anyone slide early, with the occasional exception of students like Sibylla. As they began to take off their pads and roll up the mats Aubri squatted, balancing easily on her toes next to Mr. Darrow.

"What?" he asked briskly, noticing the look on her face.

"Will she be okay tonight?" she asked.

"She should be, we still have time," Mr. Darrow said. He gestured at the bag in Aubri's hands and yelled, "Give your gear to Ms. Telfer over here on your way out!"

"Ms. Telfer?" she asked, arching an eyebrow.

"My mom's maiden name," he replied. "Don't worry about it too much, you'll have a matching license later this week."

"I will have to trust you I suppose," Aubri replied, amused.

"You don't have a choice on that. But I can appreciate your willingness to play along," he thought for a moment, then continued. "Do me a favor, keep a sharp eye out tonight anyway, yeah?"

"Of course," she replied, smiling at the two red-headed teenagers who were fighting each other to be the first to drop their pads off.

Chapter 2

By the time Sibylla was showered and changed it was early evening, the confrontation with Chad already a fading memory. Stepping out into the student parking lot she paused for a moment to breathe deeply. Cold and fresh, the air stung her lungs. Deep down she knew she was going to miss her little town and the people in it.

In just a few short months she was going to be graduated and on her way to… what? The question had bothered her since she was a freshman. While she had taken on as many advanced and honors classes as she could in preparation for doing something glorious after high school, there wasn't a plan. What was she going to do?

Miss all of this, she thought, looking at the empty parking lot and the trees beyond.

Main street was just on the other side, the tops of the little mom-and-pop shops just visible through the treetops. Sibylla knew them all, and all the people who ran them and all the people who shopped in them. Behind the school were the sprawling neighborhoods that had replaced the old decrepit homes that had been condemned to rot on the other side of the river that split the town.

In front of the school was the town's only grocery store, next to which was one of two restaurants, one laboring to call itself Italian and the other unashamedly American cuisine. She knew and loved all of it.

"You're a smart girl," her English teacher, Ms. Coleman, said practically every week. "You should leave and make a name for yourself!"

What exactly she was supposed to be doing to make that name for herself, she had no idea, and neither did anyone else. She had to remind herself constantly that she had plenty of time. Lots of people waited to go to college, some people waiting until they were in their thirties and forties. What was the rush for her? Besides, she had a strange feeling that there was something she still needed to do before she could leave, though she had no earthly idea what it could be.

"I thought you were headed somewhere?" a voice said behind her.

Gasping, Sibylla spun to face the source, instinctively snapping to a fighting stance.

"Oh my god!" she said with relief, clutching her chest.

Just behind her Aubri was leaning against the wall, hugging herself against the cold.

"Sorry," Aubri said apologetically. "I would have said something sooner, but you seemed deep in thought and I did not want to surprise you. Then it kind of just felt awkward."

"Right," Sibylla said, embarrassed. "Have you just been standing out here since practice ended?"

Aubri shrugged. "More or less I guess. I do not get weather like this where I'm from, so I like to enjoy it as much as I can."

Before Sibylla could ask where she was from, a flash of lights and a honk let her know that Kayla had arrived. The black sedan drove through the parking lot recklessly, swerving in large loops while Kayla showed off her new car, one her parents had bought for her very recently. Sibylla had already seen it, but Kayla seemed intent on showing it off to anyone with eyes.

"That's my ride," Sibylla said, a little embarrassed.

Pausing, Sibylla wondered if Kayla would mind including Aubri. It was a personal tradition, but Aubri was new in town, and it couldn't hurt to have her along. She seemed fun, if a little stiff. Then the passenger side window rolled down and Kane stuck his head out, howling like a wild wolf.

"And that's my boyfriend, Kane," Sibylla said, planting her face in her hand.

"They seem like they are fun to be around," Aubri said, watching the scene with a smile.

"They are," Sibylla admitted, feeling embarrassed, though she didn't know why.

Aubri held out her hand, "It was nice to meet you, Sibylla, hopefully, I will see you around."

"Of course!" Sibylla said, taking Aubri's hand, then gasped.

Electricity flowed up her arm the second their hands made contact, shooting like lightning into her brain and sending showers of sparks before her eyes. Aubri's eyes lit up, shining like sapphires behind her sunglasses. Sibylla's body seemed to hum with the charge, her limbs growing warm despite the rapidly dropping temperature around them. Arcs of energy chased each other in her belly and chest.

"Wow," Sibylla breathed.

The screech of tires shattered the moment like a brick through a sheet of glass. Sibylla jerked her hand back in surprise. Looking down at it, she half expected to see scorch marks.

"You are special," Aubri murmured. The sound of her voice sent a shiver up Sibylla's spine.

"Come on chica!" Kane said from the window, eyes glancing between them curiously. "Who's the new kid?"

Sibylla turned to introduce them but saw that Aubri was already passing through the door back into the school. Disappointment surged through Sibylla, but she turned back and forced a smile at Kane.

"Mr. Darrow hired her," Sibylla replied, "I guess you guys will get to meet later."

"Sweet!" Kane said, already moving on. "Get that cute behind in the car! We have a haunted pile of rocks to explore!"

He slapped the roof of the car, eliciting a strong reprimand from Kayla.

"She's new!" Kayla said angrily, "Be nice!"

Smiling, still buzzing from the handshake, Sibylla climbed into the back seat of the car.

The gate was, in a lot of ways, exactly what it sounded like: a gate. It was two doors between two posts, designed originally to keep someone out of someplace. The biggest difference was the scale of it. The massive oak planks that made up the doors were suspended between two stone towers that topped off at almost thirty feet tall. The doors were held together by thick iron bands that had been forged to look like two wolves grappling, their claws and noses touching where the doors came together.

The towers were connected by a narrow wall walk and had originally been done up to look like a museum display. There were still replicas of weapons and uniforms and armor behind thick plastic walls, but it had been some time since it had been open to the public. Curiously, there were also banners depicting battles with wolves, though it worked well with the name that was elegantly carved above the oak door: Portus Lunae, or the Moon Gate.

Needless to say, it was aggressively out of place on the outskirts of the old decrepit neighborhood that separated it from the rest of Red Falls. Howard Baft, the founder of the town and an eccentric billionaire, had transported it stone by stone from France. Why was anyone's guess, as he died the same day the last stone was placed and hadn't written down any reason for it. The displays had been put together by his estate and then Mr. Eric had taken over.

Pulling up in Kayla's car, Sibylla was reminded of what the gate was known for. Covered in ivy that wasn't native to Wyoming and seemingly always surrounded by fog, it was considered the most haunted place in town. The general desolation of the town nearby and the presence of wolves in the area only added to its mysterious nature. For most of the teens at the school, the unironically named Loup-Garou High, going and spending the night at least once was a traditional display of courage.

Sibylla had spent the night there at least two or three times a month for close to four years since she started going to L.G. High. Unlike other people, she found a strange solace while sitting in the towers or on the wall walk, feet dangling over the edge, staring dreamily at the shadows cast by the light of the moon shining through the branches. Tonight was no different, the same ivy and shadows that scared others inspired excitement in her.

"I don't get you at all," Kayla said, looking at Sibylla through the rearview mirror. "This place gives me the creeps."

"And yet, here we are," Sibylla said excitedly. "Come on chicken, let's go to the west tower. Rumor has it that there was someone who hung themselves up there. Maybe we'll see their ghost!"

"Yippee!" Kayla said sarcastically. Eyeing the towers nervously, she tapped her fingers on the steering wheel and made no move to get out of the car.

The story wasn't true, of course, there weren't any documented cases of anyone committing suicide inside the towers. Since it left France there hadn't even been acts of violence near the towers. Anything before then was a little murky, with some battles here and there, some mysterious murders, etc. Nothing unusual for a remnant of an old castle. Still, as the resident expert on the structure, she liked to mess with people as much as possible.

"You coming Kane?" she asked sweetly.

"Hell yeah!" he said with mock enthusiasm, "try and stop me."

Rolling her eyes Sibylla hopped out, making it to one of the old side doors with the keys in hand before she heard the other doors open. Stepping inside felt like it always had to Sibylla: like entering a whole new world. The west tower was mostly stairs, the steps winding up around the perimeter of the wall, pausing at landings in front of arrow slits and at the door that went to the walkway over the gate. From there it was a straight shot to the hatch that led to the tower's roof.

Tonight, like every other Halloween for the past three years, they were only going to sit on the wall walk, backs to its stones, staring up at the moon, waiting for the hauntings to happen. At least that's what the others would do. Sibylla found it was one of the few places where she could think freely, even dream. The gate was her protection from the barely controlled chaos that was her life, and she loved every stone and board.

"I swear it got colder up here," Kane muttered, pulling his coat tighter. "We're not staying here too long, are we?"

"It's just the stones," Sibylla said, closing her eyes and drinking it all in. "Perfectly natural."

"Nothing natural about this place," Kane said, peering into the shadows.

"So," Kayla said quickly, "how's the future looking for everyone?"

It was the traditional question, the one a freshman version of Sibylla had asked of the freshman version of Kayla when they had first started going.

"Football," Kane said, a smile breaking through his brooding. "I already got a scholarship."

"What?" Sibylla asked, surprised. "That's so cool! Why didn't you say something sooner?"

Kane smiled. "You've been so busy lately that I figured it was easier to wait for tonight than try and get it in sooner."

It was his first time coming out to the gate since he and Sibylla had started dating, and she had been excited to share it with him. Seeing him there, sitting next to her, their fingers intertwined, she was struck by how relaxed he looked like he belonged there with her. She snuggled in closer and looked down at their hands, and the memory of her handshake with Aubri came back. A feeling like a lightning strike, like energy surging through every cell of her body. It was something she had never experienced with Kane.

Does that mean something? She wondered.

"You gonna go with him?" Kayla asked before Sibylla had a chance to either explore the thought or push it away.

"What?" she asked, surprised by the question.

"You gonna go with Mr. Football Star here to college?" Kayla asked, "Y'all would be so great together."

Like a deer in headlights, Sibylla was unsure of what the question meant or how she was supposed to answer. A slight tingle filled her fingers and her toes, the kind of feeling she got when she was too cold.

"I-" she began, not convinced she knew what she was going to say next when she heard a sharp scraping noise from behind them.

Whipping around, she saw nothing there but Kayla's car, sitting right where they had left it. Eyes darting around, she looked for anything that could have caused the noise. Trees surrounded the gate, and there was a light breeze that would cause the branches to sway and scrape against each other. An uneasy feeling filled her guts, and the cold seeped into her hands and feet.

"What's wrong?" Kane asked, following her gaze. "Something more interesting out there?"

"You didn't hear that?" she answered, settling back down.

Looking into his eyes, she realized that he thought she was making it up to get out of answering the question.

"Nevermind," she said quietly, "it must have been the breeze or something."

"So?" Kane asked, hand going stiff in hers.

"So what?" Sibylla asked, distracted.

Her chest was feeling restricted like a band was tightening across it. As inconspicuous as possible she tried to take some deeper breaths through her nose and out through her mouth, like Mr. Darrow had shown her.

"Are you going to college with Kane?" Kayla answered, brows furrowed in confusion.

A rustle of leaves drew Sibylla's attention to the bushes across the small grass lawn behind the gate. Overgrown, the mist settled in between the weeds and bushes and trees like a thick, impenetrable blanket. The breaths were too deep to be subtle as she fought to keep her emotions under control.

Not now, she pleaded uselessly.

The anxiety attacks had been coming on more frequently, especially the closer she got to graduation. There were so many ducks she needed to get in a row, from who would take care of her brothers and her dad to what she wanted to do or needed to do or who she even was in the first place. So far she had done a good job keeping them from Kane, but of course, it would rear its ugly head the moment she had to answer about whether or not she was going to go with him.

Of course, I'm going to go with him, she thought, breathing becoming less and less stable. Right?

"There!" she shouted, her numb hand shooting up to point into the woodline.

A shape had been there, massive, its head almost reaching the lower branches of the trees. The rays of the moon had, for the briefest of moments, illuminated it. Sibylla could have sworn she had seen fur and ears and shoulders and arms. Something was out there, something huge and scary and dangerous.

"There," she said again, still pointing, unable to say anything else.

It was as if her brain had frozen in place. She could see the words in her mind, words like 'I saw something huge over there, we should probably leave' or 'Once we get out of here, I'd love to tell you what I think about our future together.' But they couldn't make it to her mouth so that Kayla or Kane could hear them.

"What?" Kane asked, an edge to his voice. "Do you want to go with me or not?"

Damn it, she thought, a tear rolling down her cheek. Just say something!

"There!" she said again, the word catching in her throat.

Not that! Something else! She thought.

"There's something…" she trailed off, sucking in air in short, haggard breaths.

Kane pulled his hand away and Sibylla collapsed over onto Kayla, who wrapped her arms around her protectively.

"What's wrong?" Kayla asked, concerned. "Sibylla?"

The only answer Sibylla could give was her sobs, fighting for what little oxygen her hyperventilating could provide. Trembling uncontrollably, she clutched at Kayla's arms, trying desperately to hold onto something real as more of the shapes and shadows appeared throughout the edge of the forest, their edges blurring through her tears.

"There!" she whispered hoarsely.

"There's nothing there Sibylla!" Kane snapped, waving at the woodline.

How can he not see them? Sibylla wondered, watching helplessly as the shapes disappeared one by one.

"It's okay," Kayla whispered, stroking Sibylla's hair. "There's nothing there, you're okay, I promise."

"This is bullshit," Kane muttered, stepping over Sibylla and charging angrily through the door. "I'll see you both tomorrow."

Crying harder, Sibylla buried her face in Kayla's lap. She had been looking forward to her night with Kayla, and spending the time with

Kane had seemed like such an absolute bonus. Now Kane was convinced that she didn't want to go to college with him, and he was going to be so angry.

"It's okay," Kayla said, "he doesn't know, it's okay."

After what felt like an eternity she started to calm down, taking deeper, shakier breaths, until she was able to sit up awkwardly, too embarrassed to look at Kayla.

"You okay?" Kayla asked, hands folded awkwardly in her lap.

It wasn't the first time she had seen Sibylla break down, but she still seemed unsure of what to do about it.

"Yeah," Sibylla wiped her eyes, still sniffling.

Looking at Kayla she could see the doubt in her eyes. Looking back over the wall she was hoping that Kane would at least be waiting down by the car. If he was waiting, that meant he was more annoyed than angry. She could handle him being annoyed, she couldn't handle him being angry. To her severe disappointment, he wasn't there.

"Can we go, please?" Sibylla asked.

"You sure?" Kayla asked, "It's not even ten yet."

Sibylla knew that Kayla was trying to be nice, but it was clear that she didn't want to stay any longer than she had to. Knowing that Kane was angry and realizing that, for the first time, the gate was a scary place, Sibylla didn't want to stay there any more than Kayla did.

"I'm sure," Sibylla said, voice trembling. "Mind if I crash at your house tonight?"

"Of course," Kayla replied, unable to hide her relief.

Chapter 3

By the time they had finally arrived back at Kayla's house, neither Kayla nor Sibylla had remembered that they needed to set an alarm to get to school on time. Sibylla woke to the thunderous knocking of Kayla's dad on the door, accompanied by his booming voice announcing that they were going to be late for school.

"Thanks for the heart attack, Dad!" Kayla snapped, clutching her chest.

"At least a heart attack would be a good enough reason for you to be late!" her dad snapped back, his voice receding with his clomping footsteps. "Now quit your crying and get moving!"

"Some kids get a nice breakfast or a happy good morning, lucky me to get you!" Kayla called out.

"Lucky to still be living in this house! Move your butt!" Her dad replied, voice still clearly heard despite the increasing distance.

"Friggin' love that guy," Kayla sighed and rolled out of bed.

Since it had been an impromptu sleepover Sibylla didn't have an extra change of clothes, so Kayla loaned some of hers. Fortunately, they were close enough in size that it was comfortable enough, though Kayla preferred being flashy and standing out. 'Making a statement,' is what she called it. Sibylla preferred not to make a statement with her clothes, but she liked wearing dirty clothes even less. Makeup was another matter entirely. Kayla's palette was a little too bold for Sibylla and took a lot more time to figure out and work around. After twenty minutes of struggling with it, Sibylla accepted defeat. She focused instead on foundation and eye shadow and moved on.

When they did manage to stumble out of Kayla's room, Kayla's dad was waiting at the kitchen counter, phone in hand. Dramatically pressing something on the screen he looked to them and back.

"You're slowing up in your old age, Red," he said with a wink.

"What was it today?" she asked, remembering the traditions that Kayla's parents followed nearly every day.

"Twenty-five minutes," he replied, showing her the screen. "Any longer and I would have notified the morgue."

"Yeah yeah," Kayla said, kissing her dad on the cheek, "if we don't head out now the school will call in a search and rescue."

After a quick hug, the two of them bounded through the front door and into Kayla's car and were well on their way, though certainly behind on time. As much as Sibylla hated being late, she had to admit that at least she wouldn't have time to talk to Kane about the previous night, something she wasn't prepared to do. Thus far she had been carried along by the adrenaline of a time crunch, she certainly didn't have the energy to think up ways to apologize for her anxiety attack.

When the old school building swung into view Sibylla was able to shove all of it to the back of her mind, a task made easier when she saw the time. Her first class would be starting in only a few minutes and they would most certainly not be able to find a parking space even remotely close to the building.

"Tuck and roll!" Kayla bellowed, slamming on the brakes in front of the school's front doors. Terrified by the noise and bracing herself against the dash to keep from slamming into it, Sibylla turned a wild, questioning eye toward her friend.

"I don't care if I'm late," Kayla declared, unbuckling Sibylla's seatbelt for her and shoving her toward the door. "Come on, you gotta move faster than that if you want to keep your record intact. See you in class!"

Sibylla stumbled out of the car and gave Kayla a grateful wave. "What would I do without you?"

"Thankfully we'll never know!" Kayla flashed Sibylla a grin and sped off toward the school parking lot.

Thanks to her time in track practice and Kayla's sacrifice, Sibylla made it to her first period just as the bell was ringing.

Her first period, her favorite class, was taught by Mr. Darrow, who had a pretty loose policy regarding most things. He probably wouldn't have even marked her tardy if she had arrived at the end of class with only five minutes to spare. He also didn't seem to care that Sibylla was in the class primarily because Kane and Kayla had also managed to take it.

Beyond the fact that it was Mr. Darrow's class, Sibylla loved his classroom. In a lot of ways, it reminded Sibylla of a museum: trinkets and artifacts from his time in the military and all the other stuff he'd collected over the years, from foreign uniforms to little statues. Everything was a snapshot of all that he had done and seen, and he had done and seen a lot. Her favorite piece was a poster of his favorite poem, "Invictus", that was stapled behind his desk. It was a declaration of being in charge of one's fate and soul, of maintaining dignity in the face of everything life had to throw at someone.

That day she didn't feel too terribly dignified, especially seeing that Kane was already seated and making a pointed effort to not look at the door or at whoever was coming in.

As soon as Mr. Darrow had released them to work on their assignment two notifications popped up in the corner of her screen. Glancing up at Mr. Darrow, she saw that he was absorbed in helping another student with a question. So she opened the app and saw that Kane and Kayla had both messaged her at the same time. Trepidation flared in her chest for the briefest of moments, Sibylla's finger hovering over the mouse pad. What would it say? Would he accuse her of faking an anxiety attack to get out of the question?

Or worse, would he ask her if she wanted to go with him to college?

There's only one way to know, she told herself, trying to cut off the spiraling thoughts. With an anticlimactic click, his message jumped into the text box at the corner of her screen.

KANE: Can I ask about last night, or are you going to fly off the handle?

Pursing her lips, Sibylla avoided looking at Kane before typing a response. Of course, he would be cautious about asking her about it, she hadn't given him the best impression last night. If only she could get her anxiety under control, she could have at least told him yes. Then he would have been happy and she wouldn't be so stressed out about it.

Besides, would it be so bad to go with him to college? It wasn't like she had any real idea of what she wanted to do anyway.

SIBYLLA: I'm fine, sorry about last night, I promise it won't happen again.

KANE: Good, because you made me feel like crap for wanting to keep dating, and that's not fair.

Sibylla was mortified, unsure of how to respond. Of course, she wanted to keep dating him, he wasn't the source of her anxiety at all.

SIBYLLA: Fair, I promise it won't happen again.

Before she could send her next message explaining how he was the only real stable person in her life, Mr. Darrow called over to her.

"Red, I need to talk to you in the hall real quick."

The class let out a chorus of "ooooh"s like she was in trouble, and she rolled her eyes. No one ever got in trouble in his class, it had to be something else. She hoped it was something super important, the last thing she needed was to leave Kane hanging again. Hopefully whatever he wanted to say wouldn't take too long. When she got out into the hallway she groaned internally.

Coach Savage, the head of the football team and Kane's mentor, was waiting for them. Standing next to him, looking about as annoyed as Sibylla felt, was Chad.

This definitely could have waited until after school, she thought.

"Spit it out, kiddo," Coach Savage said to Chad before Sibylla had a chance to say anything.

"Sorry about yesterday," he said, glancing sidelong at his coach. "I guess I had some… issues I was working through and took them out on you."

"No," Sibylla said hurriedly, surprised by his apology but not wanting to seem like she was hesitating, especially in front of Mr. Darrow. "I should have had better control. I'll do better next week, I promise."

Chad nodded but still avoided eye contact, glancing more at the coach than at her. Coach Savage looked between them and then at Mr. Darrow.

"Good?" he asked no one in particular.

"I would say so," Mr. Darrow replied.

"Good! Come on champ, you got laps ahead of you if you're late to class." He pushed Chad down the hall, flashing a smile before following.

"You okay?" Mr. Darrow asked when they had gone.

"Yeah, why?" Sibylla asked.

"You just seem a little off today," he replied, leaning back in his chair. "A little unfocused."

Damn it, she thought, not him too.

"Not a big deal," he added. "Just curious."

"I'm alright, I guess," she said. "Had another anxiety attack last night."

"Oof, those are tough," Mr. Darrow said. "I know how much they take out of you. Have you seen anyone about them yet?"

"I got it handled," she said, feeling awkward.

Fortunately, the bell rang, saving her from having to admit that she didn't, in fact, have it handled. If anything they seemed to be getting worse.

"You can always talk to me Red," he said, wheeling back into the class, temporarily blocking the flow of students trying to escape.

"Of course!" she said, sidestepping the crowd, searching for Kane. "See you tomorrow!"

"See you tomorrow Red," he said after her.

ψ

Admittedly he had ambushed her with the apology, but there had been a reason for it. It had nothing to do with Sibylla, he knew she would have taken care of it on her own time, but he needed to see Chad's face. He had been coaching Sibylla for years and knew how hard she could hit, and he did not doubt that she had broken his nose. Seeing Chad there, nothing wrong at all and nose intact, confirmed Mr. Darrow's fears.

Yanking open a drawer he pulled out a few books to reveal a paper that was wrinkled and stained. It was a handwritten list of names that he started years prior when things had seemed to begin accelerating. Writing in Chad's name he carefully replaced the list under the books and closed the drawer.

Chapter 4

Despite how tired she was, Sibylla managed to survive until seventh period, PE, her least favorite class. Not only did it come across as a waste of time, they never did anything that resembled a challenge. In fact, they never did anything at all. Coach Savage spent the period working on stuff for football and barely paid attention to what anyone did. As long as no one was getting hurt or breaking school property they barely occupied any part of his attention.

On that day, however, it was a relief to mentally check out and just walk laps around the basketball court for forty-five straight minutes. Letting her mind wander, devoid of focus or purpose, proved to be relaxing, cathartic even. She could let everything drift away and empty her mind while she walked around the court on auto-pilot. Unfortunately, it didn't last very long.

"Hey Lavigne," Coach Savage called to her, mispronouncing her name.

It was a common occurrence for most people but she didn't mind. Granted, most of the mistakes were with newer teachers who had never met her before, but she didn't mind the coach taking a little longer than others.

"Listen up Lavigne," he said, "You know I love y'all's club, right? Nothing brings me more joy than watching teachers empower members of the community and students, right?"

Sibylla nodded enthusiastically. Coach Savage was instrumental in facilitating the Fight Club, since he essentially owned the gym, as far as the school was concerned. Without his approval, there weren't too many other places for them to practice, especially in the colder months.

"Good," Coach Savage said, nodding to himself. "Then I want you to know that what I'm about to say also comes from love and empowerment, etc. Tell Darrow that, if he leaves another mess in my storage room, he'll be saying goodbye to his happy home here in my gym."

"Oh!" Sibylla was surprised. "I didn't know he stored stuff here, I thought he took it with him."

Coach Savage shook his head. "Negative, buckaroo, I told him it was fine to leave it here since he's chair bound."

Sibylla winced at the phrase. It wasn't the worst reference to someone in a wheelchair ever, she had heard worse from other students. Mr. Darrow never made any indication that being in a wheelchair bothered him, and she knew that he could handle insensitive comments. Still, it was all she could do to bite her tongue. Mr. Darrow didn't need her to defend him, and one thing she knew for a fact was that what he hated most was pity.

That being said, she didn't think it would be worth his time to have to worry about organizing the closet. Since it was probably Aubri, the new girl, who didn't put it away right. A part of her rejected the idea outright, but she ignored it and moved on.

"I'll take care of it today and let him know," she said apologetically. "I promise it won't happen again."

"Good deal Lavigne, make it quick," he instructed, the bell punctuating his point. "Can I trust you to lock this all up for me? I got practice."

"Absolutely!" she nodded.

"Good, make it happen, Lavigne," Coach Savage waved a vague hand toward the closet.

Sibylla hurried into the closet and saw that, indeed, the shin and arm pads were in a pile on the floor in the corner of the room. Confusingly, there didn't seem to be a place for them at all. Every shelf was spoken for, stuffed with baskets of different gym equipment, cones to basketballs to wristbands of different colors. Most of it Sibylla didn't recognize since Coach Savage never actually played games with their class, but she made a note of it for the next day. No reason why she couldn't coordinate something if anyone was willing. Looking at the mess, she wondered where Mr. Darrow put everything.

Following some strategic planning and the use of her organizational skills, she found a place for all of the pads in a basket that had originally held some flags for capture-the-flag, which seemed like they would be okay stuffed into a box that held the little disk sized cones that were used on the court. After shuffling some more boxes and crates around Sibylle stood back and admired her handy work. There was no way that Coach Savage would even see them in their new home. The Fight Club was secured.

Checking her watch she was surprised that the task had taken her almost 20 minutes. The gym was eerily quiet in the dark, soft November afternoon casting long shadows across the basketball court through the windows high on the wall. When she stepped out of the closet she realized that the main lights to the gym must have been shut off while she was working.

"Must be on a timer or something," she whispered to herself, already feeling a twinge of trepidation.

Her small voice seemed small in the empty gym, and the all too familiar cold pin-pricks that precipitated her anxiety attacks began filling her fingers. Though it seemed different somehow, like there was something nearby, something that her subconscious didn't like.

She rushed across the now-darkened gym and burst into the girls' locker room. Barely slowing down she crossed to her locker, thankful for the motion-sensor lights that snapped on when she entered. Working quickly she changed, her mind completely absorbed with trying to keep her rising panic under control when then the lights went off with a loud snap and plunged the room into darkness.

Sibylla froze, something inside of her telling her to stop and listen. Her nerves were tight, eyes wide open to absorb as much of the room around her as she could. In the darkness, all of the sounds her mind mentally shuffled away as unimportant came rushing to the front of her consciousness. On the other side of the locker room came the drip... drip... drip... of a leaky faucet. Above her, the heater kicked on with a whump, the sound so sudden and loud that Sibylla dropped to her knees and gripped her chest. She could feel the rapid beat of her heart against the palm of her hand, her breathing growing increasingly shallow.

The volatile mixture of perfumes, deodorant, and body odor all fought for her attention. Wrinkling her nose Sibylla couldn't imagine why she had never noticed the combination before.

"Someone needs to hose this place down," she said, her voice a barely audible whisper. "And call a plumber." After a moment she added, "I must be out of sight of the sensor, that's okay."

She took some comfort in her own words and prepared to get back to stuffing her locker. Before she had moved a muscle the lights snapped back on, bathing the room in their bright fluorescence. Sibylla blinked and squinted at the sudden light, and she froze. There, in the corner, just before her eyes had focused, she swore there had been a shape. Not just any shape, but something big. Big and fast. A shuffling noise came over the tops of the rows of lockers and then stopped, the room silent once more.

"Hello?" It came out as a worried-sounding squeak, "Is someone there?"

For a moment she didn't hear anything. Then a low rumbling growl came in response, echoing around the room as if it was coming from every direction at once. Under most circumstances hearing a growl from any room in a building would have been terrifying. There was something different about that growl though, something Sibylla had never heard in a growl before. She couldn't place it exactly, but it pierced her to the core with terror. As bad as it was, the deep silence that followed was far worse.

Hands and feet cold, her breaths beginning to hitch, she fought hard to keep control.

The football team is practicing outside the gym, she thought, unable to speak.

As an explanation, it didn't help at all. The cold was spreading to her chest now, restricting her lungs making it even more difficult to take anything deeper than short, rapid breaths.

She got to the last row of lockers and saw at the other end the blessed blue door, with the most beautiful EXIT sign she had ever seen above it. Pausing she listened, and then heard shallow, ragged breathing.

At that point she couldn't deny it, something was in the room with her, something big.

That's ridiculous, she thought, her mouth as dry as dust.

Still, she got low and launched herself at full speed toward the door. This time it was unmistakable, the sound of feet slapping against the old tiled floor, keeping pace with her, the sharp scratching of something hard on the concrete.

The thought added speed to her sprint. Her chest felt like bursting as she cleared the lockers, covering the last few feet of open space between the end of the row and the wall in mere seconds. Exploding through the door and crashing to the floor on the other side, she scrambled to her feet and spun around, backpedaling until she stood in the middle of the basketball court.

The door slowly closed, the quiet squeak of the hinges a kind of quiet protest at her aggressive exit. Nothing was in the doorway that she could see, no flash of fur or eyes or claws. The door clicked closed, the noise echoing across the empty court like a gunshot.

Breathing heavily, eyes wide, hands and knees shaking violently, Sibylla waited. There was something there, there had to be. Maybe the heater sounded like breathing? Fear must have got the best of her, that was the only explanation. With the shadows and anxiety of the night before her mind was just making it all up.

Of course, she thought to herself, frozen in place. This isn't real.

Slowly, as if in mockery of her attempts to stay calm, the door started to open on its own. Sibylla froze, eyes locked on the widening gap between the door and its frame.

There was nothing there, the door swinging open seemingly on its own. The darkness inside seemed deeper than it should be, resisting the light of the gym to hide whatever it was that was in there. A shape began to form, something like what she had seen the night before, something inhuman, wrong. Two yellow points of light appeared, near the top of the frame. Eyes, she realized with horror, staring straight at her.

"It's not real," she said, voice hitching, ice climbing up from her feet and her hands. "It's not real."

A low growl, so deep that Sibylla could feel it in her very core, echoed across the gym. Sibylla squeezed her eyes shut, willing the image to disappear, body rigid as panic threatened to overtake her. After several long moments, she opened them slowly, holding her breath in anticipation.

There was nothing there, the door to the locker room was closed, and the gym was empty.

Without another thought she sprinted out of the door to the gym, letting it slam behind her.

Chapter 5

It had taken most of the drive for her hands to stop shaking. The first few minutes were an exercise in unchecked speed and reckless maneuvering while she waited for her heart to start beating at what could be considered a normal rate. Not until she cleared the last back streets of town did she start to take control of her breathing, and then her speed. Halfway home she pulled off onto the shoulder and got out, running her fingers through her hair. For a while all she could do was pace back and forth in the snow-packed grass, the cool breeze pulling at her clothes and hair.

"There's no way that was real," she said to the empty field next to the road.

It couldn't have been, she thought.

The longer she stood in the open air, with the gray sky above and the wind rustling her hair, the more it seemed absurd. Of course, it hadn't happened, she was alone in a creepy gym after an exhausting day. If nothing else it was confirmation that she needed to do something to carve out some extra time to sleep. Shaking out her hands against the creeping cold and taking a few deep breaths, Sibylla got back in her car, feeling better.

That feeling evaporated when she pulled into the family driveway. For a moment she considered going back to Kayla's house when her dad's truck, a dented and rusty Ford, came into view at the end of the drive. Even knowing she didn't have time to spare she sat in her car as long as she could stand it, hesitant to approach the house. Her relationship with Roger was tenuous at the best of times, and it only seemed to be getting worse.

As a person and a parent, Sibylla's dad wasn't the worst, by any comparison. Kane's dad was a deadbeat drunk who openly cheated on his wife. No, Roger's biggest flaw was just being absent at the worst of times. Since the death of Sibylla's mother, Delphine, he had found himself very unexpectedly a single parent with no real idea of what to do. And he had been devastated by Delphine's death.

Sibylla didn't remember much from the time, but she could remember the doors that had once been wide open had become firmly shut. Any evidence that Delphine had ever existed had rapidly disappeared from around the house, save for whatever Sibylla had been able to hide away, which admittedly wasn't much. All that remained were hazy memories of smiles and two or three pictures, which Sibylla looked at pretty much every single day.

For his part, Roger had withdrawn into himself, becoming distant or, in most cases, non-existent. He was often away from the house for days at a time, pulling odd jobs around town or working in neighboring towns. Honestly, Sibylla had no idea what he did to earn money, only that it seemed to be enough to keep the house. There was also a family debit card of sorts, something he left behind when he disappeared that had enough on it to get gas and groceries.

Otherwise, Sibylla had become the mom of the family, practically raising her two younger brothers by herself. It hadn't been easy, they had only been a few years old at the time and Sibylla wasn't much older than they were. But she had done it. She had helped them learn how to read and write, gotten them to school on time with Mr. Darrow's help, got them fed and dressed every day, and tucked them in at night. Needless to say, there was a lot she held against Roger, and keeping the peace between them was nearly impossible the older she got.

Bracing herself she shoved the door open and tried to go as quickly as possible to her room. The goal was speed without seeming to want to run away or hide. One of the worst parts about their relationship was that Roger liked to pretend that nothing was wrong, that he could pick up and take over whenever he was home. So the less she had to talk to him the better.

"Sibylla," his low voice said from the couch, and she froze midstep. The springs in the old decrepit couch creaked as he leaned forward. "How was school?"

Such a normal, innocent question. She had asked it many times of her brothers and heard other parents ask it. Coming from her dad, like nothing was wrong, struck a chord. Turning to face him Sibylla saw that he was sitting on the edge of the couch, elbows propped up on his knees, his calloused hands resting limply between his legs. His eyes were clear and bright and completely focused on her. Like nothing was wrong.

"Fine," she replied curtly.

"You didn't come home last night," he said following a brief pause. "Late night?"

Things were now starting to come together in Sibylla's brain that she wasn't fully in control of. The anger she felt for her father, fatigue, and anxiety she had experienced over the past couple of days were combined into a concoction deep inside her that was threatening to explode. Like a caged animal, she started pacing in front of him, feeling an inexplicable nervousness just being near him.

Things clicked then in Sibylla's brain. Her and Kayla's tradition of going to the gate every Halloween was something that Roger did not particularly like. In fact hee hated it and had repeatedly told her not to go there for any reason. Despite being an ardent rule follower in most other cases, she had taken much joy in repeatedly ignoring him.

"Sort of," she replied carefully. "We had a presentation today."

It wasn't a lie, a presentation had happened that day, and theoretically, she would have spent the night before preparing for it, if she hadn't already prepared several days prior. If he picked up on it as the truth and found it acceptable he would lean back and let her go. To her disappointment, he flexed his fingers and stood, the old floor creaking beneath him.

There were many words Sibylla could use to describe her dad as a person. Words like jerk, bastard, or ghost, to name a few. But only one word truly captured his physicality: Intimidating. Standing more than a head taller than her with a chest and shoulders that defied any off-the-rack clothing, the man was a mountain of muscle. One look at his arms and hands and there was no doubt that Roger could hold his own in any confrontation. Blocking out the light from the window, he walked stiffly to the kitchen table and took a seat.

"Sit," he said when he saw that Sibylla hadn't moved.

His tone was neutral, but Sibylla bristled at his command. The urge to talk back, to tell him to screw himself, was almost too strong for her to suppress. Instead, she stalked to the table and sat down across from him. She didn't pull the chair forward though, sitting back from the table to create additional space between them. He rolled his eyes and leaned so far back in his chair that it groaned in protest. Small wonder it hadn't collapsed beneath him.

"We need to talk, Sibylla," he began, "about something important."

It soon became apparent that he wasn't sure how best to proceed, and his default in those moments was to just… stare. And the stare was unnerving. Cold blue eyes locked on hers, his face blank and impassive. He barely moved, adding to the stillness that covered the room. To most, his face was stone, unreadable, and cold. Sibylla had seen it enough times to be able to read the subtle differences though. When he was angry his eyes narrowed ever so slightly, easily missed. When he was frustrated he pursed his lips. Not much, just enough to narrow his mouth. At that moment it was clear that an internal debate was taking place.

Sibylla glanced toward the hallway that led to her room before flicking her gaze back to his. It was a flash of movement, and frustratingly involuntary.

"In a rush?" he said, jumping on the subtle shift.

"A little," she said without thinking. Nervous, the little habit of talking to herself popped up unbidden. She quickly added, "I just have a lot of work to do after the weekend."

"Well," he said with an edge to his voice, "I won't take up too much of your time."

They descended into silence again, much to Sibylla's frustration. Whatever it was that he wanted to tell her was a complete mystery, but he seemed to want to tell her less than she wanted to listen.

"It's… about your mom," he said finally, haltingly.

Unintentionally, Sibylla leaned forward at the mention of Delphine. Roger had never been forthcoming with details about what had happened to her, how she had died, or even where she was buried. Not too surprising, considering he had worked hard to erase any part of her from their home.

"Well, it's about our whole family," he continued, "we have a long…"

He trailed off and looked at his hands, eyes distant. Whatever it was it seemed to be incredibly difficult for him to get out. Tension built in Sibylla's bones and she started to shift in her chair, a gentle sway from side to side. Her fingers started tapping and she forced them into her lap to keep Roger from locking onto that as well. Tension was building deep within her core, filling her hands and feet with heat. A fire of curiosity burned within her, fueled by the growing silence. Forcing it to stay contained was difficult, but Sibylla was determined to wait as long as possible.

Across from her Roger seemed to be doing the same thing. His fingers drummed a rhythmless beat on the table, and Sibylla heard the low sound of fabric rubbing on fabric, indicating that he was bouncing his knee. As small as it was, Sibylla had never seen such a display of emotion come out of her dad before. Built like a mountain, with eyes of ice and a face of stone, it had taken her years to learn his quirks. Nothing had ever been so clear about him, and that fact ripped through the walls containing the energy that burned through her.

"What about us?" she asked, hoping to spur him into action.

His eyes flitted back to hers, coming back into focus as he returned to the present. Sibylla could almost hear the snap of his emotions locking away again. Body completely still, he stared back at her. Sibylla knew then that she should have just kept her mouth shut.

Why should I? She thought, and it stuck like a burning torch in her mind.

The idea that he would hold information back, like a hostage, made her fume. Sibylla was almost seventeen, she deserved to know something, anything, about the person who gave birth to her. After being the adult in the house for so long she deserved to be treated like one. If nothing else, Roger was the child in the room, acting out of spite and meanness. Throwing a tantrum because Sibylla wouldn't let him control her.

"Nothing," he finally said.

Sibylla grunted in exasperation and threw herself back, the chair squeaking as it slid even further away from the table. Frustration flowed through her veins like hot lava, her temper flaring up. In an instant, the energy in the room changed.

"Watch the tone," he said. He folded his arms and narrowed his eyes.

"I didn't say anything," Sibylla snapped, folding her arms.

"Watch it," he said again, eyes like ice.

"Look," Sibylla said, getting out of her chair. "You're the one keeping me from work so you can sit there and keep secrets and be weird about it."

"Enough!" he growled, getting to his feet so quickly that he knocked his chair over, sending it clattering to the floor.

Unable to help herself, Sibylla took a step forward. For a minute he stood there, body tense, massive hands balled into fists, only the table separating them. The room was deathly quiet, almost like the house itself was afraid of what might happen next.

Sibylla was tired of it all. He was the one who forced her to talk when she didn't want to. He was the one who got her hopes up about something he knew was important to her. He was the one who yanked it out of reach again, and then just expected her to roll with it. She wasn't the one with an attitude problem. She wasn't the one who couldn't communicate. The man was a mountain, pure muscle, a scary face. And yet, he was too scared to even mention her mother, to admit that she had ever been real.

"You are a coward," she said, allowing her rage to boil to the surface.

The word struck a chord. Jaw flexing, Roger's face turned bright red, almost purple. He rounded the table, closing the distance between them until only a foot of space separated them. Sibylla had to tilt her head back to maintain eye contact, but was unafraid. It took every fiber of her being to not step even closer to him as a challenge. A small voice in the back of her mind demanded to know what the hell she was thinking, but she shoved it back down.

"You know nothing," the words came out in a deep rumble. Yet, in his eyes, Sibylla could see something that he didn't want her to. Doubt.

Then he turned and left the dining room through the kitchen and out the back door, slamming it behind him.

"Because you won't tell me!" she screamed after him.

She stormed across the living room to the front door of the house. She threw it open and stalked toward a small shed that sat off to the side of the yard.

A white-hot heat tore her apart on the inside, raging like wildfire through her limbs. Her hands flexed into fists as she tried to contain it. She flung the old door open and pulled out a heavy sledgehammer that was propped up against the wall. Next to the shed was an old hardwood stump, showing the typical wear and tear of a wood-splitting platform. Screaming she swung the sledgehammer against it, again and again and again.

Beating the stump senselessly was something she had picked up a few years before, a way for her to channel her anger into something she knew she couldn't break. Or at least wasn't likely to break, since she had broken other stumps in the past, among other things. Even the handle for the sledgehammer was fairly new, one of several replacements she'd had to purchase or make to ensure the outlet stayed available. Her temper seemed to fuel some kind of energy or strength that didn't normally come out at other times.

Thump thump thump, the satisfying sound of the heavy steelhead of the sledge impacting the face of the stump synced with the blood pumping in her ears. Eventually, the sound replaced her scream, which had come down from something feral to something that sounded a little more human, before finally dissipating completely. At last her arms were too tired to support her anger and she let the sledge slide from her hands to the ground. To her surprise, she had cracked the stump. Glancing at her hands she was also surprised to see that blisters were already cracking through the callouses that she had built over the years.

"So," a voice said from behind her, "tough talk with Dad?"

Sibylla glanced wearily over her shoulder and saw one of the Ginger Twins sitting on the hood of her car, a safe distance away. He looked completely relaxed, his head propped in one hand like he was watching a river flow by instead of his sister savagely beating a stump with a hammer.

"Ginger Twins" was what she called her brothers since they both had the same vibrant and curly red hair that Sibylla did and were identical twins. Understandably, nearly everyone had a hard time telling her brothers apart, most finding it almost impossible. Making life harder for others was a pastime for them, so they often wore similar clothes or did their hair the same way. Fortunately, Sibylla had figured out her way to spot the subtle differences that gave them away and knew immediately that she was talking to Nate.

"Hardly a talk," she muttered, turning back to the stump. "Just another waste of time."

"This definitely seems more productive," he teased. "If you're done with your little tantrum, I'd love to show you something we found."

"Not now," she said, scooping up the sledgehammer with aching hands.

"Too busy, eh?" he asked, "you know that even god doesn't work as hard as you do?"

"If he had he could have finished making the world in five days instead of six," she shot back. "And yes, I am busy. Between what happened at school and Dad's BS I'm too far behind."

"Fair enough," he said, sliding off the hood of the car. "It's not going anywhere. But here's a taste."

He handed her a folded-up paper and walked past her, on his way to the barn.

"Where are you going?" she asked, looking quizzically at the paper he'd given her.

"Gotta calm dad down before he busts up the shop too much," Nate called back over his shoulder, "Hunter and I have some stuff stashed away, and let's just say it's better if he doesn't find it."

Sibylla waved him off, too distracted to ask more questions. Whatever it was was likely not going to be a problem for anyone other than them anyway. Unfolding it, she saw that the paper was a wrinkled old picture. It looked as though it had been crumpled and smoothed out more than once, and had one or two stains on it that looked like drops of water. What caught her attention, however, was who was in it.

Smiling back at the camera, standing arm-in-arm, was Delphine, Roger, and Mr. Darrow. She had known that Mr. Darrow was an old friend of the family, though she had never seen him at the house or even talking to her dad. The old picture was the first time that she had seen them all together, actually being friends. Running her fingers gently across her mom's face she was struck by how beautiful she was. It was a more recent photo than the ones she had stashed away, and the ones she had were more formal family photos, not like the one she was holding.

Then she saw that the three of them were covered head to toe in weapons: axes, knives, pistols, rifles, the works. She squinted at the dark shape that they were standing over, trying to make sure her eyes weren't playing tricks on her.

"What the hell?" she murmured.

At their feet, very obviously dead, was the biggest wolf Sibylla had ever seen.

Chapter 6

On the desk that occupied a corner of her small room was a pile of things. She knew she needed to keep track of them but not right then. It was one of many piles scattered around the room, their location in the room depicting their level of importance. Things like long-term reports, letters or cards from family, notices about upcoming appointments, etc lived in the desk pile. It kept it in her sphere of consciousness but only just, and on top of that pile went the picture.

It was something that struck her as important, but there wasn't an obvious reason why. Just a nagging sensation at the back of her mind, like a friend calling out something across the room. Over the next few weeks, it stared up at her from the top of the pile, the three smiling faces and the unnatural wolf.

Eventually, she decided to cover it up with a homework assignment that was due a few weeks away, hoping it would take it off her mind. After that she had doubled down on how much she was doing, trying to cram as much work into every day to keep her mind occupied. That had worked for a minute until the howling began.

At first, it was only once every few days. Sometime around midnight, a howl would rise out of the darkness of the woods that bordered their property. It would be lonely, long, low, and pure in its tone. And then another howl would answer it from another corner of the property, and then another. Laying in the dark, Sibylla would get goosebumps listening to the forlorn chorus. There was something comforting about it like they were singing a song just for her.

Over time she had even been able to tell a few of them apart, and every so often she would hear one of them that cracked the shell of comfort they created. Those were the ones that seemed otherworldly to listen to, and she would be flooded with anxiety and anger, a weird clash of emotions that she couldn't explain or justify.

Soon after it became every single night, and the howls picked up a new tone, something more… sinister. The howls seemed to get closer, like they were on the edge of the woods, and there were more of the 'bad' kind than the 'good'. More than once Sibylla rushed to her window and peered into the darkness. Her eyes strained to see through the shadows and what could be out there. A few nights of that and the familiar song became a kind of taunt, as if they were daring her to try to sleep.

Then the howl had come from so close that Sibylla flinched, feeling an edge of panic force itself into her mind. She was sure it had come from just under her window. With a gasp, she rushed from under her covers to, though she didn't understand why, try and catch the wolf before it had a chance to disappear. Pausing at the window, she was horrified to see a dark shape scurrying across the open lawn, clearly visible in the light of the moon. What was worse was that it was going straight to the barn, where the family cow, Sir Moo, was sleeping.

Without a second thought, Sibylla shoved on her boots and grabbed her hoodie from the floor before racing out of her room and through the back door of the house. Sprinting at full tilt she made it to the barn and slammed the door closed, latching it from the inside. It wasn't until she had latched the second door on the opposite end of the barn that it occurred to her that, maybe, it was a bad idea to be out and about with a wild wolf nearby. Alone. At night. In her underwear.

The rest of the night was spent shivering against Sir Moo, the old cow offering her just enough heat in the hay to keep from getting hypothermia. All the while she was surrounded by the intensifying howling that came closer and closer by the second, keeping her awake and miserable for the rest of the night. In her panic, she had completely forgotten to grab anything to defend herself with, which bothered her considerably. Though she wasn't sure if it was the fact she didn't have a weapon that bothered her the most or the fact that she felt like she needed one in the first place.

Hearing another howl nearby, she nuzzled deeper into Sir Moo's side, wishing that she had grabbed anything at all.

Chapter 7

The impact of a fist against her face tore her back to the present, stars exploding in her eyes. It was a not-so-gentle reminder that that night had come and gone several days prior and that she was very much so not in the best place to be distracted. As much as she wanted to be present and focused, her sleep had not improved since that night, with the constant interruption by wild animals that seemed to think that midnight was the time to sing the song of their people.

Reeling from the strike, Sibylla staggered back and tripped over her own feet, collapsing to the ground in a graceless heap, exhausted. Every part of her felt raw and used up.

"Hands up! Up!" Mr. Darrow shouted from the sidelines. He gestured with his arms up in front of his face.

Sibylla nodded, scrambling back to her feet, mind already drifting to everything other than her opponent on the mat. Struggling to stay awake long enough to make headway on homework was enough of a challenge, never mind staying awake in class. Even going to the Fight Club had almost been sacrificed to make room for studying, almost. It was the only thing left that felt refreshing and the least taxing mentally. Studying could wait an hour every weekend, she had decided.

"Katie, find a new partner," Mr. Darrow instructed, wheeling between Sibylla and her sparring partner Katie. Aubri walked behind him, her eyes fixed on Sibylla with obvious concern.

"Go try Hunter or Nate," Mr. Darrow continued, "or both at the same time. They won't be challenging but they could use a beating from a girl."

Katie nodded with enthusiasm and stalked toward her new victims, pounding her fists together. The ginger twins were shouting with every strike, throwing each other dramatically across the floor. They looked like they were practicing to be on some kind of wrestling show or cartoon, not self-defense. Rubbing her temples Sibylla spared a quick prayer, as Katie would not go easy on them.

What the hell is going on with me? She thought to herself.

"Red, what the hell is going on with you?" Mr. Darrow said, echoing her thoughts. "You come to class late, miss assignments, and practically failed the test on Friday. Now you're getting your butt handed to you left and right by people who should be a warm-up for you. Where's your focus?"

"Sorry," Sibylla said. Having known Mr. Darrow as long as she had, Sibylla knew that his tone was one of concern, not anger. He was worried about her.

At that moment Sibylla hesitated. Would he believe her? Would he tell her it was nothing or that she was overthinking something?

Of course, he'll believe you, she told herself. He had been there for her more often than her dad. At least he'll listen to you.

"It's just been hard," she finally admitted. "The local wolves have decided to serenade me at all hours of the night, so I haven't been sleeping that great for a few days now. On top of that, Nate and Hunter found this weird picture of you and my parents, standing over a wolf that looks a little too big to be real. So when the wolves aren't scaring the hell out of me, I'm thinking about how some of them could be as big as the one in the picture. Any chance you can tell me what was going on, like if it's a trick of the camera or perspective or something?"

Mr. Darrow gave her a hard look, seeming to be choosing his words carefully. Instead, he turned his attention to Aubri.

"Spar with Aubri," Mr. Darrow said, "let's see if she can keep you focused."

"What?" she asked, too surprised by the suggestion to wonder about the sudden deflection.

Looking over, Aubri was already standing up, pulling off the baggy hoodie she had been wearing since Sibylla had met her.

Underneath the hoodie, she was wearing a form-fitting shirt that was more colors than Sibylla typically saw on a shirt. The hues of greens and oranges and reds and blues seemed at first to just be a kaleidoscope of random patterns thrown onto fabric. On anyone else, Sibylla might have thought it looked gaudy or ridiculous, and she certainly never would have bought it herself. But it seemed to fit Aubri, matching her confidence and vibe. Her hair was still in its Viking braid, the sides shaved down to the skin. a playful expectancy danced in her eyes.

It occurred to her that she had been staring at Aubri's shirt longer than she needed to. Then she noticed that Aubri had also taken the sunglasses off with the hoodie, her glittering blue eyes on full display.

"You keep getting knocked down," Mr. Darrow explained, pulling her attention back to him. "You need to get your focus back."

Aubri, padded gloves on her hands and shins, bounced on her toes and punched the air lightly in different combinations. Her movements were effortless and practiced like she had been fighting since birth.

"Some advice," Mr. Darrow whispered, motioning Sibylla close. "Don't hold back, because she won't." He winked at Sibylla and rolled off the mats.

"What do you-" Sibylla started to ask but was cut off when she saw rapid movement out of the corner of her eye.

She ducked instinctively and rolled to the side, barely avoiding Aubri's onslaught of jabs and punches. For the next thirty seconds, Sibylla focused purely on dodging, so much so that at no point even considered her counterattacks. Aubri was as quick as lightning and incredibly efficient. If she had a weakness or soft spot, Sibylla couldn't find it.

"Damn," she gasped when Aubri finally let up. Aubri giggled and bounced on her toes playfully.

"You're faster than you look," Aubri said. To Sibylla's annoyance, she wasn't even breathing hard. "I'm impressed."

"No... need... to patronize," Sibylla said, trying to suck in as much air as possible between words.

Aubri giggled again and Sibylla was thankful her face was already beet red and covered in sweat.

"Your turn," Aubri said, still bouncing on her toes. Tapping her gloves together she adopted a fighting stance Sibylla hadn't seen before, standing at a half crouch and hands low, by her hips. She had an eager energy, as though she had been waiting all night for the opportunity to fight Sibylla.

Sibylla bounced on her toes, trying to loosen up and reorient her energy. Her calves and arms ached, and sweat dripped from her nose. As they circled each other Sibylla wracked her brain trying to think of something she could do that would make a dent in Aubri's defense. Aubri was fast, but she had focused on strikes, not takedowns. Maybe if Sibylla could shake Aubri's balance she could take her to the ground and try grappling. Sibylla wasn't great at grappling, but so far she was worse at striking.

It turned out to be a terrible mistake. First, it took too long to get Aubri off balance. She was just too quick and could read Sibylla's moves before she'd even tried to grab her or take her down. Then, just when Sibylla thought she saw an opening, it proved to be an inescapable trap. By the time Mr. Darrow had blown the whistle, Aubri had Sibylla's head tucked under her arm and Sibylla's waist trapped in her legs.

Rolling onto her back, chest heaving, Sibylla wondered if there had ever been a time she'd been beaten so badly. Sibylla knew she had been soundly whipped. She also knew that she didn't mind. Was it embarrassing? A little. The fact that the girl was an utter machine took the edge off, however. That and she was beaming, which made Sibylla happy enough to let it go.

"Look," Aubri said, holding up a finger. Hanging precariously at the tip was a bead of sweat.

"Wow," Sibylla said playfully, gesturing at herself. She was covered head to toe in sweat, her skin glistening in the fluorescent gym lights. "I hardly call it even."

Aubri flicked the sweat away and sat down on the pad next to Sibylla. "Maybe so, but still better than I expected."

"Gee thanks," Sibylla replied, taking a drink of water.

Looking up from her water bottle she saw that the glow in Aubri's eyes had intensified somewhat, practically glittering. To Sibylla, they seemed like sapphires in the sun, pure and translucent yet brimming with a deep blue she'd never really seen anywhere else.

"Sorry," she said awkwardly when Aubri arched an eyebrow. "I've never seen eyes like yours, they almost look like they're glowing in this light."

Aubri's smile faltered and the sunglasses came out again, much to Sibylla's disappointment.

"Hey," Sibylla said, "I didn't mean to make you awkward. I think you look better without the sunglasses though, for what it's worth."

Aubri paused, hand halfway to her face. "No lies?" she asked.

Sibylla nodded, "Yeah."

A shriek reverberated across the gym and Sibylla broke eye contact to see who had made the noise. To her surprise, Katie had Nate and Hunter by the ears, one in each hand, and was dragging them off the mats.

"Y'all should know when to quit," Katie was saying. Sibylla didn't even attempt to hide her smile.

"How long have you guys been fighting?" Aubri asked, pulling Sibylla's attention back.

Sibylla noticed that Aubri had placed her sunglasses back on the mat, next to her hoody.

"A couple of years now," Sibylla said, smiling, "Mr. Darrow has been training me and the twins over there, trying to get us into fighting shape. Which, by the way, completely failed to prepare me for someone like you. You are absolutely ridiculous."

Embarrassed, Aubri started to pull off her gloves and pads. "It's hard to explain. The easy way is that my parents liked the idea of me being a fighter, just like my brother."

"You have a brother?" Sibylla asked, trying to pick the right topic to keep the conversation going. Aubri was looking more and more uncomfortable, something about her past preventing her from being herself. When Aubri didn't answer, Sibylla switched tactics.

"Did Mr. Darrow take you on then?" she asked instead, "for the job?"

"More or less," Aubri said, relaxing with the change in topic. "Part-time, he said. Possibly running… errands from time to time."

"Part-time?" Sibylla asked. "What're you doing with the rest of your time if you're not helping out here on Sundays?"

"I thought I could spend some more time with you," Aubri replied.

Sibylla blinked, the flutter returning. "What? Why?"

"Darrow mentioned that the class is getting too easy for you. I think we could challenge each other pretty well, don't you?" Aubri replied.

"You could challenge me, that's for sure," Sibylla scoffed, "I think you'd get bored."

"You underestimate yourself," Aubri replied, "I think you would do a great job keeping me interested."

Sibylla found herself at a loss for words, unsure of what to say or do. To her sleep-deprived brain, the idea that Aubri may be flirting with her seemed ridiculous.

"Maybe we can put it to the test sometime?" Aubri asked, saving Sibylla from saying something embarrassing.

"Absolutely," Sibylla replied, thankful. A chirp from her phone drew her attention and she saw that it was Kane, wanting to know when she would be done with the fight club so they could hang out.

"Sorry," she said, "I gotta go. But I'll catch you later."

"I will hold you to it," Aubri said, smiling broadly.

I certainly hope so, Sibylla thought, blushing slightly while she rushed to the locker room.

ψ

After a few minutes everyone had filtered out, and Mr. Darrow found himself alone with Aubri, who continued to stare at the locker room door, deep in thought.

"You don't have to do that, you know," Mr. Darrow said. "Though I deeply appreciate it."

"I want to do it," Aubri said quietly. "It's refreshing to be around her, she's so… different… from anyone back home."

"I don't doubt it," Mr. Darrow chuckled. "She is a force of nature."

"Do you think it'll happen this week?" Aubri asked, looking down at him.

Mr. Darrow sighed. "It'll be Sunday at the latest, though I expect it to come earlier."

"Will she be ready?" Aubri asked, sounding worried.

"I hope so," Mr. Darrow said, an edge of trepidation in his voice. "I truly hope so. In the meantime, I need you to run an errand for me if you don't mind missing some sleep."

"Of course," Aubri said. "What do you need?"

"How do you feel about hunting?"

Chapter 8

The next night for Sibylla passed blessedly without anything happening at all. The howling of the wolves that had been hounding her disappeared as suddenly as fog in the sunlight. Sibylla barely noticed, too focused on trying to distract herself from thinking about the picture. Who could she ask for more information about it?

Asking Roger was a nonstarter, he seemed content to pretend that Delphine had never existed. Trying to pry an answer out of him would have been disastrous as their confrontation from a few weeks prior. He had been avoiding Sibylla since that argument, which suited her just fine since she was also trying to avoid him.

Asking Mr. Darrow had a higher chance of success, but Sibylla wasn't sure what kind of answer she would get from him about it, considering how quickly he had moved on when she had asked him about it the first time. She didn't think he would lie to her, necessarily, and there wasn't anything about the picture or their relationship that prompted her to think that he would.

Unfortunately, the picture couldn't occupy too much of her attention. Distressingly, Kane had seemed more annoyed with her than he had before, and Sibylla couldn't blame him. In the few weeks since their Halloween visit to the gate, they had barely seen each other outside of class. Daily she got texts wanting to know where she was, or why she was ghosting him. More than once they had talked on the phone and Sibylla had just been able to calm him down, assuring him she was falling behind on her schoolwork and needed to buckle down.

That had sparked the unforeseen argument that her school work was more important than he was, but she had been able to take his mind off of it by letting him know that she wouldn't be able to go with him to college if she started to fail her classes. That had bought her a few days at least, and she had only gotten glowing messages and voicemails from him since.

As Monday night ended, however, she knew that she at the very least needed to add in more time for him. Plus, if she did, she might be able to finally talk about the picture with someone other than her brothers.

Tuesday morning began with her door being thrown open and her brothers charging in shouting "HAPPY BIRTHDAY!" at the top of their lungs.

Their volume was on par with an explosion, sending her sprawling to the floor with a startled yelp, trapped in a tangle of sheets.

"What is wrong with you?" she gasped.

"Birthday cheer!" Hunter shouted.

"Enough to go around!" Nate added, just as loudly. "Come on grumpy pants, we got your favorite breakfast waiting for you on the table."

Checking her phone she saw it was five-thirty in the morning. She groaned and stood stiffly, noting that at least she had managed to sleep the whole night through again. The wolves had given up on torturing her, or maybe put it on hold for her birthday.

"Can I ask why you thought five was the best time to wake me up?" she yawned, following them into the hallway toward the kitchen.

"Don't blame us," Hunter said.

"Your birth certificate said five thirty, so five thirty it is," Nate added. He pulled out a chair and gestured for her to sit.

"You had to look at my birth certificate to know when my birthday was?" Sibylla asked, rubbing her eyes.

"Of course not!" Hunter said defensively. He brought in a plate of eggs and pancakes with a side of bacon. "You're seventeen, officially an adult according to North Korea."

"Yippee," she yawned. "Give Kim Jong-un my best."

"He already knows!" Nate said.

"He knows everything!" Hunter said cheerfully. "He's god!"

Sibylla groaned and pushed the plate away to make room for her head on the table.

"So I can blame him for having you two as brothers?" she asked, voice muffled.

"Sorry comrade," Hunter said sadly, "you can only blame capitalists for something like that."

"Sounds like something they would do," Nate confirmed.

"You guys are the worst," she muttered.

Having the Ginger Twins as brothers usually meant that they were thoughtful in the most aggressive, disruptive way possible. But the food smelled heavenly, and who was she to turn down food made by someone else? So she sat up and ate, trying to shake the cobwebs of sleep from her brain. They busied themselves with cleaning up the mess they'd created in the kitchen. It was pretty good.

"Y'all are going to be useless at school today," she said. "You must have gotten up early for this."

"Firstly, anything for our big sis," Nate said. He slid into the seat next to hers.

"Secondly, we never went to bed, so no big deal," Hunter added, sliding into the seat on the other side.

Sibylla glanced from side to side, feeling a sense of dread come over her, realizing what they had done everything for.

"What do you guys want?" she asked.

"Just a wee favor," Nate said, "nothing crazy."

"You want me to cover for you ditching school, again?" she asked, the pieces clicking together before they had a chance to ask.

"Nope!" Nate said then thought for a moment before adding "Well, ish." He pulled a folded piece of paper from his pocket and held it out to her. "Just hand this to those nice ladies in the office and that's it!"

"Done!" Hunter chirped.

Sibylla stared at the note for a long minute, weighing her options. They were going to stay home no matter what. It would take a miracle for her to convince them it was a bad idea, or at least it would take more time than she had. The only time she had ever actually talked them out of something dangerous or stupid had been when they had tried to tie firecrackers to Sir Moo's tail. And that had only been a success because of threats of violence and a bucket of water.

"Fine," Sibylla snatched the note.

"Thanks," Hunter said, "his Respected Comrade Kim Jong-un will be most pleased!"

"Happy birthday!" Nate kissed her cheek and then they were out the door, leaving her alone in the dining room.

Sibylla spent the next hour getting ready for school, lost in thought while she packed her backpack. Two full weeks had come and gone, and she could barely remember anything about them. Outside of her sparring session with Aubri, anyway. Holding her open backpack she glanced at its contents and realized that she had accidentally packed her hairbrush with everything else. Aubri was the only other thing that seemed to occupy her mind. A chirp came from her pocket, her phone's reminder going off to let her know that she needed to be out the door in the next five minutes if she wanted to stay on track.

Unfortunately, Roger was waiting for her when she came out into the living room. Sibylla was surprised to see him at all, as it was a rare thing to see him in the morning as he was usually at work before any of them had even woken up.

"Happy birthday," he said flatly.

"Thanks," Sibylla said, matching his tone.

"It's a big day, turning seventeen," he continued, "at least in our family it is. I, uh…"

He trailed off and looked down at his hands. Sibylla saw that he was holding something wrapped in colorful paper and bound with a purple ribbon.

"Did you… did you get me a gift?" Sibylla was surprised. Gifts were rarer than seeing Roger in the morning, even for birthdays or holidays. Even more so, considering how little they had interacted since their last fight.

"Yes," he said. "Your mom…," he trailed off. "We agreed to… Well, it's a big birthday." Without another word, he held it out for her to take, which she did after a moment's hesitation. It was the most emotion he'd shown in some time, apart from being angry. At the mention of her mom, however, her focus snapped to the gift in her hands.

"You don't need to open it now," Roger stood up, "I'll tell you more about it when you get home."

"Promise?" Sibylla said, uncertain. "You won't change your mind?" It had taken years, but Sibylla had long since learned to expect disappointments from him. With everything else that had happened between them, she was hesitant to change her mind.

Roger held her gaze a long moment before answering. "Not today, I promise."

Before she could say or ask anything else Roger walked through the front door and disappeared into the early morning light. The roar of his truck and tires crunching gravel signaled that he too had left Sibylla alone in the house. Then there was no sound except for the beat of her racing heart. The gift was heavy in her hands, in more ways than one.

Presented with the first actual connection to her mom, someone she had dreamed about meeting and knowing, Sibylla found herself hesitating to open it. A part of her was terrified of being let down by whatever lay beneath the paper, that it would be something pointless or unfulfilling. She didn't think she could handle seeing something like a "Chicken Soup for the Soul" book or a scrapbook or something.

Running her fingers gently over the paper she could feel ridges and bumps, suggesting that she was safe in that regard. Most of the newer books wouldn't have such an intense texture to it.

"I Will Always Love You" blasted from her pocket, making Sibylla flinch so hard she almost dropped her gift.

"For Pete's sake," she muttered, heart rate slowly returning to normal.

Kane had picked the song as his ringtone in her phone and had insisted it described how he felt about Sibylla. Picking specific ringtones for people wasn't something Sibylla normally did, even for Kayla, but it had felt right at the time. Since then she had been afraid to hurt his feelings by changing it back, and he liked to call it while they were together so that he could hear it. Grabbing the present from the floor with one hand, Sibylla answered her phone with the other.

"Happy birthday beautiful!" Kane sang. "It's another glorious day of your life on this Earth!"

"Thanks, handsome!" she said back, smiling.

"How's the prettiest girl in Red Falls doing on this fine Tuesday morning?" he asked.

"Running late," she chuckled, locking the front door.

"Not today you're not!" Kane said with mock sternness. "You can't be late on your birthday, physically, it's impossible! Time bends to your whim!"

"I wish," she said, starting her car.

"I know you do," he said, a smile in his voice. "I just wanted to see how far out you were, what you're wearing, normal stuff."

"Yeah yeah," Sibylla said, smiling. "I'm leaving my house now, I won't be too long though."

"Good! I have the perfect birthday planned," he said. "Presents, flowers, dinner at a fancy restaurant. You know, the works."

"Dinner? At a fancy restaurant?" Sibylla asked, looking down at her outfit.

There wasn't a fancy restaurant anywhere near town, except for one that claimed to be Italian. Still, for a birthday dinner, she didn't think it would be right to wear worn-out jeans and a hoodie. Maybe she could find time to run home after school or borrow something from Kayla.

"Yeah! Remember, I told you last week so that you'd make time for it?" he replied an edge of doubt in his voice. "Today I have to be more important than your homework!"

"Right!" Sibylla exclaimed, not remembering for a second what he was talking about. The last two weeks had been pretty hectic though, so she might have just forgotten. Guilt rearing its ugly head, Sibylla lied. "Sorry, it's been a wild morning. The Ginger Twins had me up at five thirty, I'm still waking up."

"Good!" he sounded relieved. "Alright, I gotta prep some stuff, I'll see you in thirty!"

Chapter 9

Sibylla drove in silence for a few minutes, the fields of grain and grass sliding by unnoticed as she tried to process her brief interaction with Roger.

Will he actually tell me everything? She thought doubtfully.

Glancing down, Sibylla saw that some of the fragile wrapping paper had ripped on the present. Through the tear, she could see what looked like leather peeking back at her. Fingers drumming on the steering wheel, Sibylla wondered what it could be. Something important enough that Roger and Delphine had both decided that she had to wait until she turned seventeen to receive it.

Finally, Sibylla pulled the car to the shoulder and put it in park. She looked down at the gift and ran her fingers along the smooth surface of the paper. It was old and felt brittle, probably wrapped when they agreed to give it to her. There was a small part of her that still didn't want to see what was in it, to just let it sit a little longer, unopened. A much bigger part of her could not, would not, wait.

Grabbing the edge of the brittle paper Sibylla tore it away, not stopping until she held only the book. The scent of old paper wafted to her nose, filling the car with its pleasant scent. It was definitely old. It was a beautiful book, ancient-looking and well-preserved. What caught her attention more than anything else was the title, pressed into the leather and coated in gold leaf.

The Hunter's Guide to Werewolves. Beneath the title was an illustration of a man holding a spear against a wolf that stood on two legs, almost twice as tall, its jaws open to expose sharp-looking teeth. At some point, there might have been paint or dye, but the evidence was still contained within the deeper lines of the illustration. Leafing carefully through the pages Sibylla found dozens of intricately detailed illustrations, showing everything from the anatomy of a standing wolf compared to a human to traps holding or killing them.

Turning to the first page she saw there was a list of previous owners, dozens of them. Some names stuck out, like Horatio the Weller, Diamond Lou, or Nicholas the Skinner. Others were more mundane, like Peter, Lucas, or Nathaniel. Some names were difficult to pronounce, like Enguerran and Vauquelin, or like Adlebehrt and Apelbeorht. The sheer breadth and variety were staggering.

At the very top, the first name written in the book was something that looked like it could have been Felix, though it was worn and faded. Turning to the next page she saw that the list of names continued. Her eyes drifted down the list and stopped at the last two entries. The first name she recognized, written unsurprisingly in gold ink: Howard Baft. Under his name, written side by side were Roger and Delphine. It had taken her some time to move past them, spending several minutes running her fingers along the graceful arcs of her mother's name.

Diving deeper into the book, trying to soften the dull ache in her heart, Sibylla found stunning hand-drawn illustrations. There were also a lot of handwritten notes, mostly along the lines of translations, as the first dozen pages or so appeared to be in Latin, though that was more of a guess than anything else.

It struck Sibylla as she turned each page that people had been adding to the book. After the Latin entries there were some in a language she didn't know, then in what she assumed to be German, then French, then another language she didn't know. The images too had the telltale signatures of multiple contributors. All of them were very detailed, some looking like they had been done by actual artists, others looking like the contributor was giving it their very best. Some of the earlier entries had sticky notes or note cards tucked in next to them where someone else had translated the passage.

"Tonight," she said, reluctantly putting it in the passenger seat. "It can wait until tonight."

Arriving on campus, thoughts so focused on the book and its implications, Sibylla almost missed the crowd of students milling at the edge of the school where the student lot met the building. Between her and them were three football players that she immediately recognized.

"Hey, Trey! Hey Brandon, Isaiah!" she said cheerfully, thankful for the distraction.

"Happy birthday!" Brandon said.

"Thanks," Sibylla said, eying them suspiciously. "Y'all look like you have a secret."

"I don't know what you mean," Trey said, brightening. There was a gleam in his eye that made Sibylla feel uncomfortable.

"Kane has something... special planned for you today," Isaia added, receiving a sharp elbow to the ribs.

Sibylla furrowed her brows. "Please tell me you're kidding."

The three players glanced at each other and chuckled. It could have been nerves, it could have been the fact that she had barely slept in the past several weeks, whatever it was, Sibylla did not like the vibe coming from their little group. She wanted nothing more than to get away from them.

"Prince Charming awaits," Trey said, sweeping his arm toward the school. It was then that Sibylla saw the fringes of the crowd, watching her expectantly.

"We'd love to see your face when you get there," Trey chimed in, " but we have to do something for Coach. We'll catch you on the flip side though."

"Good luck," Brandon said, "Try to enjoy it."

He gave her a quick hug that Sibylla wanted to end immediately and the three of them walked off toward the football field behind the school. Sibylla looked at the crowd, chittering away and glancing back and forth with glee and anticipation. As much as she begged him not to, Kane liked to do things big. It was his way, and she knew that.

Chances were that he would have done several smaller things throughout the past few weeks, but she'd been too busy to give him the chance. Now it was all coming out, all at once. She squared her shoulders and marched resolutely toward the door.

The students scurried away at her approach, looking for all the world like happy little cockroaches. Already Sibylla could see the birthday signs in some of the windows, and balloons drifting lazily from the front door handles. Kane liked putting people on pedestals in the limelight, it was how he showed affection. She had learned to accept that. She walked through the front doors and was confronted by what looked like half the school population waiting for her in the foyer. As one, they bellowed out "Surprise!!"

"Oh my gosh!" she said, feigning surprise. "Thank you all!"

"It's not over yet honey bun!" a voice echoed through the school intercom system.

Honey Bun was a bold choice for a nickname, certainly not one he'd ever used so far. Or even one she appreciated. She tried to relax. He had put serious effort into the whole thing, who was she to slap him down? Any other girl would dream of having this kind of attention.

What came next was Kane, carried through the crowd of students on a folding table held aloft by the football team. In one hand he had a microphone, in the other he held a rose. He threw her a wink and signaled someone Sibylla couldn't see. A moment later the beginning sounds of Happy Birthday filtered through the intercom, joined at first by Kane, then the rest of the student body.

Covering her face in her hands, Sibylla knew it was as red as a tomato. The students took it as bashful playfulness, which it was. At least a little. Most of it was straight-up horror at the scale of the presentation.

"Happy birthday baby," Kane said, kneeling in front of her. Another nickname he'd never used, mostly because she had asked him not to. He presented the rose and she took it with a sheepish grin, eliciting a cheer from the gathered student body.

"Please tell me this is all you have planned today," she said, giving him a quick kiss.

"This is all I have planned today," Kane parroted, winking at her.

"Kane!" she pleaded in a harsh whisper, keeping the smile plastered on her face for the sake of appearances. He was already disappearing into the crowd. The bell cut through the chatter of anticipation that still rippled through the students. Like an ocean they closed in behind Kane, cutting him off from any further attempt to convince him that he had already done more than enough.

Outwardly, Sibylla shook her head with a grin. Inwardly she was dying. While she had spent plenty of time being on stage at the center of attention for plays or sports, Sibylla hated it. After years of doing speeches and presentations, however, she had learned that it was simply the price to pay, an unfortunate side effect of being in high school.

Being the center of attention for her birthday, however, was mortifying.

Kayla came out of nowhere and hooked Sibylla's arm, pulling her through the milling crowd toward their first class.

"Gotta keep you on time!" she said. "How's your big day going so far?"

"Great!" Sibylla smiled at the students who jostled her, saying 'Happy birthday' before disappearing on their way to class. Leaning closer, she whispered, "It's a lot, too much."

"I tried to tell him," Kayla whispered back, "but he's convinced this is his best play."

"Please tell me this is it," Sibylla whispered back, looking over her shoulder and seeing the banner in the front hall that read 'Happy Birthday Red!'

"You're cute when you're dumb," Kayla said with a smile. "Gird your loins. And remember, he's doing something super special, so try to have some fun with it."

Sibylla tried to demand clarification but Kayla had been swallowed by the crowd before she had the chance. Unfortunately, Kayla hadn't been lying about Sibylla needing to brace herself. Horrified, Sibylla was visited by Kane in each one of her classes, each time singing a song or reciting a poem, with gifts of flowers and chocolates. He even managed to bring in a three-tiered cake for lunch, complete with sparklers. She did her best to smile and act like it was what she wanted, but it was too much attention.

There was no denying that he had put a lot of thought and effort into planning it all out, and Sibylla was genuinely impressed that he had gotten as much support as he had from the staff and teachers of the school. With all of the disruptions, they may as well have declared it a town holiday and given everyone the day off. One of the benefits of small town living, she supposed, was being able to convince educators that Sibylla's birthday was more important than academics.

Chapter 10

When the last bell rang Sibylla cut across the gym and through the cafeteria to the hall that housed Mr. Darrow's classroom. The excess attention had convinced Sibylla to gain some more time from whatever Kane had planned by finally deciding to approach Mr. Darrow about the picture again. Thankfully his door was wide open, and he didn't seem too busy, staring out the window, lost in thought. She coughed once and knocked lightly on the door before entering.

"What's up Red?" he asked, looking up from his computer. "Aren't you supposed to be serenaded by your boyfriend right now?"

"Yeah, sure," she said. She shoved her hands in her pockets and leaned against the door frame. As much as she wanted to know about the image and what it meant, the urge to discuss it had dulled somewhat.

There's no reason to rush, she thought, glancing down the hallway. The sounds of a crowd growing impatient were already drifting toward her through the closed double doors.

"I just had a quick question about something that we didn't get to finish talking about earlier, would now be a good time?"

"I'll do what I can," he said. He pulled out from behind the desk and met her halfway.

Sibylla reached into her pocket and withdrew the picture that had been haunting her for the past two weeks. Every detail of the image was familiar to her, to the point that she could probably sketch it from memory.

"What can you tell me about this?" she asked.

For a long, awkward moment Mr. Darrow only stared at the picture, almost through it. It was as if he wasn't in the room anymore, lost in thought in a memory. Finally, he reached out with trembling hands and took the picture. He sat back in his chair, the sound of creaking leather being the only sound in the room.

"Well," he sighed, "I knew that this would be coming up again. What'd your dad say when you showed it to him?"

"Nothing," she said, "I didn't think he'd give me much about it. We haven't been talking for a minute now."

Nodding, Mr. Darrow turned the picture over in his hands again and again.

"Why?" she asked when it became clear he wasn't going to be volunteering any answers.

"Damn," he said wistfully, "we were so freaking young, practically kids."

For a minute Sibylla was unsure of how to get him back to the present. With every passing second, try as she might to avoid it, she could feel irritation beginning to boil. She was tired of mysteries and riddles and waiting. Was it too much to want a straight answer?

"You caught me at a weird time, Red," he finally replied, rubbing the bridge of his nose. "This is a big day for me, and I have no idea how it's going to end. Unfortunately for you, that also means I can't tell you much about this."

Disappointment hit her like a dump truck. Deciding to bring the picture to him had been a delaying tactic, keeping back the inevitable tidal wave of unwanted attention from her classmates and boyfriend. The two weeks of staring at it had taken its toll, however, and it was impossible to keep its evidence from her expression.

"I'm sorry kiddo, I can't be the one to tell you," he said.

"Come on!" Sibylla protested. "This is driving me nuts!"

"It has to be your dad," Mr. Darrow said, holding up his hands. "I don't know what to tell you."

"Literally anything," she muttered, slumping into her desk. She rubbed her eyes with the heels of her palms in frustration. "It would be nice to know something about any of this."

A chirp came from her pocket. Sibylla pulled her phone out resignedly, expecting a text from Kane telling her to hurry up. When she saw it, however, she furrowed her brow. It was from an unknown number, which was weird enough. Stranger still was that it was a picture of a barn, her barn she realized. At the center of the photo, their backs to the camera, apparently unaware of the picture being taken, were her brothers.

"Everything good?" Mr. Darrow asked.

Before Sibylla answered, another text came in.

ANONYMOUS: The monsters are coming.

"I don't know," Sibylla said absentmindedly, trying to understand its meaning. "I think it's just a prank."

Something about it didn't sit quite right for a prank. A cold dread twitched up her fingers and toes, joined by a lump in her gut. There was something there, something dark that her subconscious didn't like.

ANONYMOUS: Wanna race for blood?

ANONYMOUS: I bet we'll get there first.

"I need to go," Sibylla said, rising from her desk. The lump had turned into ice, spreading quickly to her limbs.

"You okay?" Mr. Darrow asked, rolling forward, concerned.

"Thanks for looking at the picture," Sibylla said quickly, trying to seem normal. "See you tomorrow!"

Instead of going down the hall to the front door, Sibylla cut back through the cafeteria and into the gym, where she almost ran face first into Coach Savage's chest.

"Where are you going, Lavigne?" Coach Savage said, mispronouncing her name again.

"To my car?" she said, her jitters increasing exponentially.

"I don't think so young lady," he said, a grin on his face. "Your beau put some effort into the finale, I'd hate for you to miss it."

"Oh, right." Sibylla said, giving him her best disarming smile, injecting a light tone to her voice, "Just pretend you didn't see me, no one has to know."

Just freaking move, she thought miserably, feeling her heart rate begin to climb.

"Negative," he chuckled, misinterpreting her thinly veiled anxiety. "It's the price of love I'm afraid."

He jerked his head toward the opposite side of the gym and Sibylla sighed, shoving her phone into her pocket. Each step across the empty gym echoed like thunder, matching the sound and beat of the blood thumping in her ears. Anxiety worked its way through her veins, pulling blood from her hands and feet, goosebumps chasing it across the surface of her skin.

"You have to admit," Coach Savage said as he fell in step with her, "he's put some real effort into this."

"I know," she said, trying but failing to hide the misery she was feeling. "He's a good guy. Though I would have liked it better if he'd scaled it back a touch."

"Not really his style, is it? The kid has some pretty big feelings," Coach Savage said. "In his defense, I've never seen him do this for anyone else. That means something, doesn't it?"

She wanted to say 'It means getting home to check on the twins is going to take an eternity.'

"I guess," she replied instead. She barely noticed her fingers twitching at her side and curled into loose fists. The itch to sprint through the crowd to her car was unbearable.

They pushed through the double doors that led out into the hallway. Being small, the school had a simple layout. In the center was the main hall which housed the main office and security. At the end of the main hall was a kind of 'T' intersection, one hall going to the locker rooms and the gym, the other hall going toward the wing that had all of the classrooms in it.

Between the two halls were two double doors at the end of the hall leading to the cafeteria. The gym also had doors into the cafeteria, as did the classroom wing.

What it meant was that Sibylla could see what she was walking into as soon as she left the gym. A large crowd of students started cheering, the cheerleaders forming a gauntlet that led into it. Sibylla's heart rate went into overdrive.

"Deep breath kiddo," Coach Savage said, "godspeed."

Sibylla nodded and plastered a smile on her face that she hoped came across as genuine. The noise increased as she got closer, much to her chagrin. The morning introduction only had part of the student body present, and now the rest wanted to make up for their absence with increased enthusiasm. At the end of the gauntlet, Kane dressed as a prince, struck a pose behind a chair that was decorated to look like a throne. 'For my Princess' was painted on the white washed wood in deep red.

Wanna race for blood?

Sibylla stumbled and barely caught herself, drawing ragged breaths. Her mind was a kaleidoscope of whirling thoughts and contradictory commands, simultaneously trying to convince herself it was a prank while also commanding her legs to run. The crowd and noise filled whatever gaps were left, and for a moment she froze in place, every single one of her senses overwhelmed. It was like a computer with too many tabs open, threatening to crash.

Her phone went off again, its quiet tone seeming to cut through the cacophony of noise that crashed around her. Hands shaking so badly she almost dropped it, Sibylla managed to open it and saw another picture, looking through a crack between the old dried up boards, her brothers looking at a trunk of some kind, only a few feet away.

UNKNOWN: tick tock Red.

Chapter 11

It was a heartbeat. A fraction of a second. One moment she was standing in a crowd of her classmates.

Heartbeat.

Sibylla was sprinting across the parking lot to her car.

Heartbeat.

Driving recklessly through town, ignoring the honks of protest at her cutting people off.

Heartbeat.

She was tearing down the gravel drive that led to her house.

The idea that she may need a plan hit her when her old beat up car hit the first rock in the field on the way to the barn. The impact shook loose the grip fear had on her brain for a brief moment, reminding her that, somewhere, was a person who could be incredibly dangerous and that she had no real way of dealing with them. She slammed on the brakes, the old car skidding to a halt a few feet from the tall swinging door of the barn.

Without stopping to take a breath, her hands shaking and cold, Sibylla kicked her door open and tried to get out. Unfortunately, she had, at some point, managed to buckle herself in without realizing it. Grunting with frustration, fumbling, and cursing through gritted teeth, she managed to press the release and lurched out of the car. Not bothering to shut the door, she sprinted around the front of the car, heart pounding in her ears.

Swinging the wide door open, she ran inside. The interior of the barn was much as it always had been: littered with random boxes of rotting cardboard, moldy hay, and sacks of feed piled haphazardly in the corner. Sitting in the middle of it all, perched on an old decrepit trunk, bound together with thick ropes and gagged with duct tape, were Nathan and Hunter.

Without hesitation, she sprinted over to them and began tearing at their ropes.

"It's okay guys, I'm here," she said quickly, trying to sound much calmer than she felt.

Trying to dig her fingers into the knots, she was thwarted by the constant wiggling and groaning through their gags. After a moment she hissed in frustration and tore the duct tape off Hunter's face, eliciting a sharp grunt.

"What?!" she demanded.

"Look!" His voice was hoarse but urgent.

Sibylla realized then the error she had made. It hadn't occurred to her that she would need to look around for the person or people that had tied her brothers up. Her brothers had become her sole focus, not the danger that they were in. When she turned, all conscious thought ceased the instant her eyes landed on the threat standing at the door of the barn.

At first, her mind couldn't make sense of what she was seeing.

"You don't exist," she murmured, hands clenched into fists, fingernails digging into her palms.

It was the gate on Halloween all over again. It was the locker room at the school, haunting her. All the shapes and shadows, all the hints of something on the edge of her consciousness, all the things she had convinced herself couldn't exist, not in the real world. Not in Red Falls.

But she couldn't deny what was standing right in front of her.

Standing on two legs at almost eight feet tall, its pointed ears brushing the top of the doorframe, the thing looked like a wolf had been stretched and distorted, a nightmarish combination with the misshapen form of a man, covered in bloody sores and splits in its skin. Fingers flexed in anticipation, and great globs of drool dripped from its lips, which were stretched over its jagged teeth into what could have been a smile.

"Hello Red," a hoarse, cruel voice said above her.

Sibylla's head whipped up at the sound of her name, where another werewolf was crouched in the rafters above her. A guttural chuckle behind her and she spun again, where two more werewolves stood in the opposite door. Sibylla and her brothers were completely surrounded, cut off in a barn outside of city limits, entirely alone.

Sibylla shook violently, unable to think of anything besides being torn to pieces by mythical monsters. Small flashes of other thoughts broke through, things like how disappointed Kane looked. Or how she wished she could have made peace with her dad, or found out what was so important that he wanted to tell her. Her tenth birthday, when she had gone to an arcade. Things that didn't matter and that didn't distract her from a very obvious truth.

She was about to die.

The second werewolf dropped from the rafter, landing heavily a few paces away. Sibylla took a defensive stance, not thinking for a minute she could fight the nightmare in front of her. The monster laughed a sound like gravel being run through a blender.

Strangely, instead of invoking fear, it lit a fire in Sibylla's chest. Somewhere deep inside there was a part of her that was angry, furious even, about the situation she was in. The moment the feeling awoke in her, the werewolf stopped, a flash of confusion crossing its face. If Sibylla hadn't been so distracted by her anger at the potential of her demise, she might have laughed.

A shot like thunder exploded from outside the barn. One of the werewolves behind Sibylla howled in pain and rage, and the one standing in front of her snarled and dropped to all fours. Sibylla spun and tackled her brothers off the trunk, crashing with them to the ground when the thunder struck again. Something wet splashed across Sibylla's back and neck, unnoticed. Several more shots rang out and the werewolves, caught off balance, scrambled away from the new threat.

"Sibylla!" A rough hand grabbed her hoodie and yanked her to her feet. "Sibylla look at me!"

Sibylla opened her eyes and was shocked by her dad's appearance. Instead of the flannel and jeans she had come to associate with him, he was wearing body armor that was covered in shotgun shells and knives. In his hands, he held a shotgun, its barrel still smoking from its recent activity. He was shoving shells into the chamber, eyes darting from hers to over her shoulder.

"I don't have time to explain," he said, "I have to do this."

"Do what?" she managed to squeak out, panic and uncertainty constricting her voice.

"I have to give you the mantle," he replied mysteriously, "they want me, but they can't have the mantle." He paused, pursing his lips. "There's so much I should have told you. Get your brothers out of here and keep them safe."

Before Sibylla had a chance to ask him to repeat and explain any of it, an intense burning sensation exploded in her shoulder where his hand was touching her. His eyes were squeezed shut in concentration, his grip strong and firm, keeping her from pulling away. The heating seared through every inch of her, taking her breath away. The world around her seemed to pop with new sights and sounds and smells she had never noticed before, the sensory overload almost sending her to her knees. Then, as quick as it had come, it was gone.

Roger opened his eyes and he smiled at her weakly. A single tear rolled down his cheek.

"Do better than I did Sibby. I love you," his eyes were drawn over his shoulder and hardened in recognition. "Get them out of here!" he barked, and let go of Sibylla. Then he was gone.

Sibylla looked at her hands, confusion coursing through her like the heat.

"Come on!" a familiar voice said. Sibylla looked up and saw Aubri striding into the barn.

If she had been surprised by Roger's appearance, she was shocked looking at Aubri. Her face was covered in gray ash, applied in streaks that made it look like a fire had come through her flashing blue eyes and scorched her face. She wore body armor similar to Roger's, a strange pistol in one hand, a knife in the other.

"Come on," Aubri urged, using her knife to cut Hunter and Nate free. "We need to run!"

"What about my dad?" Sibylla rasped, finally finding her voice.

The boom of his shotgun echoed close by, joined by the crack of a rifle. Part of her wanted to follow Roger's instructions, to run away and get to safety. Fighting back was another part that wanted to grab the first thing that looked like a weapon and rush out to join him, to help him.

A growl reverberated through the air, one of the werewolves coming through the doors behind Aubri. Sibylla recognized it as the werewolf that had dropped down from the rafters. Evading Roger, it had circled back, intent on finishing what it had started. Aubri spun and her long knife spun through the air, connecting with the monster's chest. The growl ended abruptly, replaced by a wet gurgle. Without another sound he fell face first, unmoving.

"Now!" Aubri said, grabbing Sibylla's hand. "We need to go now!"

Nate and Hunter went first, coming to their senses and following Aubri's directions without further hesitation. Sibylla stood rooted to the floor, paralyzed by fear, fatigue, and indecision. The shotgun went off again, further away, and a rifle shot rang out almost immediately after. Roger needed her, he couldn't do it alone.

"We don't have time!" Aubri said, grabbing Sibylla's hand. She expected Aubri to yank her along, but to her surprise, she waited.

"Please," Aubri pleaded, "trust me."

Sibylla pursed her lips, looking away from Aubri's glowing eyes to look at the door behind her, the sound of fighting seeming to come closer. The rifle cracked again.

"I can't just leave," she said helplessly.

Looking back she saw that there was a fourth werewolf that she hadn't seen before. It was a little taller than the others, a little more cautious. It waited for the other two to distract Roger before lunging in itself. Sibylla's breath caught in her chest, preventing her from calling out. For its patience the werewolf caught a shotgun blast to its face, rocking it off its feet and sending it crashing to the floor.

Without warning all of the sounds and sights and smells assaulted her senses. She could feel Aubri's heartbeat racing through her hand. She could hear the wooden walls creaking in the light breeze. The grunts and growls of the fight outside the barn seemed like it was coming right next to her. Every grain of ash on Aubri's face stood out like she was looking at them through a microscope. Those and a hundred others fought for front-row seats in her brain, and, unable to cope with it all, her brain did the only thing that made sense: it shut down.

"Breathe!" a voice called out from somewhere in Sibylla's memory. It was so familiar, but in a distant kind of way, something that she could barely grasp. "You are okay! Just breathe!"

Chapter 12

Sibylla woke up screaming, the weighted blanket that had been on top of her flying across the room. Something like a helmet was stuck to her head and in her panic Sibylla tore it off, throwing it across the room. Whatever it was, she immediately regretted the decision. The moment it left her head she almost collapsed from the sheer weight of everything in the room.

A chaotic symphony of sound, from the thunder-like clatter of the helmet smashing against the wall to the splintering wood to the sound of her heartbeat, fought for her immediate attention. Sibylla wildly searched the room, trying to locate the helmet to put it back on, but she was too distracted by her eyes rapidly focusing in and out, trying to absorb as much visual information as possible.

Squeezing them shut she tried to feel around for the helmet, but every movement sent her sprawling and crashing around the room like a great dane puppy still learning how to walk. After what felt like an eternity she found it, but was horrified when it wouldn't fit on her head. It was misshapen and cracked like it had been involved in some kind of accident. Her ears rang in protest, too overwhelmed to process the stimuli that rushed into them like a hurricane.

Something slammed into her, and in her blind panic, Sibylla lashed out, sending whatever it was flying off her. She opened her eyes and only saw a confusing mass of shapes dancing in front of her eyes, moving with a horrible slowness and detail that only made her panic worse.

Two glowing blue orbs appeared, drifting toward her in a slow, graceful arc. Sibylla locked onto them, captivated. As they drew closer, Aubri's face materialized around them. Dark shadow emanated from the glow, and the tattooed lines on her face seemed even more distinct than ever before. Gray and blackened ash was smeared around them, making them seem even brighter in the darkened room.

Aubri kept one hand outstretched, palm forward, while the other one pointed toward her mouth. Sibylla could see every detail of Aubri's lips, every crack and line, how full they were. Slowly sounded out a single word. Focus.

Sibylla focused on Aubri's mouth, trying to zero in on what she could be saying. For a moment, it seemed as though nothing was changing. Then she could hear it, like a whisper in a hurricane.

"Breathe," Aubri was saying, "just breathe."

Sibylla tried to force regular breaths into her lungs but only seemed to choke on the air. She kept trying anyway, eyes locked on Aubri's mouth, attention focused on her every word.

"It's okay," Aubri soothed, "you are okay. I know it is scary, just breathe."

Sibylla nodded jerkily in response, relieved that Aubri's voice was beginning to drown out the noise storm that threatened to overcome her. After a few more ragged breaths, everything seemed under control. Still loud and overwhelming, but manageable.

"You are doing great," Aubri said with a gentle smile. "This is a sensory helmet, it will help."

She handed her a helmet and Sibylla snatched up and jammed it on her head, wincing at the impact.

"Easy," Aubri said, smiling. "A lot has changed, you will need time to adjust."

Sibylla nodded, peering through the face shield at her surroundings, relieved that everything seemed to be back to what she was used to. No one was moving in weird ways, colors and sounds were back to normal. It was then that she noticed that something was in her nose and reached up to grab it. Before she got halfway Aubri caught her arm.

"They help with the smells," she said, "and if you crack this helmet, we do not have another spare."

Aubri gestured to what appeared to be Sibylla's first helmet, one half of it caved in from the impact with the wall.

"I did that?" she asked numbly.

"You do not know your strength," Aubri said.

Sibylla glanced around the room and saw that she was in some kind of cabin. The walls were plain, unadorned logs, and the only furniture in the room was a wood pallet on the ground with a futon mattress. Like the helmet, the pallet had also been damaged, the frame fractured and splintered.

"Did I do that?" she asked, pointing at it. She certainly didn't remember hitting anything.

"Yes," Aubri replied, barely glancing away to see what Sibylla was pointing at.

Sibylla thought back a moment, then sat up straight.

"What fell on me?" she asked.

"I did," Nate groaned from the corner behind Aubri. He gave her a half-hearted salute. "Apparently jumping on you was the wrong idea."

"Oh my gosh! I'm so sorry!" Sibylla said, jumping to her feet.

Aubri caught her before she stumbled off balance and collapsed to the floor, pulling her in close so that their bodies were pressed together.

"Easy, easy," Aubri whispered, practically in Sibylla's ear. "You are much stronger than you remember."

Sibylla could feel Aubri's heartbeat through the hard shell armor she wore while their chests were pressed together. Along with her gentle whisper, Aubri's heart's steady cadence brought with it a little bit of peace.

"Right," she said, taking shaky breaths and stepping away. "You okay?"

"Fine," he grunted, standing to his feet. "I just got winded, nothing my superior genetics can't overcome."

The pain was clear in his voice, but Sibylla was grateful he attempted humor. At least if he was hurt, he wasn't hurt too badly. She looked around and saw that the door was open, and beyond it was Mr. Darrow in his wheelchair, and behind him was Hunter, looking pale and shaken. Sibylla couldn't even guess what she had looked like when she first woke up and immediately felt guilty.

"You okay?" she asked, trying to be reassuring.

"Uh, yeah," he said, looking away. Sibylla felt even worse.

"Are you ready to come out and join the land of the living?" Mr. Darrow asked, seemingly undisturbed by the whole show. "We have a lot to talk about."

Over the next several hours Mr. Darrow did his best to explain a world's worth of knowledge. The sheer amount of information was staggering. The best Sibylla could do while her senses fought each other for supremacy was to focus as much of her attention as possible on the main points. The first of which was that her family was part of a long line of guardians, called Sentinels and Rangers, who were tasked with keeping gates between two worlds closed and safe.

The second thing she learned was that Roger had accepted the mantle of Sentinel from Howard and had eventually gotten married to Delphine, who had become Howard's Ranger.

At the mention of Delphine's name, Sibylla was able to briefly bring her senses under control. Learning that she was a Ranger was the first new information she'd learned about Delphine in years, her dad being notoriously tight lipped about her.

"What was she like?" Sibylla asked, leaning forward.

"One of the best I've seen," Mr. Darrow smiled. "Together with your dad, they were one hell of a team."

Nate stepped in eagerly, "How many did they hunt down?"

"Probably hundreds," Mr. Darrow laughed. "To be honest it's hard to know. Roger brought me on around when you were born."

"You were a Ranger?" Hunter asked, "What was it like to hunt with Dad and Mom?"

The questions and answers had flowed for a frustratingly short amount of time, to Sibylla's chagrin. Sibylla hadn't realized how hungry she was to know about her parents, especially her mom. The desire to know more had always been there, but it had been shut down and denied for so long that her heart ached with the stories that Mr. Darrow told.

"That's about all I know about them," he said eventually, "I only worked with them both for a few years until your mom…" he trailed off.

Then Sibylla learned a third, very important piece of information: Aubri was not from Earth.

Aubri had proudly stepped in then, giving a little bow. "I am an honored member of the Sacred Legion, sworn to defend the Gates and to hunt and kill any and all Augulpor that cross my path."

Nate, Hunter, and Sibylla stared at her for a long moment, the only sound being the crackling of the fire.

"Like an alien?" Nate asked, breaking the silence.

Aubri smiled. "I am unfamiliar with the word. I come from the other side of the Gates. I am not sure if that counts as an alien."

"Sounds like an alien," Nate whispered. Hunter nodded in agreement.

"The Pure are not the only things that can cross over," Aubri continued. "I am from Laternum, the Sun City."

"Badass," Nate said.

"What are the Pure?" Hunter asked.

"They made the things that took you and your brother hostage," Mr. Darrow replied.

The events back in their barn came rushing back to Sibylla like a lightning strike. Werewolves. Werewolves had broken into her home, assaulted and captured her brothers, her dad. Vivid fear washed over her, igniting a cloud of fiery hornets in her chest. They had spoken to her, known her name even. The realization that she had been staring death in the eye gave even more energy to the hornets that swarmed her chest, and they spread up to her mind, confusing the memory. Teeth got longer, eyes darker and more sinister. The shadows they cast threatened to overwhelm her.

"Hey," Aubri said gently, kneeling in front of her, looking up into Sibylla's eyes. "You are okay, you are safe."

Sibylla nodded, chest heaving. Her hands went cold, her toes not too far behind. Nate and Hunter sat next to her, each of them taking one of her hands. The hornets calmed a little, and breathing came a little easier. Warmth flooded her limbs and her cheeks, and she gripped their hands a little tighter, not wanting to let go, though she tried to be a little more careful about squeezing too hard.

"What happened to our dad?" she croaked, throat dry. The last thing that she could remember was him facing the werewolves, completely alone.

"I did my best to help him," Mr. Darrow said, eyes dropping to his hands. "But it wasn't enough."

Sibylla remembered hearing the crack of a rifle along with the sounds of Roger's shotgun. Mr. Darrow must have been nearby, taking shots from a distance.

"Is… is he dead?" Hunter asked, voice barely above a whisper.

"No," Mr. Darrow replied. "Though I'm not sure his situation is better for it. They took him."

Sibylla's heart dropped and tears filled her eyes.

"What are we supposed to do?" she asked, "did they take him through the Gate?"

"No," Aubri said firmly. "They can't, not without you."

"You have the Sentinel's mantle now," Mr. Darrow said. "You are the only person on this planet that can open or close the Gate."

"What happens to us with him gone?" she asked. "How do we get him back?"

"That first question is a little easier to answer," Mr. Darrow answered. "Fortunately, in terms of brass tax, your situation is pretty stable."

The fourth piece of information that Sibylla learned was that her dad was doing a lot better than she thought, financially anyway.

"Your house and the land it sits on is completely paid off, the taxes and everything else being paid by Baft's estate," Mr. Darrow said, "and he was receiving a monthly stipend as well that should cover stuff like food and gas and whatnot."

The mystery of Roger's source of income had been plaguing Sibylla for years. She never knew how they were able to afford their house or bills or groceries or anything when it never seemed like he had a consistent job. Often he would leave for a day or two and then come back for a day or two. Knowing that she wouldn't have to take on a job or something to pay for everything took a huge load off of her chest.

"So it's just us then?" Hunter asked, sounding more like his age than he had in some time.

"That partially brings us to the second part of your question," Mr. Darrow said slowly. "I don't think your dad would want you to be left alone for weeks or months or however long it takes to find him, so for the time being I'll move in with you guys and keep an eye on you."

"How does that partially explain how we get him back?" Sibylla asked, eyebrows furrowing.

"Here's the deal," Mr. Darrow said after a long pause, seeming to struggle to find the right words. "We have a pretty big problem on our hands. The Pure of Red Falls, whoever they are, has been infecting people for close to a decade now. I don't know how large the pack is, but they are bigger than I care to think about."

Sibylla didn't like the situation at all. More and more it seemed impossible that they would be getting their dad back. But then Mr. Darrow told her the fifth and arguably most important piece of information.

"So here's my deal," Mr. Darrow pressed on, "I'll come live with you guys, but part of what I'm going to be doing is training you how to hunt."

"Y-you want me to hunt werewolves?" Sibylla said, shocked.

The memory of the barn came to mind, how helpless she'd felt. At that moment she knew that she was going to die, and only the intervention of Aubri, Roger, and Mr. Darrow had saved her life. Her brothers' lives. Hunting werewolves would put them at risk. Would she be strong enough to keep them safe? The thought of losing them almost reignited the panic attack, and only Aubri's arm around her shoulders kept her grounded.

"We know it is scary," Aubri said quietly.

"And we know that it's a lot to ask," Mr. Darrow added. "But if you want to save your dad, if you want to keep your brothers and this town safe, this is what it's going to take."

Sibylla unconsciously pulled her brothers into a hug. None of them seemed to know that the last thing she wanted was for them to be involved, but she knew Mr. Darrow was right. Sibylla was the thin line that protected the town from monsters that were operating just under the surface, and she would never forgive herself knowing that she could have done something but didn't.

I don't know if I'm strong enough for this, she thought, hugging her brothers tighter.

"Uh-" Nate gasped.

"Ribs!" Hunter squeaked.

"Right!" she said, face flushing with heat. She released them and they stepped away, gasping.

"You may need some training," Mr. Darrow reflected.

"No shit!" Nate gasped, hands on his knees.

"What'll it be?" Mr. Darrow asked, ignoring her brothers. "Will you help us?"

Sibylla took a deep, shuddering breath, trying to dispel the memory of the werewolves in the barn. True, she was stronger and faster with the mantle, but that first memory would haunt her forever.

I hope I'm strong enough for this, she thought.

"When do we start?"

Chapter 13

The following weeks were a confusing and frustrating mess for Sibylla. Most of the time had been dedicated to adjusting to the new world that was created by her senses. It took almost three days before she could manage to take off the sensory helmet, and even then she winced at every loud noise or gust of wind that touched her skin.

After that, it was learning how to sort through the mass of information that her brain was taking in. The first day or so Sibylla barely moved, suffering from migraines and nausea, unable to block out any unnecessary details like she had before. School was absolutely out of the question, she could barely leave her room. Mr. Darrow was forced to get assignments and tests for her, though she barely touched any of them. Even the feeling of paper against her skin and the scratching of the pencil sent her spiraling back to bed.

By the end of the first week, she had managed to at least complete some of the assignments, but she did it in the dark, though that proved to be a fascinating exploration of what her body had to offer. Using only the light that managed to sneak past her blinds and from under the door Sibylla was able to read her assignments as if it were daylight. Despite all the pain and suffering, she had to admit that it was incredible to discover that her night vision was almost as good as her vision during the day. Equally impressive was when she realized that she could smell trees through her walls or hear her brothers even though they were across the house with several walls between them.

As unbelievable as the sensations were, week two found her focusing on getting better at filtering out all of the background sensations. It allowed her to finally leave her room and go outside without throwing up or collapsing with a debilitating migraine. Sibylla practiced turning it all off or on at will constantly. Sometimes she would focus on listening to her brothers talking about some page of the book or try to isolate a particular scent like the trees or Aubri's perfume.

When she could open her blinds at night she would search the snow at the base of the trees for any signs of animals, or look for little items that Aubri would set out during the day for her to find. More importantly, learning how to control her new senses broke up the monotony of what felt like being violently sick for weeks.

The strength she was struggling to manage, which was substantially increased from before. Snapping pencils, torn paper, and broken chairs were just as responsible for her lack of progress on her assignments as the migraines. On one of the days in the middle of the third week, Sibylla managed to crush her doorknob when she grabbed it at the same time as being struck by a migraine. The silver lining was that Nate and Hunter got practice installing new door handles, on top of how to do minor repairs on furniture.

When they weren't fixing what she broke, Nate and Hunter had managed to stay busy studying the old book that Roger had given Sibylla on her birthday. Sibylla hadn't had a chance to take more than a cursory look at it before the werewolf attack, but according to Hunter, it was an absolute gold mine.

"At least the parts that we can read are," Hunter admitted.

"Half the damn thing is in Latin or French or German or some other kind of gibberish," Nate said.

Thankfully Google Translate seemed to have the answer for the bulk of it. Every day they found her and told her excitedly about some new fact that they had discovered. Werewolf bones were just as fragile as human bones, but the sternum was more dense and difficult to break. Their skulls were also tougher, especially around the forehead and jaw. Werewolves were fast and strong and tough, but not particularly agile.

Nate had also found diagrams that illustrated how werewolves fought, using their superior reach to pull in victims, or how high they could jump. They were also pack hunters, despite their territorial nature. At least the Pure were. The Infected were too impulsive with explosive tempers and were more likely to attack each other than the intended target. So it took a strong Pure to be present to keep them in line. Otherwise, they were more likely to hunt on their own.

Handwritten notes filled the margins as new Sentinels and Rangers added information or made corrections. Next to the section that detailed werewolves as pack hunters someone had scrawled "only with strong leadership. A weak leader will cripple the pack. A pack will cut out its weakness." In the section that had diagrams showing how werewolves fought, someone else had written "Disregard. Every beast is different."

All of it was incredibly useful if a little tedious to figure out, and Sibylla was glad that Nate and Hunter had decided to take it on. Their safety was paramount to her, and research was a good way for them to contribute without putting themselves at risk. Or at least that's what she had thought.

Toward the end of her recovery, there was an explosion that rattled the windows of the house. Heart thumping like a jack rabbit in her chest and ears ringing from the unexpected noise, Sibylla collapsed to the floor in the fetal position, brain overloaded by the sudden, violent injection of sensory data. After several long seconds, focusing through gritted teeth, Sibylla struggled to her feet and staggered to the window, swaying uneasily with every step. At the sight of smoke pouring out of the barn through every crack in the walls and roof, she wasted no time in yanking the window open and jumping out into the frigid snow and broken glass.

Sprinting to the barn, Sibylla saw that Aubri was already leading Sir Moo out of it, smoke following after them from the wide open barn doors. Not bothering to stop, Sibylla tore past them and into the dark roiling cloud. It smelled like burnt green wood, acrid and foul, and stung Sibylla's eyes.

Seeing was out of the question, as was breathing. One breath and her throat seized up and her stomach bucked, bile rising into her mouth. She stumbled the length of the barn, panic rising with each passing second of not being able to locate her brothers. At some point, she ran into the large door on the opposite end of the barn and kicked it open. By the time she had taken another gulp of fresh air the cross breeze had cleared enough of the smoke that Sibylla could see two still forms on the ground just off the center of the barn, next to a metal drum that still belched the black smoke. Its sides were mushroomed out, likely the explosion had taken place inside it.

Sibylla sprinted back in, throwing a horse blanket over the drum before grabbing each brother, a collar in each hand, and drug them out into the fresh air. They were so light that it reminded Sibylla of when she had first held them, back when they were infants. At the time Delphine was still alive, and the act of holding them had felt so new and exciting. As she deposited them both in the snow outside the barn Sibylla felt nothing but terror.

"Come on," she said with a shaky breath, checking Nate for a pulse. "Stay with me."

She almost laughed in relief when she felt a weak heartbeat in his neck. Without another thought she started CPR, trying to be careful not to fracture his ribs. After one breath, however, she shot back, hands darting for her mouth.

"What the hell?" she gasped, lips going numb.

In reply, Nate let out a ragged cough before rolling on his side and vomiting into the snow, Hunter not far behind. The smell of their vomit, mixed with the smoke that still billowed out from the barn, made Sibylla dry heave.

"What the hell!" she shouted, throwing a handful of snow at Hunter. "What did you guys do?"

Nate hacked and coughed some more, chest heaving as he fought for air. Hunter let out an uneven breath, spitting up black phlegm. Both of them collapsed to the snow, arms and legs twitching.

"Guys?" she said, lips still numb. Her breathing became shallow and her vision swam. "What did you… what… you… did…?"

She collapsed face first into the snow. She knew she should be concerned, but for some reason, she felt completely relaxed. Breathing became more difficult and Sibylla became light headed. She wanted to sit up, to get out of the frigid snow, but her arms and legs refused to obey her.

Dimly, she was aware of the crunching of snow as someone approached, and through the haze, Sibylla smelled the familiar sweet, piney scent of Aubri. A shadow passed over her eyes and then Sibylla was looking up into the sky. Out of the corner of her eye, she saw a dark shape, then heard the beep of numbers being pressed.

"Mr. Darrow?" the voice of Aubri asked, "I need you, now!"

ψ

Then Sibylla was looking into two bright blue orbs.

"You scared me," Aubri whispered, "you okay?"

"I'm okay," Sibylla said weakly. "Are the boys…?"

Fear prevented her from finishing the sentence. Whatever had been in the smoke had been horrible, but Sibylla had only been in it for a few moments. If her reaction had been that bad, what had happened to Nate and Hunter? They had been in the smoke far longer than she had. The thought that she hadn't been fast enough brought tears to her eyes, and she tried to sit up to check on them.

Aubri's firm hands on her shoulders kept her on her back, but Sibylla saw that she was no longer lying in the snow. She was in her room, the shades and blinds drawn.

"They are okay," Aubri said, "or at least they will be in time."

"What happened?" Sibylla asked, laying back, relieved.

Aubri sat on the edge of the bed and put her hand on Sibylla's. Sibylla's chest fluttered at the touch, and her fingers involuntarily wrapped around Aubri's hand.

"We're not sure," Aubri answered, glancing down at their hands and smiling, "though it looks like they tried to recreate a weapon from the book, and it did not go as planned."

"A weapon?" Sibylla asked, trying to ignore Aubri's smile. "I thought the book was just like a diary or something for the different Sentinels."

"It is," Mr. Darrow said from the doorway. Sibylla pulled her hand free from Aubri's and sat up. A wave of nausea rolled over her, which helped her to ignore Aubri's coy smile. "Some of the other Sentinels, most of them, made notes about different ways to fight the werewolves. Your brothers seem to have found a diagram for a kind of smoke grenade. It uses wolfsbane as its primary ingredient, which, as they found out, is toxic to werewolves and humans."

"It is why you all lost consciousness, and why you need to rest," Aubri explained, placing her hand on Sibylla's chest and gently pushing her back onto her back, sending another fluttering wave through Sibylla's chest and stomach.

Damn it, Sibylla thought, trying to be annoyed.

"Will they be okay?" she asked.

"Should be," Mr. Darrow replied. "They'll probably suffer as their bodies punish them for being stupid. You should be fine in a day or two since you now have the ability to heal much quicker."

"Good," Sibylla sighed.

"Indeed," Mr. Darrow agreed, "the next full moon is in two nights, and the three of us will be taking a little hunting trip. Who can we trust to keep an eye on the boys while we're out?"

Chapter 14

"Nope!" Kayla said loudly, turning away from the table, hands flung in the air. "No, no, no, no, NO!"

By the last 'no' she was shouting, turning in circles, gesturing wildly with her arms. Sibylla winced at the sudden increase in volume but kept her hearing sharp. Outside the wind gently rattled the sides of the barn, dead and dried things twirling and scraping in the snow. Aubri pacing just a few yards away, undoubtedly making noise on purpose so that Sibylla knew that she wasn't alone.

"I kn-" Sibylla began, reaching out to touch Kayla's arm.

"No!" Kayla shouted, jerking her arm away. "Absolutely freaking not! There's no damn way!"

Sibylla knew that when Kayla resorted to cursing that she was beginning to spiral out of control.

"There's no way!" Kayla said, raising a finger toward the table and its contents as if she could shush them.

Glancing at the table, Sibylla couldn't blame her. She had been the one to set the table up and still felt a little squeamish about it. Sitting there, in all their hideous glory, were the burnt and cracked skulls of the three werewolves that Roger had managed to kill before being captured. Their bodies had been burned while Sibylla had been going through the worst of her recovery, creating a stench that she would be happy to never smell again.

"Kay-" Sibylla began again.

"No!" Kayla said sharply, cutting her off a second time. "What kind of sick joke is this Red? First, you ghost me for weeks then you come at me with this… this… THIS." She gestured at the gruesome props without looking at them directly.

"It's not a joke!" Sibylla said for the hundredth time, frustration rising again. "It's real!"

"Stop saying that!" Kayla groaned, turning away. She was so pale that Sibylla wasn't sure she wouldn't pass out. "It's not real! It can't be real!"

Glancing back at the table, seeing a gaping hole in the middle skull where a bullet had passed through, Sibylla wished she could agree. After four weeks of experiencing the changes in her life, she had forgotten that someone else would struggle to accept the truth. Granted, she would have preferred to avoid trying to expose Kayla to the truth at all, but it had proven to be a necessity.

Since the accident, neither Hunter nor Nate had woken for more than a few minutes at a time. Sometimes they coughed up a foul smelling black foam that stained their skin and was oily to the touch. Most of the time they just lay there, still as corpses, their rattling breathing the only indication they were still alive. Mr. Darrow had said that they would recover soon enough, but Sibylla had not missed his lingering concern or his long silent stare as he watched them struggle to breathe.

Worse, Aubri was also concerned. Wolfsbane was a plant that was well known to her since it had been introduced to Earth from Laternum when the first gate had been opened centuries before. Aubri had seen many cases of accidental exposure and had even gone through it herself when she first started training.

"I was coughing and vomiting for days," she had admitted, "but I have never seen anyone react like this."

That had been enough to convince Sibylla that there was no way she could leave the house for any reason, hunt or otherwise unless someone was home to keep an eye on her brothers. Logistically the request had been problematic. Aubri was necessary as a safety net on the hunt, and Mr. Darrow was going along as the leader, intent on teaching Sibylla some lessons about the finer elements of hunting werewolves. Since Nate and Hunter couldn't watch themselves, Sibylla had stubbornly refused to take any part until they had solved the problem.

"What about a camera, like they do in baby rooms?" she suggested.

"So you can obsessively check a bright screen in the middle of the darkened woods while we hunt monsters with superhuman vision and hearing?" Mr. Darrow asked, clearly frustrated.

"Right," Sibylla said, embarrassed. "How about a babysitter?"

"A what?" Aubri asked, surprised, looking between Mr. Darrow and Sibylla with obvious concern.

"Someone, to watch kids," Mr. Darrow explained, "you wanna let some strange high schooler keep an eye on them?"

"Well… no," Sibylla replied, feeling exasperation creeping up her neck and into her face. "How about Kayla?" she said.

Mr. Darrow snorted. "Kayla? You trust her with their safety?"

"Why not?" Sibylla asked defensively. "She's been my best friend for years, and she even babysat them a few years back."

"This," Mr. Darrow said, gesturing at the still forms of her brothers, "is a little different than making sure they don't burn down the house or vandalize someone's property. They're in a coma for Pete's sake."

"Kayla knows CPR," Sibylla grumbled sullenly. "It's better than leaving them alone."

"Not by much," Mr. Darrow said, matching Sibylla's tone.

Aubri had been the first to break the sullen silence that followed, placing a reassuring hand on Mr. Darrow's arm.

"It is for one night," she said, "it will be okay."

Mr. Darrow let out a long sigh, pinching the bridge of his nose. "Fine, under one condition. You have to tell her everything."

"W-what?" Sibylla sputtered, "Why? She wouldn't believe me!"

"While small, there is still a chance of werewolves attacking this house tonight. She can't be caught by surprise," he said, "whether or not she believes you is on you Red."

It had proved to be a tall order. Sibylla had wrestled for hours trying to figure out just how she was going to present everything she had experienced to someone who firmly believed in what she could see. Whatever Sibylla did, it would have to be definitive, beyond a shadow of a doubt absolutely real.

In the end, Sibylla had come up with an explanation that covered the details that she thought would be most important or helpful and ignored the rest. Convincing her that werewolves existed would be hard enough, she didn't want to have to explain that there was a spirit that lived in the Gate or that Aubri wasn't even technically human. To that end, she had taken Kayla to where the table was set up in the barn, in the middle of the scorch marks and burnt hay that marked the epicenter of Nate and Hunter's accident.

Which brought them to Kayla pacing back and forth like a wild animal caught in a cage. It didn't take much to see that she wasn't taking it well.

"Okay," Kayla said finally, keeping her eyes clamped shut and away from the table. "Cover them up, I don't want to see them anymore."

Once the skulls had been covered, Kayla seemed to relax a little. Sibylla couldn't blame her, they were creepy and strange and unnatural. It was as if someone had taken the skull of a dog and the skull of a human and mashed them together without any care as to what it would look like in the end. In particular, the mix of canine and human teeth bothered Sibylla the most, who knew what it was for Kayla.

"This is nuts," she muttered, running her fingers through her hair.

"I know," Sibylla agreed carefully.

"Damn it," Kayla said, walking toward the door to the barn before turning on her heel and coming back. Staring at her toes, it only took a moment longer for her shoulders to slump in defeat. "What am I supposed to do? Fight them? I can't fight monsters Red. I don't do scary, horrible creatures that want to eat me. Or my family. What am I supposed to do?"

"I don't need you to fight them," Sibylla said quietly. "I just need you to watch my brothers tonight."

Kayla looked up sharply. "Your brothers? What happened to them?"

Sibylla gestured to the marks on the floor in way of explanation.

"They blew up?" Kayla asked, confused.

"Ish," Sibylla said, unsure of how to explain. "They were trying to build something and it went wrong somehow. We're still not sure."

"Are they okay?" Kayla asked, eyes troubled.

Sibylla shrugged, a vague feeling of helplessness descending over her. "Yes? I'm not sure, they haven't woken up yet."

"Shit Red, take them to the hospital!" Kayla said, horrified. "What the hell are you doing out here?"

"My best!" Sibylla snapped, anger burning the helplessness away. "What am I supposed to say? 'Hey doc, my brothers poisoned themselves making a weapon to fight werewolves, can you take a look at them?' I don't even know who the werewolves are in the stupid town, what if the doctor is one? Then what? I just gave my brothers to the enemy!"

"The enemy?" Kayla was flustered, shouting back. "Damn it Sibylla, you're not at war! You're talking about mythical creatures! They. Aren't. Real!"

She emphasized the last sentence by jabbing her finger into Sibylla's chest. Without thinking Sibylla shoved Kayla back, sending her tumbling toward the open door of the barn. Sibylla had only wanted to create distance between them, not hurt her, and immediately cursed herself for being so careless. Rushing to Kayla's side, Sibylla was relieved to see that she was okay, if not a little stunned.

"Could… could you do that before?" Kayla asked, eyes wide, taking heavy breaths.

"Not really, no," Sibylla said, offering her hand to help Kayla up.

Kayla looked at it timidly, as if she were afraid of what it might do if she touched it. Sibylla could understand why but found the hesitation still stung. After some time, Kayla took Sibylla's hand and stood on shaky legs.

"Sorry," Sibylla said, sincerely. "I'm going through a lot right now, I'm barely keeping up as it is. Everything is on me: I have to hunt the monsters, I have to rescue my dad and take care of my brothers, I have to do everything. It's hard, and I'm afraid it's not working."

"Your dad is missing?" Kayla asked, eyes wide.

Sibylla could only muster a nod in reply. As frustrating as it was to have so much push back from Kayla, she shouldn't have lost her temper. What if Sibylla had hurt her for real? Shoved her into a wall and broke a bone or worse? She wanted Kayla's help, not put her in the hospital. There was no doubt in her mind now that Kayla would refuse to help, maybe even refuse to talk to Sibylla ever again. To her surprise, Kayla nodded.

"Okay Red," she said, voice quiet, nearly inaudible to anyone other than Sibylla. "I'll watch your brothers tonight."

"You will?" Sibylla asked. "Why? Do you believe me?"

"I'm not sure," Kayla admitted, rubbing the place on her chest that Sibylla had shoved. "I need to think about it. But, if I have to think about it, I might as well do it here."

ψ

A little later Kayla watched Sibylla, the strange new girl named Aubri, and Mr. Darrow disappear into the growing darkness. Five minutes passed. Ten minutes. Fifteen. After thirty minutes she tossed the shotgun that Sibylla had provided, at Mr. Darrow's insistence, on the couch and wandered into Nate and Hunter's room. Without hesitating she swung the door open and stared at the two lumps in their beds, chests barely rising and falling, breaths coming in shallow gasps.

A black fluid that leaked from Hunter's mouth drew Kayla toward him for a closer look. A sniff was all she needed to recognize the scent. Wrinkling her nose in disgust she pulled out her phone.

"Wolfsbane," she muttered.

KAY: Update: I'm in.

She typed in a message to an unknown number, one of dozens that they used to keep people guessing. Kayla thought it was ridiculous, especially in small-town USA just down the road. Who was she to argue? His paranoid, borderline delusional, methods had kept him in operation for years.

KAY: The boys are fine, moderate wolfsbane poisoning, I have the place to myself tonight.

P: Take care of them. Now.

KAY: Done.

Kayla sighed, sliding the phone into her pocket and sitting down on the couch, she reached for the remote.

There was no rush, she would be alone for hours, and they weren't going anywhere.

Chapter 15

Mr. Darrow was tougher than Sibylla had originally thought, and she had thought he was tough, to begin with. She had been surprised when he had said that they were all going to be walking through the woods, considering she had never seen him leave his wheelchair in all the years that she had known him.

"It hurts," he'd explained, attaching his prosthetic limb to the stump of his leg. A brace had already been strapped to his other leg. "A lot. I don't like doing it, and not for long."

Yet they had been hiking through the woods for well over an hour before stopping to take a break. Sweat dripped from his nose and soaked through the neck of his jacket, but he didn't complain.

Words couldn't express her admiration for the man. Sibylla thought again about how he had helped her and her family for so many years when Roger had checked out. Mr. Darrow had gone to every major event not only in Sibylla's life but in Nate and Hunter's as well.

Looking at everything that he had done, knowing what she now knew, she realized that he had spent a great deal of time trying to prepare her for when Roger would have to pass on the mantle of Sentinel. All the hours spent in the fight club, learning survival skills and how to hunt and handle weapons, had all been his effort in making sure that she could survive.

Frustration welled up in her at the realization. Mr. Darrow had always been more of a father to her than her father. Which was worse now that she was having to take a crash course in the role that was always going to be passed to her. How much better off could she and her brothers have been if Roger had just been brave enough to tell her what was going on? If he had just done his job as a dad in the first place, instead of just letting Mr. Darrow step in the gap? Sibylla let out a heavy sigh, trying to suppress the feelings with little success.

She reminded herself that, as bad as he had been, he had risked his life fighting a group of werewolves without his powers to let them run to safety. Who knew what he was going through at that moment, waiting for her to come in and rescue him? Looking at what she had been learning and what she already knew about werewolves, he was more than likely suffering enough without her mentally condemning him for his past actions.

More than anything, she needed to focus on getting him back. They had spent too much time with her recovering and getting used to the new world she was now intertwined with. They needed to start making progress, and fast. It had already been four weeks, going on five, since he was taken. What if he wasn't even alive anymore? Sibylla shook the thought away.

He was still alive. He had to be.

"We have probably about another hour of hoofing it until we get to our position," Mr. Darrow said, wiping his face with a rag. "Aubri, go on ahead and get into position. Keep an eye on the area and text me if there are any changes."

Aubri, who looked just as good and fresh as she was when they started walking, nodded. Before they had left the house she had reapplied the same ash mix that she had during the attack on the barn. Her eyes were glowing against the gray and black that surrounded them, and Sibylla found it difficult not to stare. It was incredible how captivating they were, their depth drawing her in. Aubri winked at her, noticing her stare, and disappeared into the trees. Face flushing, Sibylla took a swig of water to hide her face from Mr. Darrow in the fading light.

"Okay Red," Mr. Darrow said, "You and me are going to head out here in a minute or two. Before that, I wanted to make sure we were on the same page about what's happening tonight. Fair?"

Sibylla nodded, "Sure."

Mr. Darrow leaned back against the tree, eyes closed and head tilted into the chilly breeze that penetrated deep into Sibylla's bones.

"I know you've been absorbing a lot of information over the past few weeks, so I'll keep this straightforward," he continued. "Werewolves are twisted and tricky, but still just biological creatures, like you or me or

Aubri. They aren't unstoppable like the movies like to say. Silver hurts them and kills them quicker, sure, but lead can do the job just as well."

Sibylla nodded. Hunter had found the same information in the book and had already passed it along. It had been a substantial relief, considering that silver was expensive and not as accurate as normal ammunition over distances, at least according to a note left behind by a previous Sentinel. Sibylla had never used silver bullets before, so she had no way of knowing how true that was.

"How good are their senses?" Sibylla asked. It was another detail in the book that she already knew the answer to. According to the text, all of their senses were exceptional, but a thought had occurred to her about something that the book hadn't mentioned. With the number of contributors being men, she thought she knew why, but decided she could add the detail later.

"Better than yours, definitely better than mine," he said, holding out his hand for her to help him up. Standing up he easily towered over Sibylla and had to have had at least a hundred pounds on her, but he felt as light as a feather as she pulled him to his feet. "Anyway, for tonight's hunt, you-"

"Specifically," Sibylla interrupted him, "how good is their… smell?"

"Smell?" he asked.

"Yeah," she said as they started walking through the trees in Aubri's tracks. She could still smell the flowers that Aubri had started wearing in her hair. Sibylla couldn't be sure, but she thought that Aubri had added them for Sibylla.

"Is it like a dog?" she asked before she lost focus.

"Like a bloodhound," he said, obviously confused. "They can smell changes in hormones if you're in the same room with them, and can follow you through the woods by singling out your scent from the scents in the forest."

"Hormones," Sibylla repeated, keeping her eyes focused out in the woods. "What about something like blood?"

"Absolutely," he replied, keeping pace with her. "If you're ever injured it would be best to cover it up with something as fast as you can.

Dirt is good, even rubbing plants or some other stronger smell that's common to the area."

"What if..." Sibylla trailed off, unsure of how to continue. As much of a dad as he was, she was finding it difficult to talk about something she didn't even want to talk to Roger about. "That's not a good option?" she finished.

"How do you mean?" he asked, still confused. "What kind of -oh."

The realization of her meaning stopped him in his tracks. Sibylla stopped but didn't turn to face him.

"Uh, I… don't…" he faltered. "I think they'd be able to…"

He started moving again, shaking his head. "I'd say you'd probably want to not… um, hunt… during that particular week of the month. Or be more… careful."

"Okay," she said, keeping in step with him.

They continued in silence for a few minutes before Sibylla spoke up again.

"What if, let's say, it's happening now?" she asked.

"Well," Mr. Darrow said, not stopping. He seemed to have thought that the conversation was leading in that direction and was recovering from his initial surprise. "We'll be far enough away from the target, and I think we're going to be downwind if the direction doesn't change. We'll be okay tonight, but in the future, we'll plan ahead."

Sibylla nodded. They continued in silence for a while, the only sound being the crunch of snow beneath their feet and Mr. Darrow's labored breathing.

"Anyway," Mr. Darrow said, breaking the silence. "Werewolves are normally excellent hunters, smart and very aggressive. These, however, are not."

"What do you mean?" Sibylla asked, surprised.

"The werewolves your dad killed at the barn aren't normal werewolves," Mr. Darrow explained through heavy breaths. "They were twisted, malformed, dysfunctional. They were certainly aggressive, but they weren't smart or coordinated. Typically, a Pure looks like a normal wolf except freaking huge."

Sibylla thought back to the photo that Nate and Hunter had given her, with her parents and Mr. Darrow standing over the body of a wolf that seemed unnaturally large.

"When they infect a human the transformation process is messy," Mr. Darrow explained. "There's never been a perfect human-werewolf hybrid that I'm aware of, and the ones that are created are unpredictable and difficult to control. It takes a strong Pure to keep even a small pack of four or five in line. Whatever Pure is working out of Red Falls has to be exceptional."

"Why?" Sibylla asked, thinking back to the four that had attacked the barn.

The three that Roger had killed had been just as warped as the fourth, but the fourth had attempted to choose the proper moment to attack. Was that significant?

"Because the three that were killed at the barn aren't the only ones I know about," he explained, pausing to lean against a tree to catch his breath. "I have about twenty names of people in town who I think might be infected. If this pack is even close to that size, the Pure would have to be incredibly smart and powerful. But that's not super important tonight."

Silently Sibylla disagreed, waiting for him to catch his breath.

"What do you need me to do tonight?" she asked.

"You?" he said, watching her carefully. "Your job tonight is to just observe."

Sibylla blinked in surprise and felt her chest tighten. "What?"

"Observe, learn," he said.

"That's not fair!" she said, loud enough to make Mr. Darrow wince.

How could he expect her to just sit there? What did he have going on that she didn't? She was strong, fast, hell, she could walk at least. How was she supposed to know if she could handle herself? How was she supposed to prove that she had what it took to be a Sentinel? How was observing someone else doing her job going to get her any closer to helping her dad? These questions and more began pouring into her mind like molten lead.

"I know you don't like it," he said, an edge creeping into his voice.

"I don't," she said, crossing her arms and sticking her chin out. "Because it's stupid and ridiculous."

"Really?" he asked, pushing himself off the tree and continuing on their journey. "Explain to me why you think that."

It was his teacher's tone, the voice he used when students became defiant or angry about something in his class. It made her furious that he was using it on her. Clenching her fists and her jaw, she stomped after him.

"Because it's my job to do this!" She said, "I'm the Sentinel. I'm the one who is supposed to be hunting the werewolves, not some -"

"Some what?" he asked, not breaking his stride.

Sibylla paused, debating what she wanted to say. She knew what she was going to say, but it was overkill. If she was going to change his mind, she would need to be smarter about it. Taking a deep breath she counted to ten before responding.

"I'm stronger and faster," she said slowly through clenched teeth. "I heal faster too."

"Interesting argument," he said, still focusing on the trail they had landed on. "But not good enough. Do better."

Sibylla bristled at the criticism. She wasn't writing an argumentative essay, or trying to describe why some dictator was doomed to fail. It was about her worth on the hunt. As far as she was concerned the ability to walk unassisted was all the evidence she needed that she should have a more active role.

"Excuse me," she muttered, "I didn't realize being enhanced with superhuman abilities and senses wasn't a strong enough argument. Please, impart your infinite wisdom and explain to me why I should just sit back and do nothing."

"I didn't say 'nothing'," he said, keeping his tone even. "I said learning. There's a difference."

"I've been hunting for years!" she protested, "you taught me! What else do I need to know?"

He stopped and turned slowly until he faced her, drawing up to his full height. Defiant, Sibylla didn't step back or back down but met his gaze.

"Here's the thing Red," he said, face expressionless. "I'm not going to give you the whole spiel on deer not wanting to tear your flesh from your bones and thus is inherently a wildly more dangerous hunt than you've been on before."

Despite his lack of expression, his voice was icy and sharp. Sibylla fought the urge to step back or break eye contact. She had seen her dad take down werewolves with a fraction of the power she possessed, and Mr. Darrow had already explained that these werewolves weren't that smart. The fact that they were dangerous was obvious, what else was there for her to know?

"Instead," he continued, "I'm going to ask you one question: what weapons do you have on you, right this moment?"

With a start, Sibylla realized that she wasn't carrying a single weapon. The conversation with Kayla had been such a source of anxiety that she had completely forgotten to bring a weapon with her.

"You-" she started.

"I am not responsible for you being prepared," he cut her off. "You've hunted enough in your life to know that you can't hunt a deer with your bare hands, much less a werewolf. Being strong and fast is great, but they are not enough."

"Where's your weapon?" she asked, the challenge clear in her words.

"At the site, where I planted it yesterday after I had done recon and gathered information on where we would be most effective tonight," he said.

Sibylla hesitated for a moment, letting his words sink in, before lowering her gaze to her boots, half hidden in the snow. How could she have forgotten something as necessary as a weapon? She didn't even have a knife with her. If there was an emergency, or if she had to fight a werewolf, she would be utterly defenseless. The idea that she was better than Mr. Darrow just because he was stuck in a wheelchair most of the time seemed utterly laughable. She was just as vulnerable as he was, but at least he had the experience to help. Sibylla had nothing.

"I'm sorry," she said quietly.

"Don't be sorry," he said, placing a hand on her shoulder. "Learn from this. Come on, we're running behind."

Chapter 16

"The key," Mr. Darrow said in a slow voice barely above a whisper, "is to remember that we are hunters hunting hunters."

Sibylla nodded, even though she knew that he couldn't see her. They were prone under thick blankets that had branches and scrub tied into them, about four feet apart. Sibylla's chin was pressed into the dirt, hands folded in front of her face so that only her eyes were visible. Mr. Darrow looked like a lump in the ground, the camouflaged barrel of a rifle protruding from the front. Even knowing where he was hiding she had a hard time seeing him.

Facing them was a large open field, devoid of any distinguishing features or character. To Sibylla, it looked no different than any of the other farms that surrounded Red Falls. Even down to the small farmhouse on the opposite side, glowing squares indicated the farmer and his wife were awake. Probably watching reruns like they had done every night for years, completely unaware that the night was going to be far from ordinary.

A thick forest of naked aspens surrounded the farm, split only by the dirt path that led up to the house. Somewhere in the trees on the far side of the field, Aubri sat waiting. For what, Sibylla wasn't sure. Somehow just knowing she was there, even unseen, made Sibylla feel more secure.

"Tonight especially…" he said, trailing off. The barrel, wrapped in strips of painted burlap to break up its outline, shifted up a millimeter for a moment then settled back into place.

Sibylla scanned the field in front of them, looking for what he had seen. A rabbit stretched out in the middle of the field, sniffing gingerly at something she couldn't see. Mr. Darrow must have seen it and thought it was their target. Having enhanced vision made spotting the rabbit easy for Sibylla, had she been looking for it. She was impressed that he had seen it at all.

"... the full moon will help peak their power," he finished, letting out a low breath.

Anyone who had ever watched a movie about werewolves knew that they were more dangerous on a full moon. The major difference between movies and reality was that werewolves typically could change at will, even during the day if they wanted to.

One thing Sibylla hadn't been overly clear on was why Mr. Darrow had thought that the farm in front of them was going to be attacked that night.

"It's the pattern," he'd replied, cryptically, and then they had descended into silence, being too close to talk much, even at a whisper.

It was one of the lessons she was supposed to learn, so she spent the first hour in the blind trying to figure out what pattern he was referring to. After sixty long minutes of trying to see every possible explanation that she could come up with, she only had one conclusion: there was a pattern. A pattern that said that the farm, sitting in peaceful silence before them, was next in line to be struck by the werewolves of Red Falls. After that, she couldn't fathom what the answer was, or if he was even looking for an answer in the first place.

After that, her mind wandered. To her surprise, thoughts of Kane came first, how she was going to try to fix things between them. The last she'd seen of him he had been standing in the crowd of students he had brought in to celebrate her birthday at school. After that, her life descended into chaos and he had been left behind. He had tried to get a hold of her a few times of course.

Well, more than a few. The first few days his messages had been rapid and angry, but she hadn't been able to reply. The screen had been too bright for her eyes and she could barely focus without going cross eyed. Eventually, she replied and tried to explain that she was sick, and he had accused her of being selfish and for not appreciating him and his efforts to make her feel special.

Then he had given her the cold shoulder, something he had done before for different reasons. Normally she would have gone to his house and tried to talk to him, but she just couldn't do it.

She knew she should have made more of an effort to connect with him, especially after she had left him standing there, alone, without an explanation. To have not even thought of calling him seemed so selfish, what kind of girlfriend was she? Was she even still his girlfriend? Worse, how was she supposed to be able to tell him that her dad was missing and that she was barely keeping her family together, much less her relationship with him?

Burying her face in her hands, she tried to think of anything she could do to make it up to him.

The problem was that she wasn't particularly good at being lovey-dovey like Kane, who always went out of his way to make her feel like a queen. How could she make him feel like he was her king?

Probably with something big and public, she thought with a shudder.

A presence cut into her mind then, bringing all thought to an abrupt halt. At first, it was nothing more than a tickling at the edge of her perception, like feeling a stray hair brush against her neck. Over the following few minutes the feeling became stronger, pressing in, becoming more obvious. Something was out there, something that she could sense coming closer and closer.

"There…" Mr. Darrow breathed, almost as though he could read her mind.

Sibylla's eyes snapped up, relieved to have a distraction. It only took a split second for her to see the shadow loping across the field on all fours. It took even less time to see that something was wrong with it. Like the ones in the barn, it was tall and lanky, but its arms and legs each seemed to be different lengths, looking stiff and jerky. At one point it even fell over like it tripped over something that she couldn't see. Possibly it just tripped on its own feet and legs. The dark fur grew patchy and uneven, and the exposed skin cracked and bled like an infected sore. Sibylla couldn't even imagine what it would be like to live that way.

Was it the werewolf that she had felt coming? So far she hadn't heard anything about Sentinels being able to sense the monster's presence. Maybe there was something in the book that they hadn't found yet.

"Ears," Mr. Darrow whispered, breaking into her thoughts.

Sibylla had a split second to realize that he was warning her before he pulled the trigger. No sooner had her hands covered her ears than the thunder of the rifle's report washed over her. A silencer had been threaded onto the barrel, which, unlike the movies, did not reduce the sound to nothing. Instead, it reduced the volume to something that was still noticeable, but less aggressive. Though to Sibylla it still sounded like a crack of thunder, ears ringing through her palms.

In front of her, halfway across the field, the werewolf had tumbled head over heels, settling into a heap of limbs and flesh. A second later, just as Sibylla was removing her hands from her ears, the rifle cracked again. Sibylla gritted her teeth and squeezed her eyes shut, the ringing bouncing around her skull.

"Damn it," she hissed, attempting to shake the bells loose.

"Sit still," Mr. Darrow ordered, lifting a hand and pointing out across the field.

The front porch lights had snapped on and the farmer was standing in the middle of it, a shotgun in one hand and a flashlight in the other. Straining to move past the tinny ringing from the rifle's report, Sibylla tried to pick up what the farmer was saying to the woman who stood behind him, just inside the front door.

"...some damn kids," the farmer was saying. "...probably plinking…"

Ears aching, Sibylla pushed her face into her hands and focused on dulling her senses, as she had been practicing for weeks. It took all of her concentration and will power, but after an eternity the ringing faded away, and only the rustling of the wind in the branches was left.

"You okay?" Mr. Darrow asked. He must have asked her more than once, when Sibylla opened her eyes she saw that he was holding up his blind just enough to see her under the edge.

"Yeah," she nodded, "I wasn't fully covered for that second shot."

"Never forget to double tap," he grinned. "Head out there and help Aubri drag it back to the woodline. Don't want to freak out the farmer with a monster body in the morning."

The body was as grotesque up close as it had been from a distance. It had the appearance and smell of a sick, mangy dog crossed with a homeless person and cheap alcohol. Suppressing the urge to vomit, Sibylla wished she had better control over her sense of smell. Even Aubri had wrinkled her nose at it, looking at it distastefully.

"A clean kill," Aubri admitted, nudging the body with the toe of her boot.

"Yeah," Sibylla agreed, trying not to stare at Aubri.

Aubri's blue eyes were luminescent as she looked admiringly at Mr. Darrow's work, her elegant hand covering her nose and mouth to keep the stench at bay. The glow from Aubri's eyes illuminated the ash war paint, giving her a mystical appearance, like some kind of ancient warrior. A look at odds with the modern body armor she wore and the rifle that hung from her shoulder. Unafraid, she stood easily, almost relaxed, over the body of the werewolf. As though it wasn't, only a few minutes before, a living nightmare capable of great violence.

Sibylla admired her confidence, how sure she was of everything that she did, and said wishing she had the same level of self-assurance. Watching Aubri crouch next to the body, searching it for clues, she seemed capable of doing anything. Fearless, willing to try anything.

"What's this?" Aubri said, pulling a piece of fabric loose with a sickening ripping sound to hand to Sibylla.

Hesitating, then feeling embarrassed for hesitating, Sibylla took the fabric and examined it closely. It was a cheaply made patch for an oil company that operated a few hours west of Red Falls, the White Rabbit Petroleum Company. The embroidered white rabbit that served as the company logo was smeared with dirt and blood, but otherwise intact.

"Looks like he worked for an oil company," Sibylla explained, "they pump a little ways from here."

Taking a breath, Sibylla crouched down and rolled the body over, wincing at the feeling of the still warm flesh and what was left of its face. Heavily distorted, the nose and mouth had been elongated, the skin stretched thin to the point of splitting, blood running through the patchy fur that sprouted at random intervals across its face. A hole the size of Sibylla's fist under its eye indicated where one of Mr. Darrow's bullets had landed. At that point, her body finally rebelled and she barely took a staggered step back before she emptied her stomach.

"It is okay," Aubri said, placing a hand on Sibylla's shoulder. "Everyone throws up for the first time."

"Did you?" Sibylla asked, hands trembling on her thighs.

"No," Aubri replied.

Sibylla looked back and saw a sly grin splitting Aubri's face. Sibylla offered a weak smile in return. She glanced back at the crumpled form and winced.

"It looks so painful," she murmured, feeling sympathy for whoever the monster had once been. "I can't even imagine what it would feel like."

"It is a much better thing to end the suffering," Aubri said.

"Should we figure out who he was?" Sibylla asked.

The idea of searching the body was repulsive, but it seemed tragic to let it die anonymously. Whoever the person was, their family would never know what had happened to them.

"No," Aubri said gently but firmly. "That would only be a distraction, the source of hesitation the next time you find yourself face-to-face with one of them."

Sibylla nodded but didn't like the idea. But she grabbed one arm and helped drag the body back into the woods. Trying not to look too closely anymore, she helped Aubri navigate around trees and rocks until they were a fair distance from the farm. To Sibylla's surprise, they stopped at a freshly dug hole. Standing on the other side was Mr. Darrow, cradling the rifle in his arms.

"Right," he said, "time to clean up our mess."

Chapter 17

Sibylla had to admit she was impressed. As annoyed as she was that she had to wait and sit doing absolutely nothing for hours, it was clear that Mr. Darrow was a man who planned ahead. Was that something that she could do? Could she study patterns and observe attacks and figure out exactly where the next werewolf was going to show up? Could she dig a grave ahead of time and find the perfect vantage point to take down the target? She wasn't sure she could. She wasn't even sure she could have pulled the trigger.

It had been surprising to feel such a strong feeling of sympathy toward something that she knew was evil, a monster that was probably going to murder the farmer and his family in their own home if Mr. Darrow hadn't intervened. Shoveling dirt into the grave, she still felt a profound sense of sadness, unable to keep herself from wondering what his family thought about his disappearance if he had one. What if that sympathy made her hesitate as Aubri suggested?

There's only one way to find out, she thought, watching the evidence of the werewolf's existence slowly disappear, one shovelful of dirt at a time.

Aubri's hand shot out and grabbed Sibylla's, shocking her out of a slowly devolving internal spiral that she had been fighting since they had finished burying the body.

"Wha-?" Sibylla said, instinctively pulling her hand free.

"I apologize," Aubri said, her eyes and smile suggesting that she wasn't actually sorry. "It is something that we do in Laternum."

"Hold hands?" Sibylla asked. Her fingers tingled where Aubri had touched them.

"With our friends?" Aubri said, "Absolutely."

For a long moment, Sibylla's mind had a hard time processing what Aubri was saying. Internally she had been wrestling with her feelings about the hunt, Kane and her brothers, and her dad. The sudden jolt felt like an emotional car crash, and she was too dazed to think clearly. It wasn't like she and Kayla hadn't held hands, she reminded herself, or that she hadn't held hands with other friends over the years.

It's just hands, she thought, remembering when she had touched her hand the first night they'd met, don't make it weird.

With another second's hesitation, Sibylla reached out and took Aubri's hand. Fingers curling around hers, Aubri settled in next to her, shoulder to shoulder, making Sibylla's heart skip a beat as they continued hiking through the woods.

"How was your first hunt?" Aubri asked, breaking the silence.

"Honestly?" Sibylla asked, to which Aubri nodded emphatically. "Kind of boring. I didn't do anything at all."

Aubri chuckled. "That is honestly what a good hunt is: boring."

"I guess I was just expecting… more," Sibylla said.

"More?" Aubri asked, "How could it be more?"

Sibylla thought about the hundreds of monster movies she'd watched growing up, where scores of brave human heroes pitted themselves in violent combat against their enemies. Buildings burned down, bullets flew everywhere from every direction, explosions threw shrapnel high in the air, and heroic music blared in the background. Compared to that, two shots in the dark were boring.

"I don't know, more of a fight?" Sibylla answered.

"In Laternum," Aubri said, "my brother thinks much like you do."

Sibylla blinked in surprise. "You have a brother?"

"Yes," Aubri said, grinning. "Cassius. He is ranked higher than I am, certainly an important man in the Sacred Legion. He is always looking for a fight, the closer the better." She thought for a moment, then added "The messier, the better."

"That's so cool," Sibylla said, "to have a brother like that. My brothers are great at being messy too."

Aubri glanced at Sibylla, eyes searching her face. Sibylla was uncomfortable, not because Aubri was looking at her, but because she realized that she didn't want her to stop.

"Your brothers are okay," Aubri squeezed her hand again, "what happened to them is not your fault."

Easy to say, Sibylla thought but remained silent.

Aubri had a capable brother, a brother who was trained and could take care of himself. Sibylla didn't know what that was like, would never know what that was like. Nate and Hunter would always be getting into trouble, blowing themselves up or someone else up or something else, always something else. Aubri would never have to live her life thinking that whatever happened to Cassius, good or bad, was her fault. Sibylla would always be responsible for them because no one else would.

"I have been curious about something," Aubri said, lacing her fingers with Sibylla's. "Why do people call you 'Red'?"

For a second, Sibylla couldn't answer. Her mouth had gone dry, and a flutter of butterflies had invaded her chest, bringing with them a flood of warmth that invaded every part of her body. The desire to pull Aubri closer, to wrap her arm around her shoulders was overwhelming, followed by an even stronger urge to find out if Aubri was as good a kisser as Sibylla hoped she was.

"What?" Sibylla asked, shaking her head.

"Your nickname," Aubri giggled, and the fluttering started all over again.

"Oh, right," Sibylla said dumbly, self-conscious about how sweaty her hand was getting. "My hair."

Aubri giggled again and Sibylla kicked herself for sounding so dumb.

My hair? She thought bitterly, that's it??

"My hair," she continued awkwardly, "since it's, you know, red and curly? I guess it stands out enough for people to notice."

Fiery red and a mess of curls and waves, Sibylla had been fighting her hair for years. It defied most attempts at styling or even coloring. Sibylla had been forced to settle for getting it to look like a vaguely styled tangle of curls and waves and had long since given up on changing the color. For the hunt, she had managed to get it into something that vaguely resembled a ponytail and had worn a beanie over the rest. Lord knew it was bright red enough to stand out in the dark.

"It was the first thing I had noticed as well," Aubri said, "I like it, it suits you."

Sibylla wasn't sure if she could blush any harder, though she strangely found herself intensely pleased with the admission.

"Thank you," she said awkwardly.

"Can I call you Red as well?" Aubri asked.

"Of course," Sibylla replied, surprised that Aubri was asking. "Most people just do, you don't need my permission."

"In Laternum, nicknames are sacred things," Aubri explained, "reserved for close friends."

Sibylla held up their intertwined fingers. "It's a good thing then that we're friends."

"Of course," Aubri said, smiling warmly. Sibylla couldn't blush harder.

ψ

They walked along after that in relative silence, the only real noise coming from the crunch of their feet in the snow and Mr. Darrow's heavy breathing coming from behind. Sibylla was impressed with his stamina, even though it was obvious it had run out hours ago. Despite his legs and injuries, he had guided her through her first hunt without exposing them to unnecessary danger or risk. While it had been boring and a little disappointing, his method of hunting had guaranteed that she would make it home to Nate and Hunter. Sibylla wasn't sure she could be as good as Mr. Darrow with that level of planning and execution, but she was willing to try.

"I'm worried about my dad," she said, surprising herself and Aubri. "I'm worried that we won't be able to find him in time, or that he's already dead, or that they've broken him somehow."

Aubri nodded. "I cannot imagine what this is like for you Red."

Aubri stopped and turned to face Sibylla, taking her other hand. She held them tightly and looked deeply into Sibylla's eyes. Aware of how close their bodies were, Sibylla's heart beat loudly in her ears. They were close enough that Sibylla could see the gold that streaked through the deep blue of Aubri's eyes and the flecks of green. Sibylla could see the detail and texture of the tattoos on Aubri's face, noticing how red they looked through the ash paint that Aubri had applied before the hunt.

"I do not know much about your father," Aubri said, her voice low and sincere. "But I see the determination and fighting spirit that burns in you and your brothers. If your father is anything like you three, then I guarantee the Infected and the Pure will be hard pressed to do anything to him at all."

To keep her tears from Aubri, Sibylla pulled her into a tight hug. To her relief, Aubri returned the hug just as fiercely, and for a long moment, they stood there, two people in the woods, embracing each other in a quiet, reassuring moment. Aubri was right, of course. As distant as Sibylla had gotten from him over the years, she knew that Roger, underneath everything, was a fighter. He had proven that when he had fought off the werewolves at the barn so that his children could escape.

"Thank god," Mr. Darrow said, seemingly unaware that he had shattered the moment. He was dripping with sweat, his face as red as a tomato. "We're almost there."

Sibylla looked around in surprise and saw, through the trees, her house. Taking Aubri's hand again, they covered the distance much faster, barely keeping up with Mr. Darrow's sudden burst of speed. He was ready to be done with the hunt.

Chapter 18

Aubri liked holding Sibylla's hand, especially the jolt of life that passed between them. A kind of purity that lived in it that made Aubri feel invigorated, connected. As soon as she had felt it she knew exactly what it meant, and couldn't wait until Sibylla could figure it out for herself. To her disappointment, Sibylla released her grip when they made it to the driveway and she saw a truck resting in the driveway.

"Who does that belong to?" Aubri asked, noticing the change in Sibylla's expression.

"My boyfriend," Sibylla replied, eyes darting to the front door.

Before they could make a move it swung outward violently, crashing against the railing as Kayla sprinted out. She practically jumped onto Sibylla, wrapping her arms tightly around her neck.

"Where have you been?!" she demanded. "I was worried sick all night! I've been trying to reach you all night!"

"What?" Sibylla asked, clearly surprised by the greeting. "Why? Is everything alright? Are Nate and Hunter alright?"

"Alright?" Kayla asked, smiling broadly. "Alright? Sibylla, they're awake!"

Aubri hadn't seen Sibylla move so quickly in all their time together. Like a blur she was sprinting through the front door, Kayla barely taking a step to follow her before she was gone. Attempting to respect the situation, Aubri followed Kayla at a more dignified pace, letting her take the lead. More than respect, however, Aubri didn't much trust Kayla, even if Sibylla did.

Why she didn't trust her Aubri wasn't sure, yet, but she knew better than to doubt her instincts. They had only met once or twice, not even exchanging a greeting the day before when Sibylla had recruited the girl to look after her brothers. Back home Aubri had a good sense of who people were and what they wanted. It was one of her talents, according to her brother, but she hadn't been able to nail down the nuances of people's behavior on this side of the Gate. Until she could, she would keep a close eye on Kayla.

Going through the front door, they found Sibylla standing in the hallway, a clear question in her eyes.

"Damn Red!" Kayla said, laughing. "You move FAST!"

"Where are they?" Sibylla demanded.

"I was trying to tell you!" Kayla said, too amazed to be thrown by Sibylla's dangerous tone. "They're in the barn! Have been for hours! Wait!"

Sibylla didn't bother waiting, taking off out the back door before Kayla could explain further.

"Wow!" Kayla said, shaking her head, a wild grin plastered in place.

"Who's this?" Aubri asked, not failing to notice the boy sitting on the couch, eyes as wide as Kayla's at having been leaped over by Sibylla.

He was familiar, she had seen him last when he had picked up Sibylla on Halloween. She had a similar feeling about Kane that she had about Kayla, and just like with Kayla, Aubri couldn't put her finger on why.

"Oh! That's Kane," Kayla said, still staring out the door. It hung loose on its hinges, the little window cracked from being thrown open violently too many times. "He's Sibylla's boyfriend."

Aubri looked him up and down with a critical eye, absorbing every detail. Hair shaggy and light brown, he had deep green eyes and a strong jaw. Physically he looked like he was capable of handling himself in a fight. Even though he had a surprised look on his face, his body was loose and relaxed. Not rigid with surprise, like she would have expected from someone who just watched the blur of his girlfriend whip over him faster than any normal human could move.

"Who are you?" he asked, tone barely polite. He sniffed once, twice, and settled back on the couch. He didn't look as relaxed anymore.

"Her name is Aubri," Kayla replied for her, "she's the one that Sibylla is crushing on."

"Crushing?" Kane said, confused.

"Yeah!" Kayla said, still staring distractedly at the door frame. "Since she's bi and all, you know?"

Kane's rigid posture hinted that he did not know that Sibylla was bi, whatever that meant. The term, among many others, that she was trying to learn, was a mystery to Aubri.

"I didn't know that, no," Kane said, releasing an irritated sigh.

"Oh!" Kayla spun to face him, her hands covering her mouth. "Please don't say anything! She hasn't told that many people yet. I just thought you knew."

"There's a lot I don't know," he said, his dark eyes flashing. "Apparently."

Standing, he was easily a foot and a half taller than Aubri, who was standing close enough that she had to angle her head up to look at him. Her throat was exposed, but Aubri had a feeling that if she looked away it would be far more dangerous. Something about him was off, but she couldn't quite explain what it was.

"Excuse me," he said in a tone that suggested he wouldn't mind moving her out of his way, maybe even enjoy it.

Aubri held her ground, consciously keeping her hand away from the pistol on her hip.

Kayla coughed nervously, and Kane broke eye contact to look at her. A second later he let out an explosive sigh.

"Please," he added. "I need to talk to my girlfriend."

Kayla sidestepped just enough for Kane to pass. As he brushed past her Aubri knew that, without a doubt, she did not like him.

ψ

Running as fast as she was, Sibylla was on her brothers before they even knew she had entered the barn, wrapping them both in a hug before the barn doors had a chance to finish falling to the ground.

"You stupid idiots," she muttered, pulling them in tight.

They returned her hug, burying their faces in her shoulders.

"We're sorry," Hunter said.

"Yeah," Nate agreed.

Another moment and a last squeeze later she released them and held them both at arm's length, searching their faces for any signs of their sickness. Since waking up they had both showered and cleaned up. If she hadn't known any better, she wouldn't have even known they had been sick in the first place.

"We-" Hunter began, cut off when Sibylla pulled them back in for another hug.

"You stupid idiots," she said again, tears flowing down her face. She shoved them away from her, fury overwhelming her relief. She had been suppressing her anger for weeks, and now it fought its way to the surface. "I pulled you out of here! I thought you were going to die!"

They stood like they had when they were younger and she had caught them eating cookies before dinner. Eyes on their shoes, hands loose and awkward at their sides, they stood there in front of her, waiting for their punishment. It was such a blinding moment of innocence that, for a second, she wasn't angry anymore. Focusing, she continued her tirade.

"What were you thinking?" she demanded.

"Well," Hunter said, "we-"

"You weren't!" Sibylla cut him off. "If you had been thinking, you wouldn't have messed around with explosives and almost killed yourselves!"

"We know," Nate said. His tone was firm, but he kept his eyes on his shoes. "We're sorry."

"You're damn right you're sorry," Sibylla said, brushing tears off her cheeks.

She couldn't bring herself to finally verbalize that she had been so afraid of failing to take care of them, that she hadn't been able to keep them safe. For years it had just been the three of them, taking care of each other, and the last thing she wanted was to lose them. But she could also see that any further anger would only serve to rub salt in the wound. They had screwed up and knew it. Not to mention that as miraculous as their recovery was, Sibylla was too concerned about their health to keep yelling at them. Sibylla took a deep breath, finally letting go of her anger and allowing relief to come flooding back, bringing a fresh round of tears with it.

"What are you doing in here anyway?" Sibylla asked, wiping her face again.

"Cleaning," Hunter replied, half heartedly lifting a broom in his hand as evidence.

Looking around Sibylla could see that they had been trying to clean up the shards of metal and plastic that littered the ground, forgotten since the accident. They had been at it for some time. Even the stray hay and broken boxes had already been cleared away. She could see that they were trying to make it right, to fix their mistake. They weren't prone to such behavior, the accident must have shaken them to their core.

"Hey guys, I-" she began, cutting herself off when she heard the crunching of feet in snow from outside the barn.

A moment later Kane walked past the ruined doors that had been yanked off their frame in Sibylla's excitement to see her brothers. Wide-eyed, he looked around the room, taking note of all of the details. All thoughts and plans about what their first meeting would be like immediately evaporated from her mind.

"What… is going on?" he asked, eyes settling on Sibylla.

He was scared and confused, that much was obvious. Sibylla realized his heart was pounding so hard that she could hear it reverberating against his ribcage like a drum. Focusing, Sibylla could easily measure its irregular beat, how it jumped when he looked at her, at her brothers. She couldn't blame him, she had just torn the door off the barn as easily as pulling apart a cardboard box. Still, Sibylla had to admit that it hurt to realize that Kane was a little afraid of her.

"Hey," she said awkwardly, feeling very small.

"What is this?" he asked, gesturing first to the broken frame, then the house. "I've never seen you… anyone… move like that. You were so fast, so strong, wha- what the hell is this?"

He had moved from being overwhelmed to sounding terse, angry even.

"Something happened…" she said, less sure than when she had been trying to figure out what to tell Kayla.

"No shit!" Kane said sharply.

"Hey!" Hunter said, stepping up beside Sibylla.

"Jackass!" Nate said, coming on line next to her. "Watch how you talk to our sister."

A look passed over Kane's face that made Sibylla want to take a step back. It wasn't the first time she'd seen it. It was a good indicator that something bad was about to happen. The last thing she wanted was for her brothers to see Kane like that. He was having a rough day, that much was obvious.

"I got this," she said quietly, "go to the house."

For a second they didn't move a muscle, the tension becoming thicker, harder to pretend it didn't exist. She took both of their hands and squeezed them gently. Nate looked up at her, eyes full of concern. Concern and pity, if Sibylla knew her brother. Hating the look, she pushed them toward the door, giving them a tight lipped smile, knowing it wouldn't convince them that everything was going to be okay. Neither of them looked at Kane as they passed, though Nate leaned to the side at the last minute, hitting Kane hard enough to elicit a grunt. They glared at each other until Nate was outside the barn.

Then she was alone.

"Explain," Kane demanded. "Explain what this is."

Something stirred inside Sibylla, but she pushed the feeling away. Kane never liked it when she pushed back. Instead, she clasped her hands uncomfortably in front of her, unsure if she wanted to tell him everything. If she did start to tell him everything but left something out, she knew that he would know. Somehow he always knew when she wasn't being completely honest with him.

"Explain!" he shouted. Sibylla flinched and dropped her gaze to her shoes. "First, you embarrass me, running off right in the middle of my birthday gift to you. Do you know how much that cost me? They're still talking about it!" Kane looked around until he found something to kick, sending an old plastic bucket sailing past Sibylla. "Then you ghost me for weeks, weeks! Me! Now you're ripping doors off hinges and running faster than an Olympic sprinter? What is going on!"

Movement behind Kane caught her eye, and Sibylla saw that Aubri was standing in the backyard of the house with her arms crossed, an oblivious Kayla chatting away next to her. Sibylla could tell by the set of her shoulders that Aubri could hear everything that Kane was saying. And that she did not approve.

The stirring within Sibylla caught fire, low at first, but it was quickly building. His tone bothered her, and she did not like how it felt. Nor did she like the not-so-subtle threat of the bucket being kicked in her direction. She needed to end the fight sooner rather than later, so in the last second she decided the truth was the best route to take.

"I fight werewolves," she said quietly.

"What?" he said, dumbfounded. "No, no you don't. Don't push that BS with me."

"It's true," Sibylla insisted, "for the past few weeks I've been training and working hard-"

"Don't lie to me Sibylla," he said, cutting her off. "You can barely throw a punch, how the hell can you fight something that doesn't even freaking exist?"

The fire was burning brighter then, threatening to overwhelm her. She needed him to understand, to say that he approved.

He wants proof? She thought. I can give him proof.

A quick look around confirmed that the werewolf skulls were still on the small table, the blanket still covering them. Without hesitating she strode over and yanked the blanket off, revealing the skulls in all their horrific beauty.

"Here, look," she said, handing one of the skulls over to him.

Taking it Kane gasped and immediately dropped it. Fragile and brittle from the intense heat of the fire, the skull shattered on the hard packed dirt floor. Face pale, almost green, he kicked the pieces away from him as if scattering them would erase what they had been. Then he was furiously wiping his hands on his pants.

"What the hell was that?" he demanded.

"The skull of a werewolf," Sibylla said.

"What?" he asked, horrified. "There's no way that's real."

"They're all real," Sibylla protested, gesturing at the others.

Kane rubbed his eyes with the palms of his hands and then seemed to remember the skull and shook his hands away from his face.

After that he paced in small, furious circles, muttering to himself. Sibylla waited on pins and needles, not sure what he was going to do or say next.

"Look," he finally said. He turned to face her, squaring his shoulders, keeping his distance from the remains. "This is nuts, right?"

"Yeah," Sibylla said carefully. "It's pretty wild."

"Yeah," he said, taking on a more gentle tone.

Approaching her slowly, taking a wide circle around the bone shards on the floor, holding out his arms. Relieved, Sibylla crossed the room to meet him. The fire within her had died down completely, leaving in its wake a deep desire for something normal. Relieved at his invitation, Sibylla met him halfway, falling into his familiar embrace.

It was the side of him that she had been drawn to in the first place when they had first met. Kane could be incredibly kind and gentle and thoughtful and vulnerable. Memories of quiet evenings on her favorite bridge, of picnics out in his backyard, of gentle kisses under the bleachers at games.

"It's just been a lot, you know?" he murmured into her hair.

Sibylla nodded, burrowing deeper into his chest, inhaling his familiar scent of spray on deodorant and the detergent his mom used when she washed his clothes.

Of course, he was under a lot of stress. She could say with confidence that she had no idea what he was going through anymore, they hadn't talked in weeks after all.

"Between your birthday, which, I have to say, didn't go quite as well as I'd hoped," he continued, attempting a joke.

She could understand that she had run off on him without an explanation, right at the peak of his plans. Anyone would be upset by that.

"And then I haven't heard from you at all," he said, pulling her tighter. "And now this stuff about werewolves? What am I supposed to think?"

That was true, it was a lot to take in all at once, and she had pretty much ambushed him.

"Hold on," he said, pulling his phone out and stepping away from her. "It's my parents, I have to take this."

Without wasting a moment he was out of the barn, wandering a dozen yards away. Crossing her arms against a sudden chill, Sibylla focused on what he was saying, watching the way his shoulders were tense and rigid.

"I know, I'm sorry," he said, staring into the distance. "I know I wasn't supposed to go out, but Kayla called me and I thought I would try and get some answers."

He paused and nodded. "I'm worried about her, about us. It's starting to feel a little one sided, you know? Like I'm the only one who cares about us like I'm the only one putting in the work. Honestly, I'm worried there's someone else."

Wincing, Sibylla looked away and tried to stop listening, wandering back into the barn.

Someone else? She thought, why would he think I'm cheating on him?

She had just told him the truth, but maybe it wasn't enough. Admittedly, fighting werewolves was pretty fantastical, but between that and cheating on him, which one was more likely? As far as she was concerned fighting werewolves was the answer, but evidently, she hadn't done enough to put his mind at ease.

Then she thought of Aubri, how flirty she was, how it felt to hold hands. Even the memory sent a flutter of butterflies in Sibylla's chest and ignited the electricity. Was Aubri the other woman? Sibylla hadn't thought so, but what would Kane think if he had been there earlier, or if he had seen how much Aubri flirted with her? Then she realized he probably wouldn't have noticed, since she still hadn't told him that she was bi.

Here she was, practically dating Aubri and her current boyfriend didn't even know that she played both sides of the field. He would be devastated if he found out that she had kept something so big from him. Crossing her arms over her stomach she felt lower than dirt, definitely not worthy of someone as good to her as Kane had been. He deserved better than that.

"Hey," Kane said from the doorway. "I need to go. Turns out when you run out on family breakfast without warning your parents they get a little pissed. Stuff is bad enough right now, I didn't realize that dropping everything to see you would add fuel to the fire, you know?"

"Everything okay?" she asked, concerned. "What's going on at home?"

"I don't want to talk about it," he said, fidgeting. "Not right now anyway. See you around Red. Get some sleep though, you look tired."

With that, he was gone. No hug or kiss. Just gone. It stung, but she tried to convince herself that she had deserved it. If she could have secrets, so could he. Kane would tell her when he was ready, just like she would tell him when she was ready. Walking out the door she watched him get into his truck and drive off, not bothering to spare Sibylla a second glance.

"A massive prick," Nate said from where he was seated next to Hunter against the wall of the barn.

Sibylla wasn't surprised, she had heard them whispering to each other whenever Kane was talking.

"Y'all aren't that great at following directions," she said flatly, not wanting to deal with their judgment. What did they know?

"We know," Hunter said.

"But we had something for you, something that could cheer you up," Nate continued.

"Especially with dickface coming by for a visit," Hunter added.

Sibylla sighed and pinched the bridge of her nose. She considered reminding them for the hundredth time that his name was Kane, but, just like the other times, they would ignore her.

"What is it?" she asked warily.

They had played a similar game when she was younger, and on more than one occasion she had ended up with something like slugs and snails in her tiny fist. Once they had even used a snake.

They took her to a corner of the barn behind Sir Moo's stall and showed her a footlocker covered in chunks of dirt and bits of hay. The top had been wiped clean, showing the painted initials "D.L."

"What's this?" she asked, kneeling in front of it.

"It was mom's," Hunter said, "once we opened it we thought you would prefer to have it."

A tear formed at the corner of her eye, and she quickly wiped it away. She owned precious little of anything that belonged to her mom, and now she had a whole box. Pausing just long enough to give them both a hug, Sibylla wasted no time popping the footlocker open, an excited smile splitting her face as she looked over its contents.

"This is perfect," she whispered.

Chapter 19

"You are sure you want to use those?" Aubri asked, not bothering to hide her skepticism.

Sibylla spun a revolver around her finger several times before sliding it into the leather holster hanging from her hip. It was one of many weapons she now had with her that Aubri was clearly not a fan of. On her left hip was a sawed off break-barrel shotgun with the name "Clacker" carefully engraved in flowing script on its side. Hanging below that was a tomahawk, and across her lower back was a long knife. Holding her belt up were suspenders that held another set of throwing knives. All sharp edges were coated with silver, and everything was well worn and taken care of.

None of it had been touched in well over a decade, at least until the twins had cracked it open. Wasting no time, Sibylla immediately dove into searching everything, barely taking the time to examine each object before reaching for the next in her excitement. At first, she had been surprised at how old fashioned everything was. None of it looked like it had been made in the last hundred years, and Sibylla hadn't found anything that explained why.

When she had thought about it though, it had made some sense. Everything was simple, less prone to failure. Plus, revolvers never jammed, at least according to Mr. Darrow. If a round didn't fire, just cycle through to the next. All of it focused on distance as well, easily thrown and recovered, everything razor sharp and dependable.

"Without a doubt," Sibylla replied confidently.

"You realize that there are far better choices than those at your house?" Aubri asked, probably for the tenth time.

Aubri wasn't wrong. They had found at least two gun cabinets with rifles, shotguns, and handguns, all of which were much more modern than what Sibylla was carrying. Sibylla didn't care. She had never felt closer to her mom than in that moment, standing in the woods, preparing for a hunt, sure that she was making the right choice.

"I know," Sibylla said, doing a practice quick draw. "It's a little late though, don't you think?"

Unlike the first hunt, they were working between the full moons instead of during them, to try and catch the werewolves at their weakest. What that meant was Sibylla had precious little time to practice with her mom's gear and absorb as much information as possible.

In a few short weeks, she tried to learn everything from tracking to reconnaissance to setting traps. By no means an expert, Mr. Darrow still felt confident that she could handle it without him. Instead, he had chosen to stay behind and keep an eye on the twins. Nate and Hunter had also proven to be invaluable, adding more details and context to what she knew about werewolves. By the time she stepped out the front door that morning with Aubri, Sibylla felt as though she could handle anything.

Now it was just her and Aubri, patrolling the vast expanse of the Wyoming wilderness. Alone. Several hours away from anyone else. Possibly for days, depending on how long it took for a werewolf to show up. Aubri said the tracks were fresh enough, but that didn't mean that the werewolves would be predictable enough to follow a pattern or to rely on that one trail out of the hundreds that crisscrossed the wilderness around Red Falls.

"I do not like this location either," Aubri said, looking both directions down the trail.

Sibylla had set them up on a blind corner in a trail that had a fairly steep cliff on one side and a substantial slope on the other. Based on what Mr. Darrow had told her about ambushes and what her brothers mentioned from the book it was a natural choke point. A natural choke point meant that the enemy could only go one direction into what was called the 'kill zone.' Sibylla had even dug a 'rolling trap', something she had pulled from the internet. It was the size of the target's foot: they stepped in, slipping between two rollers that had sharpened stakes stuck into it. It would keep the werewolf in place long enough for Sibylla to take it out.

All of it was Sibylla's attempt to get the same level of detail that Mr. Darrow had achieved on the first hunt. Sibylla had done the research, she had followed trails and found tracks, and had set up a trap. The only thing she needed now was a werewolf to come around the corner.

"I know," she said, trying to quell her rising annoyance with Aubri's negative comments on every part of her plan. "But it'll work, I know it will. They come through there, step on that, and then it's just a matter of taking it out." She pointed at each element as she explained her plan again. "It's simple, and simple is what it should be. Plus the added benefit of being nowhere close to a house."

"We are also upwind, we won't be able to smell or hear them coming," Aubri said as though she hadn't heard Sibylla.

"It'll work," Sibylla snapped. "Trust me."

Aubri took a long look at her, weighing her reply. "Okay," she said finally. "Where are we going to observe the trap?"

Sibylla wasn't sure Aubri was completely on board, but she could work with that. It only took a few more minutes to finish hiding the trap and work their way up the slope to a cluster of boulders that jutted out twenty yards from the trail. Sibylla took the first watch, keeping her eyes glued to the curve of the trail, hoping that something would come by soon so that she could prove to Aubri that it was a good plan.

Aubri, for her part, lay on her back on the boulder, seeming to absorb the rays of the sun. After a minute a smile spread across her face, and she sighed contentedly.

"What's up?" Sibylla asked, eying her from her boulder. She couldn't help but notice the curve of Aubri's lips, or how the tattoos on her face framed her eyes. The ashy paste she smeared around her eyes before every hunt contrasted beautifully with her olive skin, which seemed to glow in the sun. Even the way her hands lay on the rifle resting across her chest was graceful.

"Your world is beautiful," Aubri murmured. "I've never seen anything like this."

"Y'all don't have cold or snow in Laternum?" Sibylla asked, forcing herself to watch the trail.

"In some places," Aubri said. "They are too dangerous for initiates into the Sacred Legion to travel to."

"Huh, I never thought..." Sibylla trailed off, feeling a familiar sensation.

It was the same feeling she had had on the first hunt, just before the werewolf had shown up. Unlike the first time, Sibylla could almost feel the werewolf through the ground, like every time its foot touched the ground an electrical pulse was sent to her brain. She couldn't even smell or hear them yet. Whatever this new ability was, she certainly liked it.

"What is it?" Aubri asked, already crouching with her rifle on her shoulder.

"A werewolf," Sibylla said, excitement and adrenaline surging through her. "Listen," she said, turning to Aubri. "When it comes around the corner, it has to be me who takes it down, okay? Don't step in unless I ask you to, okay?"

Aubri hesitated, clearly not comfortable with Sibylla's request.

"Please," Sibylla pleaded, feeling the werewolf coming closer with every passing second. "I need this."

"Okay," Aubri relented. "I will only step in if you ask. That is my promise."

"Deal," Sibylla agreed eagerly, turning back to watch the corner. Any second the werewolf would be in sight, and Sibylla would be the one to take it down.

To her surprise, it wasn't a werewolf but a hiker who came around the corner, dressed in expensive flannel and hiking boots, carrying a pack on his back and a walking stick in each hand. By all appearances, he was just a tourist out for a hike in the wilderness of Wyoming. Before Sibylla knew what she was doing she was sprinting down the hill, shouting for the man to stop. Foot hovering mere inches over the trap Sibylla tackled the man to the ground, landing in a heap of twisted limbs and hiking gear.

"What the hell?" the man demanded, struggling to get away from Sibylla and get back on his feet.

"I am so sorry!" Sibylla exclaimed. She hauled the man to his feet and started brushing dirt from his shirt.

"Is this how someone is treated just trying to get in a peaceful hike?" the man demanded, slapping Sibylla's hands away. He brandished one of the walking sticks, waving so that Sibylla had to take a step back. "Explain yourself!"

"I am so sorry!" Sibylla said again, still trying to figure out how she could have gotten it so wrong. What were the odds of running into a random hiker on that particular trail? "I thought you were…" She trailed off, not sure how to explain that she thought he was a werewolf and had been ready to kill him without hesitation.

"Well?!" the man demanded.

"I thought you were a… uh…" she stammered, backing away. Maybe if she stayed away from town for a week she wouldn't have to run into the man by accident.

"She thought you were me," a brutal voice spat.

Sibylla's eyes widened as she looked over the hiker's shoulder and saw the deformed shape of a werewolf lumbering into view. It was just as twisted as the one that Mr. Darrow had shot, but taller even as it staggered forward on bowed legs. Drool dripped in massive globs from its jaws, mixing with blood from the splits in its lips. It flexed its clawed fingers in anticipation, coiled like a spring.

"Hello Sentinel," it said, the words barely formed through its warped teeth.

"That's… That's a…" the hiker sputtered, fear radiating from him in waves.

Without another moment's hesitation, Sibylla yanked the hiker back and behind her with one hand and drew her revolver with the other. Up close the werewolves moved much faster than Sibylla would have thought, her first two shots going wide before she was knocked to the ground. Scrambling, she fired point blank into its shoulder, eliciting a howl of pain and forcing it to loosen its grip on her.

Kicking away she fired three more times, all three hitting its arm as it sacrificed the limb to protect its chest and head. A terrifying click let Sibylla know that her revolver was empty. Shoving it back into her holster Sibylla yanked the tomahawk loose in time to be tackled again. Even with a useless arm, the werewolf was proving to be more than just problematic. Gripping the tomahawk tighter Sibylla worked her arm loose and swung wildly, trying to connect with anything at all. With the other hand, she palmed his throat, forcing his snapping jaws away from her face.

After another useless swing, Sibylla remembered Mr. Darrow's advice: don't get stuck on something that wasn't working. She released the tomahawk and pulled out a knife and started stabbing and hacking wildly, not slowing down or stopping until, howling with rage, the werewolf rolled off her. It staggered to its feet, its good hand trying to stymie the flow of blood from its wounds. Covered in foul smelling blood, Sibylla released a howl of her own, her vision slowly turning red.

She threw the knife as hard as she could, snatching up the tomahawk and sprinting forward, leaping onto the werewolf. Any semblance of training had evaporated. The only goal that mattered was trying to tear the life away from the monster before it had a chance to do anything else.

It took a few minutes to realize that it was no longer moving.

"I think… I think you got it…" the hiker said weakly from behind her.

"Right," Sibylla gasped, fighting for air.

Then she looked down and saw what she had done. Looking at the gruesome remains, the torn skin and muscles and fractured bones, it was all Sibylla could do to not vomit. There was no way that she could have done that, was there? She wasn't a violent person, the kill should have been quick and clean. It should not have been that messy.

"Oh my god," she said, body beginning to shake, the realization of what she had just done sinking in.

The werewolf, while technically a monster, was also a human. It was someone's son or brother or father. An image of Roger came to mind, and the thought that she had just killed some little girl's father… she wanted to throw up.

It attacked you first, she reminded herself, trying and failing to comfort herself.

The problem, she realized, was that killing someone else's father or brother or son was part of her world, her calling. Why hadn't it occurred to her that, beneath their twisted and pained exteriors, there was a person? She hadn't even hesitated.

It attacked you first, she thought. You killed him out of self defense.

The monster's chest rose slightly, and a choked gurgle escaped from its cracked muzzle.

"Oh my god," she whispered, icy panic shooting through her. It was still alive.

It couldn't be alive. The hatchet was edged in silver, and the wounds were a bloody mess of torn flesh and broken bone. Blood spurted and leaked from dozens of gashes, its legs, and arms beginning to twitch. Growing louder, the werewolf began to weakly thrash around on the trail, too confused to attack her or run away. There was no reason why it should still be alive, why it should be suffering.

It is in pain, she thought dully, the only thought that penetrated the thickening cloud of panic that paralyzed her. She should do something, anything. Her body would not respond.

"I must say, Sentinel, you are not as good as we thought you were…"

A cacophony of grotesque noises, tearing and popping and cracking, told Sibylla that something was wrong before she turned around to see the hiker shedding his skin like dirty clothes. His bones and joints popped seemingly at random, out of order, as they grew and changed position, elongating and twisting him into his true form. All the while his yellowing eyes never left hers, and the terrible grin never left his face.

Backpedaling from the new threat, Sibylla had just enough time to draw and aim Clacker before the ground suddenly disappeared beneath her foot. Horrifying realization flooded in as her left foot slid between the two rolling pins, the spikes penetrating deeply into her thigh. Her momentum carried her further, tearing at her leg before she came to a sudden, jarring stop.

At the same time, her hands spasmed involuntarily, pulling the trigger before she had a chance to correct her aim, the silver pellets flying harmlessly into the air, the single shot shotgun useless. Pain, magnified by her now unchecked senses, cascaded up her limbs and into her spine, numbing her brain to the threat that slowly stalked forward.

The hiker chuckled darkly, the sound like crushed glass on sheet metal, an ugly smile plastered on his face, a confident gait pulling him forward. Sibylla couldn't think past the searing pain until he loomed above her, his shadow blocking the sun. The sudden hopelessness of her situation pierced the agony. Still, she wasn't going to just give up, was she?

No, she thought, grimacing as she willed her spasming and jerking hands toward one of the few knives she had left.

It took enormous effort, but she was able to work it loose from its sheath, all the while the hiker observed her with obvious amusement. Terror at his apathy settled on Sibylla like a heavy weight, pushing out any rational thought she may have had left. Hands shaking violently, the knife clattered uselessly to the dirt.

"Worthless," the hiker growled.

Reaching down he tore Sibylla from the trap, leaving behind a dark red pool of blood and bits of her flesh. Sibylla screamed, pain arcing through her like frozen lightning. Darkness threatened to overtake her, black shadows creeping into the edges of her vision. Gasping, she saw the hiker rear his arm back, claws outstretched.

Thunder cracked, echoing in the surrounding forest. The hiker's hand relaxed, dropping Sibylla. Landing on her bad leg Sibylla blacked out, her last view being the hiker collapsing lifeless to the ground. When she regained consciousness she was screaming, her hands scrambling clumsily in an attempt to stop the blood flowing from her leg.

Then Aubri was at her side, swiping Sibylla's hands away to get a better look at the wound. Eyes flashing, she unclipped a small pack from her vest and opened it, dumping its contents on the ground. Working quickly she applied a tourniquet to Sibylla's upper thigh, cinching it painfully tight.

"I need to stop the bleeding," she said when Sibylla tried to loosen it. "Trust me."

"Trust you?" Sibylla hissed in pain. Aubri was tearing away what was left of her pants, yanking loose bits of fabric that had been stuffed into the wound by the spikes. "What were you waiting for?"

"You," Aubri said, voice quivering slightly. "You wanted to handle it, you wanted me to wait for you to ask me to help."

Finding what she was looking for Aubri pulled the cap off a small red cylinder, revealing a short needle.

"What's that for?" Sibylla asked through gritted teeth.

Her entire body was rigid, pain cascading over her. She could not think of a time when she had experienced pain like what she was experiencing at that moment. It made it impossible to focus, lightheaded as she was from blood loss. Sights and smells and sounds and flavors and feelings consumed her, overwhelming her. All at once she could see every painful detail of the mangled werewolf and could smell her blood mixing with the horrific odors emanating from the sores and infections of the Infected.

Some of the werewolf blood must have gotten into her mouth because something tasted as bad as the smell that hung in the air like a sticky cloud. Stomach spasming, she vomited, Aubri turning Sibylla's head to the side so that she would throw up in the dirt instead of herself. The only thing that she could feel was the feeling of her skin, torn and tearing, her muscles trying to operate normally despite their destruction.

In that moment she would have given anything for it to stop. Gritting her teeth she grabbed Aubri's leg, fingers digging into the muscle as pain wracked her body. If it was painful for Aubri she didn't show it, continuing to work as quickly as possible.

Aubri plunged the needle into Sibylla's good leg, the penetration barely registering through the rest of her pain. Immediately a blessed numbness flowed through her like a river of cool water. Sibylla stilled, laying like a corpse on the ground.

"What was that?" she mumbled. Her lips felt numb and clumsy.

"For the pain," Aubri replied, hands dancing over the wound, searching it, trying to decipher the extent of the injuries.

Sibylla barely felt it, registering dimly the pressure and tugging. Satisfied, Aubri pulled a small canister from the pile on the ground, showing it to Sibylla. "This is called a Second Skin. It will create a temporary bandage that will flex and stretch with the muscle."

"Right," Sibylla murmured, barely noticing the can or the sensation it caused when Aubri sprayed it on. The only thing that penetrated the fog spreading through her brain was the vibrancy of the sky. Of colors in general. Everything appeared to glow in a way she had never noticed before.

"Am I okay?" Sibylla asked, eyes losing focus.

"Yes," Aubri said quickly, blocking the sun as she leaned over to search Sibylla's eyes.

Aubri's eyes were so clear and fierce. Sibylla could have looked into them all day, noting the swirling of blues with eddies of gold, as if Aubri's eyes were actually water, not solid color like Sibylla's. She liked that.

"Did you know your eyes are like the sky?" Sibylla said, words slurring slightly. "Very pretty. Like water."

"Thank you," Aubri replied, smiling weakly as she stuffed the supplies back into their pouch before clipping it back onto her vest. "You can tell me all about it when we get back."

"He's still alive," Sibylla said, trying to gesture to the mass of flesh and bone that was the first werewolf.

"We need to get you back," Aubri said, ignoring her. "Before the medicine wears off."

Vaguely, Sibylla felt that there was more to the statement than Aubri was letting on like it wasn't just the medicine wearing off that concerned Aubri. Fortunately, the medicine pushed the thought back with little effort. Sibylla had never felt more relaxed in her entire life. Aubri easily scooped up Sibylla and cradled her in her arms.

"You're really strong," Sibylla said, impressed.

"Thank you," Aubri said again, moving quickly, eyes darting to every tree and rock on the edges of the trail.

Clouded as her brain was, Sibylla couldn't figure out what it was that Aubri was looking for. Everything was so peaceful. So quiet.

Sibylla leaned her head on Aubri's shoulder, exhausted. Sleeping seemed like the best idea in the world. So inviting.

"Stay awake Red," Aubri pleaded, squeezing Sibylla's arms in an effort to wake her up.

"Right…" Sibylla murmured, eyes already closing again, darkness descending. She knew, deep down, that Aubri was right. There was something else there as well, something she couldn't place. How was she supposed to stay awake? "Ask me something…"

"What is your favorite flower?" Aubri asked without hesitating.

Sibylla tried to think about that, but couldn't remember any flowers at all. Closing her eyes, she just felt so tired.

"Silvery Lupine…" Sibylla replied. Then she giggled uncontrollably. "Like a blue wolf. Sort of thing…"

Aubri didn't find the answer particularly funny. In fact, she seemed even more concerned than she had a moment before. Their speed increased and Aubri stopped searching the trees and the rocks. Jostled slightly, Sibylla felt a shadow of the pain returning, and she furrowed her brows irritably at the intruder. She nuzzled deeper into Aubri's neck.

A dark thought occurred to her then, anchored firmly in the sea of tranquility that covered her mind. Was she dying? The thought created waves of worry, and panic started to reach her. How would she know? Strangely, Sibylla couldn't remember what had happened, why Aubri was carrying her in the first place.

"Am I dying?" she asked Aubri, voice weak.

"No," Aubri said, breathing heavily. "I wish you had chosen a site closer to home though," Aubri added, trying to make a joke. "Just stay awake, I promise I will get you home."

Sibylla faded out then, the world shrouded in darkness. When it came back she was in the back seat of the car, the pain returning rapidly. Groaning, she tried to shift, but every new position generated another wave of pain crashing down on her. Giving up she slumped back, closing her eyes to the painfully bright light streaming through the window.

"Stay awake!" Aubri shouted from the driver's seat. "Please, please just stay awake!"

The car jolted and Sibylla blacked out again.

Chapter 20

Gasping, Sibylla snapped awake, leaping to her feet. She couldn't understand her surroundings, a multitude of images and sensations rattling around in her brain. The snowy path, blood everywhere, her leg in tatters, the fear.

The fear. It snaked through her instantly, seizing her limbs and mind. Feet numb, shaking uncontrollably, Sibylla collapsed to her knees, gripping her ears in a vain attempt to keep out the sound of the bloody gurgling of the Infected as his life slowly flowed out of him. Or the sound her mom's tomahawk made when it tore into his flesh and cracked his bone, splattering her face.

Clawing at her ears, gritting her teeth, and squeezing her eyes closed, she was confronted by the face of the hiker as he held her off the ground, his oozing hand wrapped around her throat. A sharp ache gripped her leg at the memory, and it all combined into the constant hacking and chopping and gurgling of the Infected.

"Sibylla!"

Sibylla gasped and rocked back, her back slamming into something solid. Gripping the blankets beneath her she looked around the room wildly, trying to identify who or what was in the room with her, half expecting to find the hacked remains standing in her doorway. Instead, she saw two blue eyes, blazing through the darkness that had a firm grip on her mind.

She launched herself across the room and wrapped her arms around Aubri, squeezing her tightly. Aubri returned the hug, stroking Sibylla's hair.

"You're okay," Aubri whispered.

"No, I'm not!" Sibylla hissed, the full understanding of the images snapping into sharp focus. "I messed it up, I messed it all up, everything!"

Hot tears flowed down her cheeks and she made no attempt to stop them. It had to have been one of the worst hunts in the history of the Sentinels. Not only had she completely failed to kill either of the werewolves, she had been dumb enough to stumble into her own trap. What if she was crippled? The idea sent a flood of fresh tears and sobs wracked her body. Now there was no chance at all that she was going to be able to save her dad, keep the Gate closed, or fix the werewolf crisis in Red Falls.

Shuddering, Sibylla was assaulted once again by the images of the bloody mass that she had made out of the first werewolf. She had lost control, had hacked at it wildly, and had caused it to suffer needlessly because of her incompetence. Worst of all, she felt a deep regret for having attacked it in the first place. Despite knowing that it was an evil, twisted creature, one that killed and attacked without remorse, Sibylla felt guilty. Did they deserve to die?

Not like that, she thought, fresh tears beginning to flow. She sagged to the floor in defeat.

"It's okay, just breathe," Aubri said, sinking to the floor with her, and she kept saying it until Sibylla finally calmed down.

Taking a deep, shuddering breath, Sibylla shifted and laid down, laying her head in Aubri's lap. Stroking her hair, Aubri started humming a song that was unfamiliar to Sibylla, but it's warm tones and gentle notes were comforting. Images of grassy fields and sunshine pushed away the blood and horror. They stayed like that for a while, until the tears had dried and her heart rate returned to normal.

"Better?" Aubri asked gently.

Sibylla nodded gratefully.

"What was that?" she asked.

"My mother used to sing me to sleep," Aubri said, "it is one of my favorite songs."

"Are there words?" Sibylla asked, curious about Aubri's upbringing.

"Yes," Aubri smiled. "I will teach it to you sometime."

"I'd like that," Sibylla said, looking up.

Aubri smiled back and continued humming. After what felt like too short a time, the door opened and Mr. Darrow wheeled in, taking in the whole scene in a glance.

"Rough wakeup?" he asked.

"Something like that," Sibylla said, reluctantly sitting up. "I couldn't stop thinking about…" she trailed off, afraid it would bring the memories back.

"It's called a flashback," Mr. Darrow nodded, "it feels like you're trapped in the worst moment of your life, right when you think you're about to die. I've had them for years, mostly from my time in the army."

"Do they go away?" she asked, horrified to think it might happen again.

Mr. Darrow smiled apologetically. "They haven't for me, but I promise it'll get easier. Whenever it happens just remember to keep breathing and stay grounded, in through the nose, out through the mouth. And find someone you can talk to about it. Keeping it trapped in your head can make it so much worse."

Closing her eyes Sibylla squeezed Aubri's hand. She wasn't encouraged by the thought, but there wasn't much to do about it at the moment. The first thing she needed to do was admit to him that she had failed her mission. Miserably.

"I… the hunt…" she started, not sure what to say. Disappointing him was the last thing she wanted to do, and admitting that she had almost sent her spiraling again.

"I know," Mr. Darrow said gently. "It's okay. Everyone's first time out is hard, no matter how good your training is. You survived it, you can learn from it and do better on the next one."

Sibylla nodded but, once again, did not feel encouraged. Remembering how mangled her leg had been and looking at the thick bandage that covered the damage, she couldn't think of a way she could be better. Sure, she had learned valuable lessons. Now, however, she was handicapped. All the knowledge in the world wouldn't help her if she couldn't physically put that knowledge into practice.

"It is true," Aubri said. "On my first mission, my hands shook so badly that I couldn't reload my weapon properly. If my brother hadn't been there, I would have died instead of spending two weeks recovering."

Sibylla was surprised at that. The idea that Aubri wouldn't be one hundred percent proficient at everything she did all the time seemed laughable.

"I know this is hard," Mr. Darrow said, leaning forward in his wheelchair, "but we need to talk about what happened."

A deep knot of dread built in her stomach, and she felt cold. It struck Sibylla that she hadn't actually had an anxiety attack in some time and that she almost couldn't remember what it felt like. Mr. Darrow noticed her slight shiver and nodded knowingly.

"That's the adrenaline kicking in again," he said, flexing his own hands. "Your body is preparing for a fight. Trust me, I don't want to push you on this, but the sooner we can move past it the better, right?"

Sibylla hesitated, taking a deep breath through her nose. The last thing she wanted was to relive any of it. Aubri wrapped her arm around her shoulder, pulling her in close, a quiet reminder that she would be there for her. Sibylla smiled weakly, the small gesture giving her the strength to move forward.

"Right," she said finally.

"I want to know, first of all, if you know what went wrong?" Mr. Darrow asked.

Sibylla snorted. "What didn't go wrong?"

"Specifically Red, I'm looking for the big things," Mr. Darrow said, staying serious, his tone quiet but firm. "Don't get lost in the small details, think about the source of the problems."

Hesitantly, Sibylla thought back to the hunt, looking at all of the things that hadn't been as good as she had been hoping.

"I'm looking for four," he said, giving her a hint.

"The location was bad," she answered slowly, "I couldn't see them coming. The weapons were bad, they take too long to reload and brought me too close to the werewolves..." That one stung a little. As much as she hated to admit it, she should have kept her distance. "The trap was..."

Then she looked down at her leg, nervous about what she would see there. To her surprise, it wasn't even bandaged. The skin had closed up completely, though it was covered in a spiderweb of angry looking scars and gouges. It had healed completely, but it was far from pretty.

"What's number four?" Mr. Darrow asked, redirecting her focus.

Sibylla tried to think of the fourth thing he was looking for but was increasingly more distracted by the memories threatening to break her to pieces again. Aubri kissed the top of her head. It wasn't much, just a quick peck, but it offered Sibylla a warm spot to cling to.

"I rushed it," she said finally. "I rushed in when the hiker came in. I didn't even think about it."

"Good," Mr. Darrow said, "I know you will no matter what I say, but don't let these things drag you down. Think about them, consider them, solve them, and move on. Okay?"

Sibylla nodded, wiping away another tear. Hopefully, it was the last one, she hated crying in front of people.

"Aubri said that you could feel them coming?" Mr. Darrow asked. "Sense them?"

Sibylla thought back to the beginning of the hunt and even the first hunt with Mr. Darrow. On the first hunt, it had felt like a tickle on the edge of her perception. This time was different, however. She had felt it through the Earth, like a strong electrical pulse. What had been the difference between the two? Was the hiker closer to the Pure than to the outright Infected?

"Something like that," she said slowly. "I felt connected to them somehow, like we were all on a tightrope and every step they took came straight to me."

Mr. Darrow furrowed his brow and knitted his fingers together, deep in thought. Aubri too looked tense, her eyes glued on Mr. Darrow as if she could read his mind if she tried hard enough.

"Is there something wrong?" she asked, confused.

"I'm not sure," Mr. Darrow said cryptically. "It's unusual. I certainly have never heard of a Sentinel being able to do that."

"It is the same in the Legion," Aubri added, "I have never met anyone who could do that."

Sibylla looked between the two of them, hoping they would give more information, but when none seemed forthcoming, she sighed.

"This is frustrating," she said.

Mr. Darrow nodded. "It's going to be tough, Red, for a while."

"Can I see my brothers?" she asked, wanting to change the subject before she spiraled a third time in five minutes.

"When they get home," Mr. Darrow said, snapping back to the room.

"Home?" Sibylla said, looking back and forth between Aubri and Mr. Darrow. "Where are they?"

"School of course," Mr. Darrow said as if it were the natural answer. "Y'all still need to pass high school."

Thinking back, Sibylla realized that her brothers couldn't be in school. She had left for the hunt on Friday.

"What day is it?" she asked, growing more concerned by the moment.

"Wednesday," Mr. Darrow said casually.

"I've been out for six days?!" Sibylla said, horrified.

Mr. Darrow looked at her sympathetically. "There was a lot of damage to that leg of yours Red, there was no way you were going to school in the shape you were in."

Sibylla slumped back into the bed, horrified. Granted, she had been missing a lot of school since she had taken on the mantle, so another week wasn't too bad. Yet she found herself deeply disturbed that, once again, she had been down for the count for an extended period of time. More and more it seemed as though she wasn't worthy of being the Sentinel.

"They'll be back in a few hours," Mr. Darrow continued, looking at her closely. "In the meantime, I'd like you to come with me to the Gate. It's time you got in touch with Yadder."

"Yadder?" Sibylla said, confused. "Who's Yadder?"

"Yadder is your Keeper," was all that Mr. Darrow would say about it, so Sibylla assumed she would have to wait to meet them to know more.

Leaving her room turned out to be more difficult than Sibylla had expected. Even being alone in the room was daunting, so much so that she asked Aubri to stay while she changed. Aubri had turned away at Sibylla's insistence, even though it felt silly to Sibylla to request it. She had changed in front of Kayla and other girls numerous times on trips or at the school gym, but the idea of Aubri seeing her naked made her blush far too much. Anyway, it was a welcome distraction from the nerves of leaving the house.

Chapter 21

Strangely, the drive to the Gate had been uneventful from beginning to end. Nothing at all happened. They didn't even talk while they drove. Yet something felt wrong to Sibylla. The silence was strange enough. Mr. Darrow didn't offer up any sage advice, and Aubri didn't throw out a flirty comment.

Worse than the silence was the sudden presence of werewolves when they entered the town. Peering into the sparse traffic on the sidewalks as people went about their daily business Sibylla couldn't see anyone that looked like a werewolf. No one even looked at their car as they passed. But they were there, somewhere. In the dark shadows between the buildings, or peering through the darkened windows of houses, Sibylla could feel them all around her. It had been a staggering experience and almost sent her into another anxiety attack.

Fortunately, their presence began to subside once they had passed over the river that split the new town from the old and had disappeared completely once they had parked in front of the Gate.

"Soooo…." she said slowly, turning to face Mr. Darrow. "What do I do? Is there a spell or incantation or something?"

Mr. Darrow laughed nervously. "Nothing so mysterious. Just open the door and walk through."

Sibylla looked at him doubtfully.

"That's it?" she asked, almost disappointed. "That's all I have to do?"

"That's it," Mr. Darrow nodded. "Too easy, right?"

"Yeah, right," Sibylla murmured, looking at the Gate nervously.

"Good luck," Aubri said, putting a comforting hand on Sibylla's shoulder.

Sibylla nodded and took a shaky breath. Stepping forward she felt a warm reassurance emanating from the Gate's oak panels, helping her step with more confidence. When she found herself standing arm's length from the iron handle that would allow her to open the Gate's heavy doors, she hesitated.

Stop being childish, she chided herself.

Sibylla nodded to herself and grabbed the handle.

When she stepped forward she found herself in a completely different place than she was expecting. Instead of the lawn on the other side of the doors, she found herself in a giant, ornate library, surrounded by what seemed like an unending array of shelves full to bursting with books of every type and shape. A dome was an impossible distance above her, made of colored glass that cast the space in bright, vibrant pigments. Spiral staircases led up to higher levels that contained even more books and shelves. In front of her was an open sitting space, filled with chairs and tables.

Stranger still was the only other person that was occupying the space. Though 'person' wasn't quite right. Ancient looking, despite the appearance of youth, the creature possessed an air of timeless wisdom. Standing taller by almost a full head than Sibylla on slender goat legs, it blended the elegance of a human with the grace and wildness of a woodland creature. Its legs were covered in a coat of a mixture of deep brown and warm gray.

Its eyes stood out more than its wide deer-like ears, or the curling horns, more even than the crown of flowers that was set upon them. The color of warm amber, they were ancient and knowing, hinting at the faun's true age, which Sibylla couldn't hope to guess. When they rose to greet Sibylla, they moved with such grace and nobility that Sibylla felt that it would be more appropriate for her to bow than do anything else.

"Hello," Sibylla managed to say when the faun was standing before her, its hands folded in front of it. "I'm Sibylla."

"I know," the faun said, a smile spreading across their perfect face. Sibylla almost couldn't look at it. "I am Yadder, the Keeper of the Portus Lunae. Come," they beckoned toward a table that seemed to rise out of the colorful tiles that covered the floor. "We have much to discuss."

"What is this place?" Sibylla asked, taking a seat across the table from the faun.

"This is the grand total of my knowledge," they answered, looking around at it like it was nothing more than a trivial scene.

Sibylla tore her eyes from the books and shelves and colorful light to look at Yadder with surprise.

"All of this?" she said, waving at the books around them, "is everything you know?"

"A representation of it, yes," Yadder replied, "I have been alive a very, very long time."

"No kidding," Sibylla said, impressed. Then she immediately felt silly for being so cavalier. "Sorry, I don't really know what to do here."

Yadder leaned back in their chair, still smiling. "It's nice to finally meet you. How are you doing in your new… role?"

Dropping her gaze to the tabletop Sibylla didn't want to answer the question. So many people were relying on her to be something that she was increasingly feeling like she couldn't be. It had been weeks since Roger had gone missing and she had taken on the mantle of Sentinel. What did she have to show for it? A mangled leg and almost zero progress.

"By your demeanor, I can assume that it has not gone well?" Yadder asked gently.

"No," Sibylla said with a heavy sigh. "Not good at all."

"Well," Yadder said, reaching across the table and taking Sibylla's hand. Their hand was warm, covered in lightly colored fur that was soft to the touch. "Tell me about it, about everything. I am here to offer advice, and I can't do so without a complete picture."

Maybe it was the warmth of the faun's touch, or being surrounded by the evidence of their experience and knowledge, but Sibylla told Yadder everything, down to the last detail. Everything from recovering from the onset of her new senses and abilities to her brothers gassing themselves to the first hunt to her disastrous second hunt and everything in between. Yadder listened intently to every detail, making Sibylla feel like she was having a conversation with a kindly grandmother, not the most elegant looking creature she had ever seen.

By the time she was finished, Sibylla felt a little better, like a great weight had been removed from her shoulders. Yadder didn't seem horrified or disappointed by anything that Sibylla had told them, much to her relief. Instead, they squeezed her hand gently.

"It would seem that you are in over your head," they said, voice soft. "But I can tell you that you are doing quite well for someone in your position."

"Really?" Sibylla asked, surprised.

"Oh yes," Yadder replied. "I have been tied to this Gate as a Keeper since the Roman empire. I have seen hundreds of Sentinels and Rangers come and go, failing and succeeding as they went. Even your father had a hard time with his first few hunts."

"He did?" Sibylla asked, thinking back to how he had taken on four Infected without his powers, successfully killing three of them before he was taken.

"Oh yes!" Yadder laughed. It sounded like sleigh bells in the winter, and Sibylla couldn't help but smile. "His first mission was quite the disaster, only slightly worse than your own."

"Really?" Sibylla asked, feeling a little encouraged.

"More interesting, though," Yadder said thoughtfully, "is your ability to feel werewolves when they are nearby."

"Is that not normal?" Sibylla asked, feeling trepidation building.

"No," Yadder replied. "In all my years I have yet to meet a Sentinel or a Ranger that has been able to do such a thing. That is something unexpected indeed. I am curious what makes you so special, though I would have to search the entirety of my knowledge to even begin to guess why something like this would even be possible-"

Yadder stopped suddenly and laughed again. "Forgive me, when I get excited I begin to ramble. Feel free to stop me, otherwise, you would find yourself trapped in that seat for years listening to me talk."

"It's okay," Sibylla smiled. "You have a pleasant voice."

Yadder hesitated for a moment, deep in thought. After a moment, they rose from their seat. "I am curious if you would like to try something, as a kind of experiment."

Sibylla stood quickly, almost knocking her chair over. "What kind of experiment?"

The room shifted and changed, the bookshelves disappearing, the walls fading like smoke. They reformed themselves as a large round room made of stone, with three long tapestries hanging from the ceiling high above. The tapestries were embroidered with images, one of a man in heavy armor, a shield and sword in his hand. One showed a man in shadow, with a hooded cloak that hid his features, a bow in one hand, and a quiver on his back. The last showed a man with stone tools in his hands, surrounded by fire.

"These," Yadder gestured to the tapestries, "are the Sentinel, the Ranger, and the Keeper. Together, they bring balance to the Gate. With each role comes different capabilities. The Sentinel is strong, with endurance and sharpened senses. They are expected to open and close the Gate, the first line of defense. The Ranger is quick and agile, with strong sight, smell, and hearing. They work as the second line of defense, catching anything that can get past the Sentinel. The Keeper can heal the Gate and the other two, and provide advice and counsel."

Sibylla looked at each tapestry in turn as Yadder spoke, overwhelmed by the beauty of their craftsmanship. Everything in Yadder's world glowed with elegance and timelessness.

"I think perhaps the reason you're struggling now is that you are wearing the wrong mantle," Yadder said.

"You think I should be a Ranger?" Sibylla asked, surprised.

Yadder nodded thoughtfully. "I do. It may well be that you are better suited to its responsibilities, as that is what you find yourself occupied with. I am curious as well if it would sharpen your ability to sense the werewolves. That is my experiment if you are willing to try."

"I think that could be worth a try," Sibylla said, starting to feel a glimmer of hope.

Maybe being faster and more agile would give her the edge she needed. Having the abilities of the Sentinel had no doubt saved her life, but if it was the wrong mantle it was the same as trying to drive a screw with a hammer. It was possible, but not quite the best way to do it, with more opportunities to mess up the project.

"How do we make it happen?" she asked, excited.

"Simple," Yadder replied, gesturing to a table that hadn't been there before.

On the table was a longbow and a quiver of arrows. To the right of it was the shadow of a hammer and chisel, to the left was the shadow of a sword and a shield. Sibylla felt something latch onto her hip and something tugged at her back. Looking down she saw a sword hanging from her belt and a strap across her chest.

"All you have to do is place your sword and shield on the table, and pick up the bow," Yadder explained.

"Don't I need to pass on the mantle to someone else?" Sibylla asked, unbuckling the belt as she talked.

"You could," Yadder replied, smiling. "But you would need to find someone else who would take on the mantle, and then wait the same amount of time to recover as you did."

That was true. Sibylla had been useless for a month after receiving the mantle, and there wasn't anyone that she wanted to experience that. Aubri was already skilled and powerful in her way, Mr. Darrow was in a wheelchair, and there was no way she was going to subject her brothers to the experience.

"What happens to the mantle then?" she asked, placing the sword in its place on the table.

"I take it on," Yadder replied, "as I did with the mantle of the Ranger."

"Do you normally take on the full mantle if no one is using them?" Sibylla asked, curious.

"Yes," Yadder said, "it is necessary to maintain balance, and it gives me the chance to be ready and able, should the security of the Gate be breached."

That made sense as well. Sibylla pulled the shield off and placed it on the table next to the sword. Before she touched the bow Yadder stopped her.

"Before you take on this new mantle," they said, "understand that you are also giving up the ability to open and close the Gate. Only a Sentinel can accomplish such a task."

Sibylla thought about that for a moment. It seemed important, but in the few months she had been a Sentinel, today was the only day she opened the Gate. It didn't seem like a terribly important ability that she would need to hang on to.

"If I did need it open, what would I need to do?" she asked, just to be safe.

"Ask me," Yadder smiled broadly.

Nodding, Sibylla grabbed the bow. The moment her hand touched the wooden shaft she found herself back in Red Falls, standing on the other side of the Gate. Her leg felt amazing and the world seemed more vibrant than it ever had before. The sudden rush of sensation was intoxicating, not nearly as overwhelming as it had been the first time. On the other side of the Gate, she could hear Aubri's breathing as though she were standing right next to her. The creak of the leather seat on Mr. Darrow's wheelchair, and the brush of his sleeves against the chair's handles, told her where he was before he even rounded the corner.

"How'd it go?" Mr. Darrow asked when he rolled into view.

"Exciting," Sibylla replied, flexing her hands, a smile splitting her face from ear to ear. "I can't wait for the next hunt."

Chapter 22

"She's sniffing around," the Pure said, voice low and dangerous.

Chad nodded, barely listening. The Pure was paranoid, borderline delusional. From what he had seen, Chad was convinced their pack was strong enough to handle anything Sibylla and her little crew had to offer. Considering she hadn't even been able to take on two of the most recent Infected without help, almost crippling herself in the process, what was the Pure worried about? They had even gone so far as insisting on everyone backing off.

No more attacks.

No more hunts.

The burden it placed on the pack was immense. The Infected were hard enough to control when they were allowed to satiate themselves on the full moon around Red Falls in shifts and rotations. Now they were impossible, constantly whining about the damndest things. Chad had already killed one daring to shove him during their most recent confrontation, ripping its throat out with his teeth. Thinking about the warm blood dribbling down his chin and the thrill of the kill made him forget the Pure was still speaking to him.

"Are you listening to me?" they growled, yanking Chad off his feet, holding him aloft by his neck.

"Yes," Chad said through gritted teeth.

He hated having to answer to anyone, Pure or not. The game was the game, however, at least that's what Savage always said. Playing it kept him alive, even if he hated every second of it. Cold yellow eyes peered out from under the old leather hood, searching Chad's face for further defiance. Satisfied, they dropped Chad, who collapsed to his knees, gasping for air.

"Do you know why I called you here?" the Pure sneered, turning their back on Chad.

Back on his feet, bristling, Chad replied, "Because of my good looks?"

Without warning the Pure spun, planting their foot into Chad's sternum, sending him crashing to the ground.

"You're my problem child," the Pure snarled. "Too arrogant for your own good, acting impulsively like a pampered puppy."

Scrambling to his feet, Chad considered challenging the Pure. Charging, jumping on his back, ripping their throat out with his teeth. Nothing would make Chad happier than watching the life draining from their eyes. The thought was so enticing, his claws peeling through the skin of his fingers on their own, and he took a step forward. It was a bad idea, and Chad knew it. As much as he despised the Pure and their old-fashioned bullshit, he knew that they were dangerous.

"I want you to listen closely," they said, voice full of gravel and menace. Unable to help himself, Chad took a step back. Sensing Chad's fear, the voice advanced on Chad until his back hit a tree. Seeming to grow with every step, the Pure towered over him. "Leave… her… alone."

Chad hated the explosion of fear in his chest, hated how much he wanted to run. Of all the Pure's experiments, Chad was the closest they had come to creating another Pure werewolf from an Infected. He shouldn't be afraid, not ever. Especially of the old bag of dust towering over him.

"Say it!" the Pure roared, grabbing Chad by the front of his shirt and yanking him into the air. Chad growled back and released his claws, trying to claw through the muscle and bone of the massive forearm, creating deep gashes that healed before he had finished making them. The Pure slammed him into the ground, rattling his teeth and bones.

"Say it!" the Pure snarled, bringing their face close to Chad's. They sniffed and sneered. "A scared little welp. Worthless."

Face burning, Chad willed his lungs to fill with air. The Pure's fist was slowly driving it out of him, adding pressure to the point he wasn't sure his chest wouldn't collapse. Part of him wanted to spite the Pure and force them to crush his ribs. The other, much stronger part, wanted desperately to live.

"I'll leave her alone," he whimpered, furious at how weak his voice sounded in his own ears.

The Pure released him and wiped their hand on their cloak as if touching Chad had made their hands unclean. "Get out of my sight, or I'll do myself a favor and kill you."

Chapter 23

The excitement at the acquisition of her new mantle proved to be short-lived. After telling Mr. Darrow about her conversation and change with Yadder, Mr. Darrow produced a list of names for her to look at. Yellowed and wrinkled with age and extensive handling, the list had about twenty-five names on it. Written in a combination of pencil and pen and in different colors, it was obvious that he had been working on it for some time.

"It's the people on campus I suspect are werewolves," Mr. Darrow had explained. "I've spent a couple of years working on it, there's probably more that I've missed."

Some of the names Sibylla hadn't even recognized, probably having graduated before she got there. The implications were chilling, to say the least. There were people in their community who were secretly werewolves, roaming among the population like cancer, probably turning more people into Infected. Things could get out of control rapidly.

"I need you to be my eyes on campus and check on these names," Mr. Darrow had said, "Hopefully your unique talent will make it easier to figure out who they are."

Sibylla had readily agreed, feeling more confident than ever in her role. Theoretically, her connection with the werewolves was stronger, so identifying who they were wouldn't be a problem at all.

At least that's what she had thought at first. After a few weeks at school, roaming through the crowds of students and checking on the names, not only was she unsuccessful, Sibylla was bored. Bored and frustrated.

They were certainly there, she could feel them as soon as she got into town. The problem was that the connection didn't act as a divining rod as much as it was a vague feeling. She had no idea how far out it went, or how to train herself to get it more specific and accurate. So every day she wandered around campus between classes, finding the students on the list, trying to get them alone to see if she could tell the difference between a human and a werewolf.

It was impossible.

Not only were people very uncomfortable with being cornered by a girl in the hallway for no apparent reason, she couldn't tell if there were werewolves close enough to skew her perception. In her frustration, she had returned to using the sledgehammer to beat down the stump just outside her house, though the frequency of having to replace the hammer and the stump increased substantially.

To make things worse, Kane was different around her. When they did hang out together on campus he seemed sullen and detached, barely talking to her at all if he could help it. Any time she tried to get him to talk to her about anything deeper than class or a vague greeting he ignored her or changed the subject.

When they were together she tried to hug him more or hold his hand as much as possible in an attempt to show him that she still cared about him. Nothing seemed to work. She may as well have been holding the hand of a corpse with how little he reacted to her. Her frustration there went into the stumps as well.

Not being able to locate Roger also fed into her growing feeling of helplessness. There wasn't any evidence that he was even in Red Falls, much less still alive. Knowing that, if he was still alive, he was suffering at the hands of some of the most vicious monsters Sibylla had ever heard of was enough to get her searching for something other than a stump to hit with a hammer. Fortunately, she had found a steel I-beam in the barn that served the purpose well.

To top everything off, something was wrong with Nate and Hunter. They were having trouble sleeping, looking more and more pale and haggard every morning. Their moods fluctuated wildly, going rapidly from happy to angry to sad to happy again from moment to moment. If they were making any progress at all with the book they refused to talk about it, refusing to share anything that they found, if they found anything at all. The only thing that seemed to be good with them was their appetites. They ate constantly it seemed, when they weren't fighting each other or Sibylla.

"We're fine!" Nate had snapped that morning, not bothering to use silverware while he devoured the pancakes she had made.

"Nothing wrong with us," Hunter had growled, rolling his eyes.

"Easy," Sibylla had replied, more concerned than angry. "I'm just worried about you two, that's all."

"Whatever," Nate huffed, shoving his plate to the middle of the table and stomping off through the front door.

Sibylla had stopped Hunter before he joined him, hoping that he would be more reasonable when Nate wasn't there. Hunter had a tendency to mirror his brother's attitude and behavior, but when they were apart he could be reasonable.

"What's going on?" she asked.

"It's just… nothing," he said after a long pause. It was obvious he wanted to tell her what was going on, but something was holding him back. "Yeah. It's nothing."

Sitting in the cafeteria at school, Sibylla tried to distract herself with the list, hoping it would reveal some detail that she had missed in the few hundred other times she had read it over. It had proven to be a useless exercise, considering not one person so far had proven to be a werewolf as far as she could tell. Most of the names had question marks next to them anyway.

Kane sat down next to her. Immediately she knew something was wrong.

A sniff was all it took to tell he was sweating more than usual, and his heartbeat was through the roof. She could hear it through the crowd of students that surrounded them in the cafeteria.

"What's wrong?" she asked.

Kane took a deep breath before answering. "Have you been talking to football players?"

Sibylla glanced at the list and realized more than a third of the names were on the football team. How had she missed that?

"Yeah, but it's not-," she started, seeing the look in his eye.

"Why are you talking to them at all?" he cut her off. "Looking for a new boyfriend or something? Trying to get dirt on me?"

Horrified, Sibylla stammered to give him an answer. How could he think that? The old feeling of fear and anxiety began creeping up through her fingers.

What else could he think? She told herself, you haven't told him anything about what you're doing, and he hasn't seen the list or anything.

Remembering the piece of paper in her hand, she realized that she didn't want to tell him about it at all. The idea that she was cheating on him being his biggest concern when she had told him what her life was, seemed so ridiculous she didn't think he deserved to know anything about it at all.

Thus far she had not told him about the list or what she was doing around campus.

"It's nothing," she said, folding up the list.

Kane saw it and tried to snatch it out of her hands. Moving much faster than he did, she pulled it away so all he grabbed was air.

Instantly she knew that it was a mistake.

"What is that?" he demanded, face turning a bright red.

"It- it's nothing," she said.

In reply he held out his hand, fingers beckoning. Sibylla dropped her eyes to the table and placed it in his hand. Kane took a minute to read it over, face turning white with rage.

"Do you think..." he said quietly, "that these people are werewolves?"

Sibylla looked around, not wanting to meet his gaze.

"Sibylla, for fu-" his mouth snapped shut. Without another word, he crumpled the paper into a ball and threw it on the floor.

Then he was up and moving through the crowd toward the exit. Sibylla chased him, a knot forming in her gut. It hadn't occurred to her that she would be crossing a line somewhere. If she had realized that there were so many football players on the list she wouldn't have pushed so hard to talk to them. Dodging the other students easily she quickly caught up to Kane as he was going out into the student parking lot.

"Kane!" she said, grabbing his shoulder. "What's going on?"

Shrugging her off Kane spun to face her. "I'm done!" he shouted. "I'm done with this! You're done, we're done! I'm done with your secrets!"

Taking a step back, Sibylla was shocked. "What are you talking about?"

"What are you talking about?" Kane mocked her tone. "What do you think I'm talking about? When were you going to tell me about your dad missing?"

"Well, you know," she stammered, caught off guard. "You've had your stuff, I didn't want to add to it…"

"What, you think I'm too weak to handle it?" he demanded.

"No, not at-," Sibylla said, taking a step back. She had never seen him so angry.

"You know who can't handle anything, you!" he shoved a finger in her face. "You haven't asked me once about my life over the past two months! Did you know that my parents are splitting? Or that I've been crashing at friends' houses for the past two weeks? The same friends who you seem to think are monsters?"

"Kane-" Sibylla began, shocked.

"Not only that," he said, glaring at her with such an intensity that she had to look away, "when were you going to tell me you're bi?"

Sibylla froze, mind grinding to a halt.

"Who told you that?" she asked, voice barely above a whisper.

"Why? Are you going to deny it?" he asked, arching an eyebrow.

Sibylla looked down at her feet, feeling too small to even continue talking. Of course, she wanted to tell him, she had just been waiting for the right time. Even if that meant waiting a few days or weeks or months. Or years. The point was that she was going to do it in her own time and in her way.

Who had told him? She thought. The person she had told was Mr. Darrow, not even Kayla knew.

Cheeks and ears burning, tears rolling down her cheeks, she risked looking up. Immediately she regretted it. Throughout their relationship, she had seen many emotions cross his face, from happiness to anger to irritation. For the first time, she found disgust staring back at her.

"You know what the guys say about that?" he asked, sending another wave of terror crashing over her.

Had he really told the team? She thought, mind racing as she realized that most of the school must know by now.

"They say that you're bi because I'm not good enough for you, that I can't satisfy you," he said when she didn't answer. "Do you know how embarrassing that is? Of course not, you'd have to care first. Whatever, we're done. You're just… too damn complicated for me."

Stunned, Sibylla watched him walk away. Too many thoughts and emotions were cascading through her mind to allow her to even try to chase after him. Guilt, that she hadn't trusted him with her secret. Sadness, that he had just ended everything. Horror, that the entire school knew the one secret, the one part of her she wasn't ready to share with them. Anger, that Kane was the reason that the entire school knew that part of her. Disgust, that they talked about her ability to be satisfied.

She needed to know how Kane found out, to try and figure out who she could trust. She would start with Mr. Darrow since he was the only person she had told about it.

Turning around she almost screamed. Standing behind her was Chad, with dark rings under his eyes and a big grin on his face.

"So dramatic, am I right?" he asked, jabbing a thumb at the corner Kane had disappeared around.

Sibylla frowned. Chad was the last person on the planet she wanted to talk to. "He's… got a lot on his mind."

Chad rolled his eyes. "Please. He's as bad as…" he trailed off, taking a deep sniff of the air, leaning in closer. "A girl on her period."

He winked at her disgusted expression and walked past her, pausing when they were shoulder to shoulder. So close Sibylla noticed for the first time an ugly spider web of scar tissue across his face, divots indicating where pieces of his face had been torn away. It was faded, but as close as they were it was obvious.

Their eyes locked and Sibylla saw that his were a sickly yellow, spiderwebbed with purples and reds. Sensing her hesitation, Chad broke off and sauntered across the parking lot with a laugh. Gears began turning in her brain, trying to fight through the shock of a breakup and Chad's wildly inappropriate comment. Two memories hit her at the same time: the first was what Mr. Darrow had said about a werewolf's sense of smell. The second was Roger shooting one of his werewolf attackers in the face at close range with a shotgun.

Could Chad be a werewolf? Thinking back to the list she realized that his name had been the most recent addition. Spinning, she saw him tearing out of the student parking lot in his beat up jeep, howling at the sky and laughing maniacally.

Chapter 24

Vaulting over the other vehicles in the parking lot, Sibylla yanked her car door open hard enough to bend the handle. Wasting no time she began the chase after Chad, expecting him to already be on Main Street on his way out of town. To her surprise, he had stopped at the end of the street, waiting for her.

Stomping on the gas she followed him as he led her through the heart of town, zipping in and out of traffic and barely avoiding pedestrians. Sibylla had to slam on her brakes more than once, her reflexes taking over just in time. No matter how far behind she fell, however, Chad waited for her. Always just far enough ahead to keep her going.

You should call Mr. Darrow or Aubri, the thought occurred to her as she swerved around yet another pedestrian. You shouldn't be doing this alone.

Sibylla shut it down. She was a Ranger, and she was determined to see what she could do. Not to mention she knew for a fact that she was chasing down a single werewolf. No tricks, no ambushes. Confidence as intense as her anger surged through her and urged her on. Soon they were outside Red Falls, driving down the two lane road that led away from the town, past her house, and deeper into the Wyoming wilderness. It wasn't long before trees were whipping, the speedometer climbed higher and higher.

"Come on," she urged the old beater to stay in the race.

Despite her urging it became clear that she wasn't going to be able to keep up with the jeep.

"Damn it!" she shouted, slamming the wheel.

What were her options? Briefly, she wondered if she could shoot out the tires or maybe even hit Chad before he pulled too far ahead. As much as she would have liked to be able to do something like that, she doubted even with her new abilities she could pull it off. Knuckles white on the wheel, sun flashing through the thickening canopy above, Sibylla willed Chad to crash. It was the only way she could get the confrontation she craved.

Without warning a dark shape flew from the speeding jeep. Sibylla was too shocked to react immediately, realizing that Chad had leapt from a vehicle easily going upward of 90 miles per hour. The jeep, driverless, swerved off the road and careened into a ditch, ramping up into the air and crashing into a tree. Slamming on the breaks she cursed herself for taking too long to react, overshooting the wreck.

Protesting, the car groaned to a halt just off the road. Without wasting a moment Sibylla was out the door and rounding the back of the car, wrenching the trunk open. Keeping her weapons close by had become a habit, even when on campus. Aubri had even shown her how to hide a knife on her person so that she always had at least one weapon within arms reach at all times.

As much as she loved the idea of her mom's original kit, Sibylla had no idea how the woman had made it work. In the weeks since her last hunt Sibylla had ditched the heavy revolver and throwing axes in favor of two .45 caliber 1911s and lighter throwing knives. She liked Clacker, but it being a one shot wonder was something she didn't much care for. Instead, she had found a pump action version that was a little bigger, but slinging it across her back wasn't too much of a hassle, plus it freed up space for another pistol. Since she liked the name, she had christened the new shotgun 'Clacker' in honor of her mom's original weapon. The 1911s didn't hold many more rounds than the revolver, but they were easier to load and the heavy caliber had some serious stopping power.

Weapons settled in place, she pulled on the last piece of new kit that she had adopted: a form fitting vest that had a flexible mesh inside that allowed freedom of movement. Better still, it could stop knives and slow down claws, something inspired by Aubri's protective armor. The quality wasn't nearly as good, but it was better than nothing.

A long, low howl, not far off, told her that she was taking too long to get in the game. She sprinted back to where she thought she had seen Chad jump from the car, passing the still smoking husk of his jeep impaled on a tree. Searching the ground, the trees, and the shadows and back again, it didn't take long for Sibylla to see deep gouges in the trunk of a tree. The snow around it had been thrashed into muddy slush, shoe prints leading deeper into the woods.

Another howl cut through the dark silence. Goosebumps covered her arms and the hairs on her neck stood up. She was very aware of how chilly the air was, and how it penetrated her clothes and made her legs feel stiff. The wind blew gently through the branches, shaking a few leaves loose. Her eyes caught every shift in the shadows, every sound in the brush. Little creatures, barely disturbed by the sudden violence that had taken place, flashed past her, the pitter-patter of their paws in the soft snow as loud to Sibylla as a human foot on a wooden floor.

Moving forward she found more footprints, and there were scratches in the bark of the trees and broken branches. Something told her that it was suspicious how easily he had made it for her to follow him, not just through the woods but from the school as well. The feeling got much stronger when the tracks circled a cluster of trees and then disappeared.

Where had he gone off to? She thought, her chest tightening.

He was close by, she could feel him. Cursing the vague nature of the ability, Sibylla turned in a slow circle. Eyes wide and heart beating in her ears, Sibylla searched desperately for any more signs in the snow or the trees. Nothing. It was as if he had just vanished into thin air. Closing her eyes she leaned on her other senses. At first, there was nothing different. The window became sharper, the brush of branches against each other more defined. A hint of body odor and sweat hit her, mixing in with her own scent. More than what she could hear or smell, she could feel a disturbance in the air above her, something shifting silently in the foliage of the trees.

Werewolves of any kind were aggressive hunters, that had been made very clear by the book. One of their more common ways of attacking was to go high, a tactic made simple by their powerful legs. That meant that, in the woods, full of tall trees, he wasn't going to attack from the ground. The information was passing through her mind when a glob of saliva landed on her shoulder, thick and reeking of decay.

Chad was right above her.

In that moment or possibly in the next, her life could end.

Distorted, the sound of cracking twigs and branches reached her ears. Death was already in mid-flight, rushing at her like a missile of muscle and teeth. Time distorting around her, Sibylla tilted forward in a somersault.

Chad, surprised by her move, crashed unceremoniously to the forest floor, a jumble of legs and arms. Sibylla was shocked to see that he wasn't fully changed, still looking almost human despite the longer legs and arms. And the fur, she noted when he stood up.

Without hesitating another second she had her two pistols in her hand, pulling the triggers until both guns were empty, fourteen silver tipped rounds in all. The sound was deafening, leaving a disconcerting ringing in her ears. The smell of cordite wafted through the air. Too close to miss, all fourteen rounds had found their mark in Chad's chest.

Shocked, Sibylla stared at the still form laying in the snow. It had happened so fast that she hadn't even had a chance to fully process what she was doing. Sibylla looked at the two pistols in her hands, their slides locked back, smoke drifting in silvery ribbons from the mouths of their barrels.

"I did it..." she said quietly, the realization rising in her like wildfire. "I did it!"

The sound of her elation felt hollow, echoing back to her through the snow and the trees. As excited as she felt, something still felt... off. Like what she had done had been wrong. But how could it be wrong? Chad was a monster. Not just any monster, a monster who had kidnapped her dad.

What if he had known where Dad is? She thought to herself, horrified. She had just killed her only lead in his kidnapping. Yet, somehow, it was more than that.

Before she could consider the issue further, a groan grabbed her attention. To her horror, Chad rolled over and staggered to his feet, shaking his head aggressively.

"Those... pack a punch..." he chuckled dryly, chest heaving as he fought for air.

Sibylla's hands dropped to her sides, useless.

"You… you're not dead," she gasped.

Turning to face her, he pointed to the silver shards protruding from his chest. "Some upgrades. We aren't as defenseless as we used to be."

A vest, she realized. He was wearing a vest. It was why he wasn't fully changed. He had stopped the change halfway, maximizing his protection and the use of his strength and powers. And she was holding two empty guns.

Chad exploded forward, his jaws inhumanly wide and full of jagged teeth. On instinct Sibylla twisted away and tried to pull the trigger on her guns, forgetting in her terror that both were empty. She thudded to the ground with a whump, the air driven from her body by the impact.

Claws digging into the dirt to slow his momentum Chad swung around for another attack, a wicked grin on his face.

Keep them moving, keep them guessing, the thought came in the form of Aubri's voice, some of the advice she had given Sibylla during their numerous sparring sessions.

He's expecting you to run or stand your ground, she thought, eyes locked on his as he scrabbled at the ground to get his momentum back. Running would only expose her back to him, and chances were that he could outpace her. Standing her ground was just as dangerous. By the time she reloaded, he would be on her. Despite the fear pulsing through her bones, Sibylla knew that she couldn't run.

Once again the world slowed considerably, time coming to a crawl. Whipping the empty pistol in her left hand forward toward his face, her right hand dropped the other, sliding one of the throwing knives free of its sheath on her hip. Sidestepping his lunge she grabbed his outstretched hand and pulled him forward, using his momentum to take him off balance. With the other hand, she thrust the throwing knife deep into his stomach, just under his vest.

He stumbled forward with a grunt of pain and disappeared into the scraggly brush behind Sibylla. The forest stilled, becoming quiet. It seemed as though everything was waiting to see what would happen next. Like they wanted to see if she was going to survive. Once again, for a brief moment, Sibylla considered calling up Aubri to come help her.

I'm a Ranger, I can do this, she thought to herself. I have to do this. Alone.

After a deep breath, she followed Chad through the brush, unsurprised to find the area empty. Picking up the pistol closest to her, her hands shook so much she dropped a new magazine twice before sliding it home. Then, the chase was on, and come hell or high water, she was going to find Chad. She was going to finish the hunt.

The deeper into the woods she went the more oppressive the silence became. Every so often there was the crack of a twig or the crunch of snow. Always from different directions and distances, as though he was everywhere at once. He was playing with her, he had to be. Taking her head on had been too much of a challenge, so now he was stalking her while she stalked him.

There was a faint crunch to her left and she spun to face the sound. Chad propelled himself through from a bush, his jaws snapping, clawed fingers grasping, drool and spittle flying from his mouth. Too close for Sibylla to react properly, his claws dragged across the front of her stomach, yanking her off her feet. Then he was gone.

Staggering to her feet, Sibylla fired blindly after him. When it was clear he wasn't immediately coming back, Sibylla glanced down at the front of her jacket, expecting to see her entrails spilled over the ground. Relief flooded her when she saw that her vest had done its job.

"You're gonna regret this," he growled.

Turning, she saw him standing only fifteen feet away from her. Underneath his skin, she could see the bones and muscles rolling and snapping and reforming. He was fighting the change, and losing.

"So far I'd say I'm not the one regretting all of this," she said, feeling the weight of the pistol in her hand. "Besides, you tried to eat me."

Chad let out an airy, gurgle kind of noise and she realized he was laughing. It was disconcerting, and Sibylla shifted uncomfortably. He could cover fifteen feet in a flash, probably before she could get her gun up to get off a shot. Still, she had been surprised at how fast she had moved so far, maybe she had a chance.

The chuckle continued as he reached up and tore away his vest, letting it drop at his feet. Then, like smoke in the breeze, he was gone. Sibylla's heart stopped, and her brain ceased to function at the same time. She had never seen anything move that fast.

Sibylla barely ducked the strike in time, diving to the right to get out of the way. It was a mistake, she realized immediately. He had followed his first strike with an upward swipe of his opposite hand, catching her in her abdomen, and sending her spinning uncontrollably through the woods. Her flight came to a jarring halt against a tree, sending her crashing to the forest floor in a heap. Pain flashed through her leg and shoulder. If she had to guess, there was a good chance she had broken her leg and dislocated her shoulder.

"You make this easy, you know," he said. She could hear him sweeping aside trees and bushes, looking for her. "Honestly, when the Pure told me to leave you alone, I thought it was because you were dangerous or something, they were so… emphatic. But after all this? I don't see it."

She rolled onto her stomach and waited. Her nerves were tight enough to snap, and it was all she could do to not hyperventilate, her body convulsing with the effort as his heavy footsteps drew nearer and nearer.

Thump… thump… the sound of an easy, unhurried pace.

Tears started to roll down her cheeks now as she struggled to keep her emotions in check. It was impossible.

Thump… thump…

Grabbing her injured shoulder, he yanked her onto her back. She yelped in pain, her arm numb and useless. Chad seemed to be expecting to find her helpless and afraid, ready to give up. As if she was supposed to go quietly.

Instead, he found himself face to face with Clacker, and at this range, there was no way she was going to miss. Silver pellets riddled his body at high velocity. With a roar of pain, he was jerked off his feet, his clawed feet and hands scratching at the ground as he convulsed in pain.

Staggering to her feet Sibylla awkwardly pumped Clacker one handed, releasing the empty shell and sending it smoking to the forest floor. Stumbling over to his convulsing body, Sibylla made sure she stayed out of arm's reach. Propping herself against a tree, she leveled Clacker at his head.

"You're a dick," she spat.

Chad let out a weird, unearthly, unnatural chuckle through a mouthful of spit and blood.

"And you should know better than to play with your food." She began to squeeze the trigger but stopped, remembering that he was her only chance of finding out what had happened to Roger. As much as she wanted to end it right then, as repulsed as she was by the twisted form at her feet, she knew what she had to do.

"Do you want to live?" she asked.

"Now who's playing with their food?" he muttered, spitting blood.

"I'm not playing," she said, "I'm giving you a chance to survive tonight."

Chad snorted and winced. "You would let me live? You?"

Sibylla took a deep breath and nodded. The idea made her nauseous, and she couldn't even imagine what Mr. Darrow or Aubri would say if they heard her make the deal, but she wasn't about to throw away the chance to learn anything about Roger. Even if it meant letting a lowlife like Chad survive.

"I'm not giving you shit," Chad growled, choking on blood.

"Really?" Sibylla said, feeling her already fragile patience begin to crack. "Not even to save your own life? You don't even know what I'm going to ask."

Chad shook his head aggressively and tried to sit up. Wincing, he laid back down.

"I just want to know what happened to my dad," Sibylla said quietly, hoping he couldn't hear the quaver in her voice.

Chad snorted, his lips curling back in a wicked grin over his yellowed fangs.

"Daddy's little girl," he said mockingly. "Wanting to get the big man back in your life…"

"No, that-" Sibylla said.

"Daddy, I need you!" Chad snickered. Blood oozed from his chest. "I'm too scared to do this alone!"

"That's not what I-" Sibylla said, getting angry.

"Please, Daddy!" Chad said, cutting her off again. "I'm too weak!"

"Stop it!" Sibylla growled, heat growing in her chest.

"Too scared!" Chad continued, voice gaining an edge of accusation.

"I'm not scared!" Sibylla shouted.

"Too stupid!" Chad jeered. "Too incapable, too fragile!"

"I'm warning you!" Sibylla hissed, finger tightening on the trigger.

"You can't do it!" Chad snarled, "You couldn't do it on the trail and you can't do it now. Face the facts Red: You. Can't. Do. It. Not without someone holding your hand and cleaning up your mess."

A crack like thunder filled the air. Chad's head snapped back, bone and flesh and blood splattering the snow behind him. Gritting her teeth Sibylla racked back the slide on Clacker, ejecting the spent casing and slamming another one into the chamber. Then she pulled the trigger again. And again. Until she finally heard a click.

Chapter 25

Hands shaking, Sibylla swung the car around in a wide arc, tires slipping off the pavement into the snow that lined the road. The sun hung low in the sky, casting its fiery light onto the road in wild, dancing shadows.

Like a dark fog, the moments since Chad's demise had been difficult for Sibylla to grasp. Even as she drove, all she had were flashes of memory: the bark of the shotgun, the blood, and brain covering everything, digging a hole, throwing up, burying him, and getting into her car. It seemed as though it had only taken a few minutes, not a few hours.

For a time she just drove, not paying attention to the passing forest or farms, not even sure of where she was wanting to go. All she could think of was the shock of confusion on Chad's face, there for a split second, frozen in time by her adrenaline. Then… nothing. A grotesque mask of pulverized flesh.

Swinging the car to the side of the road she barely cleared her door before vomiting again. There was no doubt about it, Chad was dead, and she had been the one to kill him. She knew that his death was essential. As a werewolf, he was a cancer, a disease, a threat. Evil incarnate. An evil that her parents had fought their whole lives to eradicate.

That's what Mr. Darrow had been telling her for months. That's what Aubri had been telling her for months. Killing Chad had fit in perfectly with the plan that she had been following since the day her dad had disappeared and she had discovered that a fairy tale was a nightmare in the flesh. He had belittled and mocked her, calling her weak and fragile. She should be overjoyed with the act of proving him wrong.

Yet, she felt horrible. As much as she understood everything about what he was and what she was, she felt miserable at the realization that she had just… ended him. Woozy, she staggered back into her seat and rolled the windows down, letting the cool breeze fill the small space. More than anything, she felt guilty. Despite having every right to do what she had done.

"He was a monster," she muttered, closing her eyes.

Hearing it out loud did little to help smooth her conscience. The words felt disingenuous. Did she feel that way? Did she believe that he was a monster? One of them had almost torn off her leg and killed her if Aubri hadn't been around to help. If Mr. Darrow hadn't been present, she had no doubt in her mind that the first Infected would have killed everyone in the farmhouse.

Eyes snapping open, Sibylla realized with another wave of horror and guilt that she had just removed her only lead for finding her dad from the face of the Earth. Pulling the trigger could have just set her back weeks, maybe even months. Why had she done that? Because she was angry? Groaning, she wished that Mr. Darrow had trained her on how to question someone, or how to keep her head when someone was trying to convince her to take theirs.

"Stupid," she moaned, digging the heels of her palms into her eyes. "So, so stupid."

Something within her stirred, something that she didn't recognize immediately. A heaviness settled on her, a yearning for something that she couldn't understand. It wanted something. It wanted to get out. Back rigid, she gripped the steering wheel tightly enough that she could hear the groan of the rubber coating beneath her fingers. An intense feeling that she wasn't alone, that something was there, just behind her, just out of sight, overwhelmed her.

Gritting her teeth, she forced herself to look in the rearview mirror. Nothing was there, but her brain persisted. There was something, there had to be. Then she looked at herself and saw something in her own eyes, a roiling of colors like food coloring being mixed.

What is that? She thought, panic rising.

A song played, making Sibylla jump high enough that she hit her head on the ceiling. A quick search revealed the source of the song to be her phone. Rubbing her head gingerly she saw that it was a text from Mr. Darrow.

Mr. Darrow: Meet me in Old Town, just off main.

Furrowing her eyebrows, Sibylla wondered if Mr. Darrow had texted her by mistake. Since the first hunt he hadn't taken her anywhere, training and teaching her at the house.

Sibylla: Where's Aubri?

Mr. Darrow: Aubri is working on a separate assignment with your brothers. Don't ask, I'll tell you later. Just get to Old Town. I have a lead on Roger.

Sibylla's heart skipped a beat, a ray of hope burning brightly within her. Maybe she hadn't screwed anything up by killing Chad after all. Throwing the car in gear, she took one last cautious glance in the mirror and was relieved that her eyes were back to normal.

ψ

Mr. Darrow slid the phone into a concealed sleeve in the center console. It was an old habit he had picked up in the early years of hunting. If he went missing, the sleeve was waterproof and the console was fire resistant. The GPS on his phone would give anyone looking for him the best opportunity to at least find the vehicle, something that had saved his life on more than one occasion.

Keeping the truck in gear, he constantly checked his surroundings, keeping a close eye on corners, doorways, and windows. Normally he would have scoped the area out better and picked a location with less potential for surprises, but the lead had happened quickly and he had been forced to be more reactive than he would have liked. He wondered if maybe he should have questioned it more, but the last thing he wanted was to have the chance to save Roger and miss it because he was afraid to take risks.

Earlier in the week he had placed a short range tracker into a teacher's bag on a hunch. He had been acting strangely for days, becoming broodier and more confrontational as the full moon approached. A werewolf of any kind couldn't hide its true nature during a full moon, and a smart werewolf knew what to do to keep people from noticing. Which was the only explanation he could come up with for missing the signs for so long. So he followed the teacher until he stopped in front of what appeared to be a random house.

With Aubri occupied, Mr. Darrow had been forced to call in Sibylla, despite his reservations. Worst case scenario, he just got her hopes up for nothing, but she got a great lesson in tracking out of the deal. In the best case scenario, they were one step closer to finding her dad. It was a chance he was willing to take.

A flash of red and blue lights jerked him back to reality, and he cursed himself for getting lost in thought in such a dangerous situation. Turning awkwardly in his seat he saw that it was Deputy Tate, one of four law enforcement officers in Red Falls. With a sigh of relief, he tucked the pistol back in its holster and kept an eye on the car parked down the road, making sure it wasn't getting ready to move while he was distracted.

"What can I do for you John?" he said when the deputy arrived at his window.

Deputy Tate looked startled, lowering his sunglasses to look at Mr. Darrow.

"Mr. Darrow?" he said, "what're you doing out here?"

Smiling easily, Mr. Darrow waved vaguely at the dilapidated buildings that surrounded them. "Taking in the sights. It's good for a history teacher to keep in touch with old places."

"You don't say," Deputy Tate said, glancing down the street. "Well, I hate to bother you, but we got a call of a shifty character in the area and, well, you know I wouldn't be doing my job if I didn't check up on everything."

"Not a problem," Mr. Darrow said, "more than happy to comply."

Deputy Tate sighed with relief. "Thank you so much. If it's not a horrible inconvenience, I have to go through the whole song and dance. Do you mind, uh, stepping out of the vehicle?"

It was a strange request, but Mr. Darrow wasn't in the mood to argue. Tate had been in Mr. Darrow's class a few years prior and had been a pretty good student, if a little absent minded and prone to getting into trouble off campus. Mr. Darrow had helped him prepare and train for becoming a deputy, helping him study and prepare for the physical fitness test. The sooner he went through the motions, the sooner he could leave, hopefully, before Sibylla arrived.

"Not a problem John," he said, unlocking his door and turning to get his wheelchair.

"Swell," Deputy Tate said, smiling strangely. "That's just swell."

Chapter 26

Back at the house, Aubri did a slow sweep around the border of the property, keen eyes piercing the growing darkness easily. A few weeks back she and Darrow had noticed some changes in Hunter and Nate, and both she and Darrow had been concerned. They were showing signs of Umbra Lupus, a sickness found in those who had been infected and were soon to experience the Change.

The revelation had created a dilemma for Aubri: if they were going through the Change, what was she supposed to do about it? With anyone else, the answer was clear. There was only one cure that she knew of, the only sure method of preventing the suffering that came with the Change. It had been drilled into her every day since she had started training with the Sacred Legion: they had to die.

It was an act of mercy, everyone said so, even her father, one of the gentlest warriors she had ever known. Killing the Infected had never brought her any joy, knowing that they were mere victims. The Pure, however, she longed to have the opportunity to kill. They were the ones who caused it all. They were the source of the Infection, passing it on indiscriminately. Worse yet, they may have somehow passed it on to the two most important people in Sibylla's life.

Anger burned in her at the thought. It was difficult not to see it as a personal failure, as she had promised to keep Sibylla's family safe. Not only had they been through enough at the hands of the Pure and his ilk, but they were legitimately good people. More than that, she felt a bond with Sibylla, and she didn't want it to be compromised by her inability to protect her family. If they were important to Sibylla, then they were important to Aubri.

A flash of light drew her attention to the barn, where she could just barely see the silhouettes of two people entering. She wished she had the vision of Sibylla who, with the mantle, could probably see who it was and their hair color from that distance. As it was, the most she could tell was that they were at least too small to be Changed.

Checking her rifle to make sure a round was chambered, she took off running, keeping low and silent as she approached. Taking them unaware would be the best case scenario. If they were going through the Change they would be too distracted by the pain and the flood of urges to pay attention to their surroundings, but it was better to play it safe. She didn't want to risk having to look them in the eye when she took them out.

It didn't take her long to reach the door, slowing down to tiptoe through the shadows. She could easily hear the growling and yelping long before she arrived. Heart sinking, she knew what that meant. Somehow the Pure of Red Falls had gotten to the brothers. The 'how' was less important than the 'what' she knew needed to happen.

She did a quick inspection of her armor, making sure everything was strapped securely in place and ready to be used. Truthfully, her heart wasn't in it. Killing Nate and Hunter felt wrong, no matter what she knew she needed to do.

Would that be good enough to explain to Sibylla?

Taking a shaky breath and gritting her teeth, she shouldered her rifle, kicked the door, and rushed in.

Chapter 27

Driving down the main street of Old Town, Sibylla realized that she had no idea where she was supposed to meet him. Glancing down the darkened alleys and side streets, she kept an eye out for his truck. She wondered what his lead was, or who it was. Hopefully, it was strong enough to help her feel a little less guilty about wasting her opportunity with Chad.

There was no shortage of werewolves around her, she could sense them everywhere, in every direction. With every passing street, she grew more and more concerned and anxious, turning off her headlights and driving by her night vision alone. After a while she pulled into an overgrown driveway and shut off her car, peering in every direction, looking for a sign of where he could be.

Briefly, she considered texting him, but a nagging feeling told her that it would be a bad idea. She could find him on her own. Old Town wasn't that big, and she would have more luck on foot. Pausing, she tentatively sniffed at the air. A hundred different odors hit her at once, and she worked to separate and identify them, looking for something familiar.

It didn't take long to realize it was impossible. The sheer number of scents was something that she wasn't experienced enough to sift through to find the one she needed. Instead, she pulled out her phone and turned on the phone tracking app, quickly locating Mr. Darrow's phone, which thankfully wasn't too far away.

Before going to investigate, she took a minute to quickly reload each of her weapons, topping them off, just in case. Using them again so soon tied her stomach in knots, and she hoped that whatever lead Mr. Darrow had found would be simple and bloodless.

Just before closing the trunk, Sibylla noticed a package that Nate and Hunter had snuck into her gear bag.

It was wrapped like a present, with a folded note taped to the front. Smiling at the shoddy folds and tape job, she opened the note.

"Hey Red, these payloads are way better, courtesy of N. and H. under the supervision of Mr. D. Let us know how these little powder puffs work. Happy hunting!"

Tearing the paper she found a cardboard box with a handful of cylinders that looked like oversized glue sticks. A crude drawing of the different steps on how to use them had been put on one of the cardboard flaps.

"So you did it," she said, cautiously picking up one of the cylinders.

They had successfully replicated the wolfsbane grenade, then given them one of the dumbest names they could have picked. Briefly tempted to put them back in the car, she rolled her eyes and tucked two of them into her pocket. If Mr. Darrow had supervised them, then there was a good chance they weren't going to just explode in her pocket. Not to mention how disappointed they would be if she didn't use at least one of them.

Closing the trunk carefully, she started jogging down a side street, following the tracker as it took her over a few blocks, over fences, and through the overgrown yards. A sense of unease grew, wondering where on earth he was. Moving quickly, sacrificing some of her stealth in favor of speed, it didn't take her long to find Mr. Darrow's car, tucked away in a backyard on the edge of Old Town, only a block or two away from the Gate.

That's odd, she thought, sniffing carefully before moving closer.

Nothing was out of place, no signs of struggle in it or on the ground around it. Some of the scents were strange to her, and some smelled vaguely like a werewolf. Which wasn't a big surprise, considering how often he was probably hunting during the days and nights she was training at home.

By all appearances, Mr. Darrow had intentionally parked behind the house, and then gone inside, tracks from his wheelchair leading from the car to the back door, disappearing into the deepening shadows of the house. The presence of werewolves all around her grew stronger, intensifying her feeling that something was wrong. Clenching her hands into fists, then relaxing them over and over, she wondered what she needed to do next.

Chiding herself for being silly, she strode forward into the house. Of course, there were werewolves all around, they had to be stashed away somewhere and she had felt their presence a few weeks before when she'd gone to talk to Yadder. Mr. Darrow was too smart to be caught off guard, she reassured herself. More than likely he was inside, trying to figure out what was taking her so long to link up with him.

Despite being able to see in the dark, the house gave Sibylla goosebumps. It wasn't a complicated layout, and, like every other house on that side of the river, it wasn't very large. Sibylla had expected to find Mr. Darrow in the front room, peering through the shuttered windows at some house across the street, but the tracks that cut through the thick layer of dirt on the floor veered down a narrow hallway.

Heart pounding in her ears, Sibylla walked down the hall on shaky legs, pausing at the first two doors in the hall, listening intently. The house was as still as a tomb, only adding to her increasing heart rate.

Where the hell is he? She thought, swallowing hard before heading to the last room at the end of the hall. It struck her how quiet everything was. There were no bird songs, no barking, just the breeze as it whistled through the cracks between the boards that covered the windows. It didn't feel much different than what she would have thought a ghost story would feel like if she were in one.

In the last room, she found something unexpected. The sliding doors that normally covered the closet had been torn off, and a hole had been ripped into the floorboards. Each of the houses in the neighborhood had been built using the same cookie cutter design, including a crawl space.

Looking down into the hole, someone had tunneled up under the house and had ripped open the floor as an access point. It made sense, it would let them move around the neighborhood without being seen. She wouldn't be surprised to find that every house on the block had a similar tunnel dug under them. Then she saw that the tracks made by Mr. Darrow's wheelchair disappeared right over the edge.

That's not right, she thought. She wiped her sweaty palms on her pants and gulped again.

The tunnel was almost completely black, even to her eyes. It gave off the appearance of an unending void, like a black hole in space. Gripping the splintered edges of the floorboards, she tried to force herself to go in. It was obvious that Mr. Darrow was in trouble, something had happened to him between his texts and her getting there. Focusing, trying to hear over the thunder of her heartbeat, she thought she could hear something like conversation. It was too far away to hear clearly.

"Come on," she pleaded with her body. "Just go."

The floorboards groaned in her hands. Below her, the open maw of the tunnel loomed. It was more than just being too dark to see in. What was she going to find on the other side? Mysterious words continued to drift up, enticing her, and drawing her in. Somewhere down there was Mr. Darrow, and there was a good chance he needed her help. A smell like wet dog drifted up to her, a sickening smell mixed with rot and blood.

When Sibylla was younger, on the bad days, she used to hide from her dad. It had been around the time her mom had died, and Sibylla hadn't realized that she needed to protect her brothers, to raise them. One night Nate had broken something, a lamp maybe, Sibylla couldn't remember. Roger had dragged him to his room, slamming the door behind them. Sibylla had stood in her room, staring down the darkened hall, frozen in fear as she heard the slap of Roger's belt.

In that moment she had been too scared to act. For days afterward she had been too ashamed to look Nate in the eye. Never again, she swore, would she stand by if there was even a slight chance of protecting him or Hunter. Mr. Darrow wasn't her brother, but if he needed help, Sibylla was determined to be there to help him.

Letting out an exasperated breath, Sibylla released the floorboards and slid forward, landing heavily on her feet. Somehow the tunnel was even darker now that she was staring it down. Squinting into the deep shadows, all she could see were the claw scratched walls that were illuminated by the fading light from above. Otherwise, there wasn't enough light in the tunnel for her to see more than a few feet in front of her. Sliding Clacker from its holster with one hand and pulling one of her knives out with the other, she closed her eyes and listened.

There was a faint breeze in the tunnel, carrying the voices along with it like ghosts.

Great, like it's not hard enough, Sibylla gulped. Horror movies scared the hell out of her.

Taking a deep breath to quell the growing anxiety that threatened to drown her, she took her first step into the darkness. Sibylla moved slowly, tracking her progress by keeping the outstretched tip of her knife hand dragging along the surface of the wall and looking behind her on occasion. The tunnel curved slightly, so it didn't take long to lose sight of the light, plunging her into complete darkness.

Slowly, painfully, her anxiety morphed into hysteria. It was all she could do to keep from hyperventilating or running back screaming. The voices grew louder, rising and falling as the speakers argued. She froze, her heart thundering in her ears, making it impossible to hear what was being said clearly. Dust trickled from the ceiling, tickling the back of her neck. Flinching violently Sibylla swung in a circle, waving her knife wildly in the dark. It was a miracle she didn't pull the trigger of the shotgun in her panic.

"I can't die down here," she whispered harshly, the sound of her voice like a hiss in the inky blackness that surrounded her.

Get a hold of yourself, she thought, trying to chide herself into calm. Then she realized that she didn't know which way she was supposed to be going. What if she got lost, or there was more than one tunnel? The voices echoed in every direction in the darkness, their unintelligible mutterings further confusing her sense of direction. She took a gasping, explosive breath and took off running.

At that moment she didn't care which way she ran, she just needed to run into something that had light. Her anxiety gave her wings, and she flew down the tunnel, eyes wide, tears streaming down her face. It took less than 30 seconds before she ran into the not-so-soft dirt wall that signaled the end of the tunnel.

Like a bird hitting a window, she sat down hard, blinking stupidly at the black mass in front of her, decorated with swirling stars. Had she gone back to the beginning, or had she miraculously gone the correct direction?

In response to her unspoken question, the ceiling above her creaked loudly, drawing her eyes sharply upwards. A hole had been torn in the floor of the house above her, and for a moment Sibylla's heart fell. She had gone the wrong way and would have to brave the tunnel once again. Then the voices came again, louder than before, clearly now.

"Come on boss," someone said, their voice high pitched and nasally. "This guy won't break."

"Yeah," someone else added, sounding eager. "Plus, we need some fresh meat."

Sibylla shuddered, grasping his brutal meaning. Slowly, quietly, she holstered Clacker and her knife. Judging the distance to the lip of the hole, she wondered just how high she could jump. It was maybe fifteen feet to the edge of the hole, another three to the floor. Grunting, she jumped just high enough to grip the edge of the hole, determined to use the crawl space as additional cover. The last thing she wanted to do was be in the same house as whoever was speaking.

Hoisting herself up, she saw that the dirt from the tunnel had been shoved into the crawl space, filling it up to the joists.

So much for staying out of the house, she thought, feeling strangely excited.

Gripping the edge of the tunnel, Sibylla pushed off and pulled up at the same time, sailing straight into the nearly identical master bedroom of a new house. To her surprise, the room was not unoccupied. Halfway to landing, she saw someone standing in the doorway, their back to the room as they watched the proceedings down the hall.

Chapter 28

Her landing, as silent as it was, was still loud enough. The boy turned, and Sibylla saw that it was a boy named Alan. He had been in a few of her classes and was far from being a member of the football team, favoring more intellectual activities over sports. Yet there he was, yellowed eyes staring back at her, one of them. Sibylla couldn't begin to fathom why or how he had become an Infected, but those questions weren't the most important ones she had to deal with.

For a long, tense moment they stared at each other. Alan looked tired, and like he had been crying.

Why would he be crying? She thought, drawing a blank.

Her hands drifted toward her knife, every muscle in her body tense, ready for his attack. Killing him was the last thing she wanted to do, but he was in her way, and she needed to find Mr. Darrow. Tears or not, Alan was still a threat.

"I'm sorry," he said, voice barely above a whisper.

Sibylla expected that to be the opening line to his attack, that he would change and alert the others to her presence, anything that would result in her finding herself in a life-threatening situation. Instead, he bowed his head and walked past her, climbing down into the tunnel and disappearing from view. The scene was so unexpected that she almost snorted in surprise.

An infected just… let me go? She thought.

"You can't eat him!" someone said, pulling Sibylla back into the world she was expecting to find.

"He's our teacher for shit's sake!"

Sibylla's heart lurched. They had him then, they had Mr. Darrow.

"Now now," came the reply, the smooth edge in the voice raising goosebumps all over Sibylla's body. "Calm yourself young one." Sibylla recognized that voice too. "We are past the time of splitting hairs for the sake of some outdated, human morals." She had heard it a hundred times on and off the field. "A meal is a meal, no matter who it comes from."

It was Coach Savage.

Sibylla reeled at the realization. The Pure was Coach Savage? One of the teachers at her school? How many football players had he turned? How many students had he turned? Teachers?

As quietly as possible she took a shaky breath, trying to derail the chaotic train of thought. She needed to focus on what was going on in front of her, on what was going on with Mr. Darrow. As slow as she dared, Sibylla eased around the corner, staying low to the ground, until she could see into the house's tiny living room.

A dark rage roared through her when she saw Mr. Darrow strapped into his wheelchair, blood trickling from his nose and lip, bruises covering the side of his face. The swelling had already closed one of his eyes, the other shining bright and clear as it stared down Savage, who stood in front of him. His shirt was torn, showing deep gashes across his stomach and his chest.

Impulsively, Sibylla reached for one of the powder puffs. Nothing would make her happier at that moment than watching Savage choke to death on wolfsbane and silver. How dare they think they could lay a finger on him? She would kill every last one of them if she had to. She wanted to. They all needed to die, as slowly as possible. A trembling finger drifted toward the safety pin.

Hold on, she thought, struggling to control herself.

A plan. She needed a plan. Mr. Darrow himself had drilled that home since their first hunt together. Going in there guns blazing was a good way to get them both killed, achieving nothing.

"You plan on eating me?" Mr. Darrow said, slurring slightly through his swollen lip. "How many people have you eaten Billy?"

Sibylla heard the uncomfortable shift of fabric from out of view. Billy, Sibylla knew Billy. He had been the one to protest eating Mr. Darrow in the first place.

With effort Sibylla tore her eyes away from the scene, looking for a way to get in and out without everything going tragically wrong.

"Come now," Savage said soothingly. "You're not the Pure here, little human. You're nothing more than a crippled thorn in my side."

Sibylla winced, eyes darting around frantically, searching for some way that would work. Peering into the room across the hall, she saw that the ceiling was partially caved in. That was something.

I can make a distraction… she thought, mentally going through what was available.

"Little old me?" Mr. Darrow asked, sounding amused. "I would have thought a Pure could have handled me a long time ago. You must not be as strong as you say."

Maybe, if she could start a fire or make a noise, she could use the ultra good senses of the werewolves against them, drawing them out.

"I am hundreds of years old," Savage said dismissively. "I have fought and killed hundreds of Rangers and Sentinels. I have nothing to prove."

"Hundreds of years eh?" Mr. Darrow said thoughtfully.

When they investigated the disturbance, then Sibylla would already be across the hall, climbing into the attic. With any luck, she could drop right next to Mr. Darrow, grab him, and run out the front door. No violence or death was strictly necessary. Taking a deep breath, Sibylla looked around the room for anything that looked combustible. To her dismay, there was nothing. The furniture in the room had been shattered to bits or removed, and nothing was left behind for her to use. Quickly searching her pockets, again she came up empty.

The only thing she had immediately in her hand was the powder puff.

Nothing like a little bit of wolfsbane to get their attention, she thought.

Leaning around the corner, eye barely passing into view of the room, her hand drifted to the pin that would ignite the little device.

"Stop!" the command had been roared out, but not by Savage.

Sibylla flinched so hard she almost dropped the powder puff. Heart beating wildly, she glanced around the corner of the door frame and saw that Mr. Darrow was looking right at her. It was nothing more than a glance, but it was unmistakable nonetheless. He didn't want her to intervene, though Sibylla couldn't imagine for a second why that would be the case. Bloody, bones broken, he wasn't capable of making the call himself.

He's too worried about me, she thought, the anger returning. I can handle myself, I don't need him to rescue me.

"Hundreds of years," Mr. Darrow repeated. "You wouldn't happen to be the legionnaire who was there, are you?"

Savage nodded. "We stopped the first wave of werewolves to ever cross over into our pathetic little rock."

"Interesting," Mr. Darrow said, looking over at Sibylla again. In that moment she saw some internal debate resolved in his mind, and she knew she wasn't going to like it.

"I don't suppose a human could challenge a Pure for supremacy of the pack?" he continued.

"Me?" Savage said, amused. "Many a... less handicapped man has attempted to do so. I'm not too sure that you would want to fight me Darrow."

Mr. Darrow barked a laugh, making Sibylla flinch. He couldn't be trusted to make his own decisions.

I need to move and move now, she thought desperately.

Yet no matter how hard she urged herself to make her move, Sibylla remained rooted in place. The scene before her played out like the climax of some terrible play, and she had no control over how it would end. A terrible realization spread through her like ice water as she realized that it only had one way to end.

"I think you're nervous," Mr. Darrow said, leaning back in his chair.

"Please," Savage replied easily.

"Isn't it strange," Mr. Darrow pressed on, looking for all the world like he wasn't facing down the jagged jaws of a Pure werewolf. "That in the ten years since that night you haven't made a single move against Roger?"

Some of the other people in the room glanced at each other. It was clear that, like Sibylla, none of them knew the true history of the werewolf infestation of Red Falls. She had no idea what had happened ten years ago, though something vague tugged at her memory. Whatever had happened, the change in Savage was much more obvious.

"You know why," he said, a dangerous edge in his voice.

Mr. Darrow clicked his tongue. "Come now, a Pure as powerful as you? That shouldn't have slowed you down. What with your impressive record fighting and killing Rangers and Sentinels."

"Enough," Savage said in a low growl. His shirt stretched against his back as his muscles grew.

"You know what I think it is?" Mr. Darrow said, leaning forward conspiratorially.

Stop, Sibylla begged.

"I think it's that tasty little snack you were trying to bring back," Mr. Darrow whispered, raising an eyebrow.

It was going to be any second now, Sibylla could feel it. The tension was building like pressure in a pipe bomb. An angry, helpless tear rolled down her cheek.

Please, she begged her body, do something.

"Come on Savage!" Mr. Darrow shouted like he was waiting for Savage to take his turn in a game. "Let's go! Let's play!"

With great effort, Savage stood where he was, breathing heavily. "No," he breathed, his voice a dangerous whisper. "You are more valuable to us alive."

"So you are afraid of a lowly cripple!" Mr. Darrow cried out in triumph. "You and every one of the bitches in here! All of you malformed degenerates, blindly following this old fool like he's some kind of prophet because he's less deformed than y'all are."

A low growl passed over the room like a wave. Wet popping and a sickly ripping noise filled the air as the far less controlled Infected began going through the change. Savage didn't move a muscle, letting it happen around him. His eyes remained locked on Mr. Darrow, who stared back easily. The chaos of horror surrounded them, but they didn't see it or acknowledge it. A smile spread across Mr. Darrow's face.

"I think I'll challenge you," he said. "I think I'll win."

In one swift, gruesome move, so fast that Sibylla almost didn't see it happen. One second he was whole, in one piece, a living person.

The next second his bowels were spilled across his knees, blood pouring from his abdomen. A mad howl filled the room, a bloodlust sweeping through the Infected, sending them into a destructive rage. Savage's chest heaved, gulping in air as he stood in the middle of the chaos, his eyes still locked on Mr. Darrow.

Sibylla was swept up in the chaos wanting to howl herself, to release the rage and the turmoil broiling in her core. Fingers digging into the drywall, cracking it in her fists, Sibylla couldn't look away. Mr. Darrow, the closest person to father that she'd had for years, who had trained her, mentored her, built her up in the worst moments of her life, sat dying in front of her, and she had let it happen.

Coward, she seethed. Do something. Do anything. Don't you dare let him die alone.

"Savage!" she screamed, stepping into the hallway.

She could smell his blood as if she were standing right next to him. Tears streamed down her cheeks now, but she barely noticed them. Willing her senses to stop, she tore her eyes away from her dying father and focused them like lasers on Savage as he turned slowly to face her. A wild rage filled his eyes.

"You," he growled, the low rumble rolling over her.

She wasn't afraid. She was too angry to be afraid. She was going to tear out his intestines and choke him with them. And she would watch the light drain from his eyes with glee.

She screamed, feeling something dark and dangerous awakening within her.

"R-run…" Mr. Darrow gurgled, blood pouring from his mouth.

He's out of his mind, she thought, holding her ground, feeling strength and adrenaline surging within her. Running was out of the picture. She was going to fight and kill every werewolf in that room.

"I have waited two thousand years for this," Savage said, flexing his shoulders, "I will not let you ruin this now."

Time began to slow as she took her first step forward, not bothering to draw her weapons. Savage transformed before her eyes, not with the violent, grotesque popping of bones and flesh like the Infected. He simply turned, his humanity fading in an instant, and transformed into the largest wolf Sibylla had ever seen, his long deadly claws digging into the old wooden floor. His eyes were as clear and blue as they had been as a human, fixed on her like a homing missile.

Two thousand years or not, Sibylla didn't care. With god as her witness, she was going to end his miserable life.

Something clattered to the floor, a new noise like metal on wood. Tearing her eyes away from Savage, Sibylla had just enough time to see that Mr. Darrow had dropped something. It was an oversized glue stick, a perfect match for the one that she still held in her hand. The realization hit her at the same time the powder puff exploded, engulfing the room in a black cloud.

Chapter 29

Screaming, stumbling, tears streaming down her face, Sibylla jumped back into the tunnel, her last view of the room being a shadow looming out of the dark cloud, eyes glittering through the flying wolfsbane. As Sibylla sprinted recklessly the length of the tunnel, she ignited another powder puff and threw it over her shoulder. It popped loudly as she climbed out, followed closely by an agonized howl. Limbs feeling heavy and numb, a realization that she didn't know where to go struck through the haze clouding her thoughts.

Helplessness threatened to overwhelm her, forcing her to stop and overthink at every corner and doorway her every decision. Where was she going? What was she going to find when she got there? What was she supposed to do next? These questions and countless others crowded her brain, making coherent thought impossible. There weren't any answers for any of them, just a feral desire to get as far away as possible from the corpse that was her mentor and friend.

The only breaks in the haze were when she ran into werewolves, the Infected fully changed and racing to hunt her down. Then a kind of wild rage and dangerous anticipation took control. The first one happened when she burst through the front door, surprising both of them. Fortunately for Sibylla, she was able to recover faster, yanking Clacker from her belt and shooting the monster point blank in the face. The second encounter was only a few yards later, with the same general effects. Using the shotgun felt unnatural, unnecessary.

Like a wild animal trapped in a slowly closing cage, she whirled from street to street, moving randomly and taking down targets of opportunity as they arose, not bothering to really aim or even to reload once the last shell had been ejected. Survival itself wasn't her focus. She just wanted to get away, to escape the sudden, brutal reality that she was on her own. No backup, no savior, no one. Aubri wouldn't be there to help her this time, and Mr. Darrow had no more advice to give.

The answer presented itself when she rounded the corner of a fenced in yard and found herself on the edge of Old Town. Directly in front of her was the Gate, as inviting as a fire on a cold night. Wasting no time, feeling the close proximity of her pursuers, hearing their snapping jaws and growls growing ever louder, Sibylla sprinted toward the Gate not bothering to slow down before slamming into it.

To her surprise, it didn't budge. She had been counting on it opening for her, allowing her to cross over to another world, to safety. Instead she found its wooden boards unyielding. Her brain shut down even further, and the primal animal within clawed its way to the surface. Somehow that seemed more terrifying than facing Savage and his pack.

Spinning so that her back was to the Gate's rough surface, Sibylla's mind raced desperately to understand why it wasn't opening. Then she remembered that only Sentinels could open the Gates from the outside and since she was a Ranger, she was on her own without the ability to do more than hope that Yadder was just on the other side, ready to open it for her.

The main street that ended at the Gate was rapidly filling with Infected who were racing at full speed toward Sibylla. She could see the spittle and anticipatory drool flying from their mouths as they sprinted on their hands and feet. Drawing both of her pistols she started firing wildly into the oncoming horde. There had to have been at least thirty werewolves coming in, with more on their way. Panic seized her, flooding her limbs with ice. Her hands were shaking so badly that she dropped a magazine while she attempted to reload.

I'm not going to survive this, she realized. Darkness closed in on the fringe of her vision, a low growl rising.

"Yadder!" she screamed, "I need you!"

A much larger werewolf rounded the corner, easily outpacing the Infected. Its jaws were snapped shut, eager anticipation and rage glinting in its red rimmed eyes. Savage. The beast within Sibylla was snapping with excitement.

"Yadder!" Sibylla screamed again.

Savage leapt through the air, clawed fingers outstretched, jaws open wide. Just before he made contact something grabbed Sibylla's arm and yanked her out of the way. Savage's jaws snapped shut against the boards, his claws digging deep gouges into the wood. Before he had a chance to recover Yadder slammed the door closed, sealing it shut with Sibylla safely inside.

Gasping for air, Sibylla lay on the cool floor of the library. Mind racing, she fought for control against the enraged disappointment that thrashed within her. Whatever it was had been too excited to take on something as dangerous as Savage, and had almost fought its way out of Sibylla's control. The feeling was foreign and terrifying, so much so that she didn't even feel Yadder pull her off the floor.

"Sibylla, what happened?" Yadder asked, concerned.

The thought brought everything she had just seen and experienced back to the surface, temporarily silencing the darkness. The death of her mentor, of the person who was like a father to her, played out in a constant loop in slow motion, her adrenaline even slowing down the memory. Worse was her complete failure to do anything to prevent his death. She had just stood there, watching it happen without doing a thing.

"Are you okay?" Yadder asked gently.

Sibylla realized that she had started sobbing. Tears gushed freely down her face, streaking through the layer of dirt and grime she had collected running through the tunnel.

"No," she whimpered, curling into a ball on the floor. "Mr. Darrow is dead."

Gently, Yadder placed a hand on Sibylla's shoulder. They didn't say anything, letting Sibylla cry without interruption.

"He's dead because of me," Sibylla sobbed.

"That's not fair," Yadder said firmly. "I'm sure you did the best that you could."

"I-I didn't do anything!" Sibylla said, pulling herself deeper into a ball on the floor. "I let it happen!"

Yadder kept their hand on Sibylla's shoulder a little longer before gently but firmly pulling Sibylla off the floor, standing her on her feet. Sibylla felt a finger lift her chin and she opened her blurry eyes, sniffling and shaking so hard she thought she might collapse again. Yadder's eyes were unlike anything Sibylla had ever seen before. Deep pools, they reflected back to Sibylla countless years of wisdom and sorrow, of experiences that Sibylla could never hope to understand. Slowly she calmed down, feeling it all fall away.

"Mr. Darrow knew what he was doing," Yadder said, their voice low and soothing. "It is okay to mourn his loss."

"If I wasn't so damn useless," Siyblla sniffed, pulling away.

That was what she was feeling at that moment: useless. What good was being a Ranger, of being trained and armed, if she couldn't even save the one person who meant the world to her?

"I should have been able to get in there and out again without any problems," she said, feeling a burning heat rising within her. "I'm a Ranger damn it, I should have been able to do something, anything at all."

Yadder watched her closely, hands folded neatly in front of them. Sibylla knew what they were thinking. They were thinking that Sibylla was weak. Why wouldn't they think that? So far Sibylla had only managed to kill one werewolf, injure a few more, and allowed her mentor to die. Now she was hiding inside the Gate, too terrified to leave or face the truth: she couldn't do it.

"I can't do this," she growled, picking one of the books off the shelf and throwing it across the room angrily. "I'm not good enough to do this!"

Picking up another book she sent it sailing after the first book, then she threw another, and then another, before she screamed and shoved the whole shelf over, scattering the remaining books across the floor. Then she was racing down the aisles, tearing books off the shelves at random, throwing them violently to the ground. Yadder followed close behind, stepping over the books without pausing to pick them up.

"I should have done something!" Sibylla cried out. "Why am I so damn useless!"

How was she supposed to continue on, now that Darrow was dead? She had no idea. He had been teaching her so much, but there was so much more that she still needed to learn. Years of experience and learned lessons that he still needed to impart. Gone. In the swipe of a claw, it was all gone, like a wisp of smoke. And Sibylla had done nothing to stop it.

After a few more minutes of throwing things and breaking everything in her path, Sibylla slid to the floor, feeling utterly defeated. Next to her, Yadder did the same, stretching out their goat legs. For a long moment, neither of them spoke. Yadder seemed content to let Sibylla work through her emotions on her own.

"I'd do anything to bring him back," Sibylla said quietly, barely above a whisper.

"I know," Yadder said softly. "Truly, as much as you are progressing, there is still much for you to learn, and your training is far from complete. With Mr. Darrow gone, I'm afraid that you are in over your head once again."

"You have magic, right?" Sibylla asked, turning her bleary eyed gaze on Yadder. "You could bring him back?"

Yadder smiled mournfully, providing Sibylla with her answer. Of course, there was nothing they could do. Dead was dead. Yadder couldn't change that any more than Sibylla could.

"What am I supposed to do now?" she asked, voice flat.

She looked over and realized with a start that Yadder had burn marks up and down their arm. Beyond that, the skin was shriveled, looking more like the mottled skin of a raisin, the smooth skin that Sibylla had been used to seeing. Even the thin fur that covered the arm was wispy and brittle.

Yadder followed Sibylla's gaze to their arm and smiled. "Don't worry, I am a soul trapped in the vessel that is the Gate, which will keep me immortal until the Gate is either destroyed or I am released. Without its healing power, any exposure to the outside world at all will result in time catching up to me. It'll be healed in a matter of minutes, that's all."

"So," Sibylla sniffed, wiping her nose with her sleeve, "you really are just trapped in here? Forever?"

Something dark passed over Yadder's eyes. "Yes, unfortunately. This is and will be my life forever."

"Seems like a bum deal, why did you choose it?" Sibylla asked. She couldn't think of any scenario where she would find herself wanting to be in Yadder's position. Even if it meant that she could destroy all of the werewolves in the world, why would she want to sacrifice her eternity?

"It wasn't my choice," Yadder said sadly. "I was tricked, betrayed, by someone who said I could trust them. I suppose it's okay, this place isn't so bad. But sometimes I wish I could be free of all of this, to walk the Earth one more time."

Sibylla thought about it for a long moment, trying to comprehend what it would be like to have someone like Kayla trick her into being trapped in the Gate forever. It didn't seem like that bad of a place, but not having the choice at all seemed too harsh.

"There's no way for you to get out of here?" Sibylla asked.

"It's a dangerous prospect all around," Yadder replied, "as you can see, I can only survive out there for a few minutes, and it's pretty painful. I would need to find a way to heal quickly and constantly. Even with improved healing and strength... it isn't enough to keep me safe out there."

The kind of power or magic that was holding Yadder in place must have been incredibly powerful if two of the three mantles attached to the Gate couldn't free them from it. It was a welcome mental exercise, and Sibylla put all of her energy focusing on it, not wanting to think for a moment about what happened just a few hours before. What could she do to help Yadder get out? Then it hit her like a freight train. Not only would it help Yadder, but it would also help Sibylla escape the role she was not meant to be in in the first place.

"I'll give you the third mantle!" she practically shouted, leaping to her feet. "You can have the Ranger too!"

"What?" Yadder said, surprised.

"Come on!" Sibylla begged, beginning to pace around the library. "Why not at least try, right? It helps us both out!"

"What are you talking about?" Yadder demanded, rising to their feet. "How does this help both of us?"

"Look," Sibylla said, excitement growing as the idea took shape. "I just watched my mentor get murdered, murdered, right before my eyes. And I wasn't able to stop it from happening. My dad has been missing for months, and I'm no closer to finding him than the day he was kidnapped. I'm not cut out for this, no matter how hard I try. I keep screwing it up. You," Sibylla said, whirling on Yadder, "you have been alive for centuries! You've seen good and bad Rangers and Sentinels, you've seen how hunts are supposed to go! Between the two of us, you are absolutely more qualified than me to do this job! Plus, with all three of the mantles, even a Pure like Savage couldn't stand up to you. I'll bet you could kill every werewolf in this damn town by yourself in a matter of weeks!"

Yadder held up their hands in motion to calm Sibylla down. "You can't do this, it is far too much responsibility for one person to carry."

"Please," Sibylla said, reaching out and putting her hands on Yadder's ageless shoulders. "Between the two of us, I keep screwing this up. I can't be responsible for more people dying. Not to mention it'll give me an opportunity to right the wrongs of your past, you know? Give you the chance to get out of here, and finally live a life that isn't tied to the Gate. Let me give you that chance. Please."

Yadder brushed Sibylla's hands off their shoulders, eyes troubled, deep in thought. Inwardly, Sibylla hoped Yadder would take her up on the offer. The thought of leaving the Gate, of going back into the world with her powers and responsibilities and expectations made her want to curl into a ball and hide away forever. If she couldn't keep Mr. Darrow safe, how could she keep anyone safe? The risk was too much for her to handle.

If there was even a single percentage point that Yadder could bring peace back to Red Falls, Sibylla decided that it was far better to give them that chance than to keep stumbling around, pretending she knew what she was doing. Maybe they could even track down where exactly the werewolves were keeping her dad.

Thinking of Mr. Darrow and her dad brought back a flood of sadness, and Sibylla fought it off with some difficulty. It was a bad time to mourn. She had already cried and sobbed and wailed. If she needed to do more, she would do it at a different time. And she could trust Yadder with finding Roger. They had to. He was the only thing their family had left anymore, and there was no chance that she could do it without Mr. Darrow.

"Okay," Yadder said resolutely. "If this is truly what you are wanting, and I can't dissuade you, then I will accept the responsibility of the third mantle."

Relief flooded Sibylla. "Thank you so much, I can't tell you how much weight this takes off my shoulder."

Yadder gave her a little smile. "Of course. All you need to do is place your bow on the table."

The room had transformed in the blink of an eye to the room with beautiful tapestries, the table that had once held the bow and the sword and shield now empty.

"Place your bow on the table, and I will take it on," Yadder instructed, now wearing a shield on their back and a sword at their side.

On the other side, a hammer hung from their belt, looking ancient and worn. Looking down at her hand, Sibylla saw that she was once again carrying the bow. Without any hesitation, she strode to the table and threw the bow onto it. She knew it was the right choice. It would be better in Yadder's hands than her own.

The bow absorbed into the table immediately, reappearing in the faun's hands. Yadder brushed their fingers lovingly along its curves as if they were greeting an old friend.

"Come now," they said, striding toward a door in the wall that hadn't been there a moment before. "Let's go say hello to our werewolf friends."

Sibylla tried to take a step but almost collapsed with the effort. For months she had had superhuman strength and senses, able to do things no other person could do. Now she felt like she was moving in a pool full of jello. Her limbs felt impossibly heavy and moved like they were in slow motion. Her senses were so dulled that she could barely hear Yadder over the rushing in her ears. She was normal again. Just like everyone else.

Thank god, she thought.

Hurrying to catch up, Sibylla was breathing heavily by the time she made it to Yadder's side just as they opened the Gate. For a long moment, blinking rapidly at the sudden burst of light, Sibylla realized that Yadder had hesitated, gazing at the open ground beyond it. Then they stuck their hand tentatively out into the open air of Earth. Sibylla heard a low hiss escape Yadder's lips and saw some smoke rising from her rapidly burning hands. For a moment she was devastated, thinking that maybe it hadn't worked. Or, worse, that she would need to take back the Ranger mantle.

But then the smoking stopped, and the skin returned to the same pale color it had been before. Smiling broadly, Yadder stepped out into the air, leaving the Gate for the first time in hundreds of years. Sibylla followed, smiling just as brightly as the faun. It felt amazing to have given Yadder the opportunity to finally be free. Then she saw the thirty or forty werewolves that stood in a half circle around the Gate, waiting for them to come out.

A surge of excitement covered Sibylla from head to toe.

Finally, she thought, these werewolves will realize the mistake they made by being in my town.

Towering above the others, Savage stood in the middle of the half circle. His eyes were as wide as dinner plates, fixed on Yadder. It brought no small amount of satisfaction to see his reaction. Death was coming rapidly, and he knew it, could sense it coming.

Good, she thought, a smug smile spreading across her face.

"You…" Savage said, taking a step closer.

It occurred to Sibylla that something was not quite right. Was that fear in his eyes?

"It worked…" Savage continued, the look of disbelief dissolving into relief. "It worked!"

"Yes," Yadder said, barely able to contain their excitement as they took a tentative step forward.

Then they rushed each other, but instead of leaping into a fight to the death as Sibylla hoped they would, they embraced. Embraced and kissed.

"No…" she said, a confused horror filling her mind. "No, no, no."

Yadder pulled away from Savage, turning a wicked smile toward Sibylla. "For hundreds of years, I've been separated from my mate. Thank you so much for being foolish enough to give me the strength to finally be reunited. I am not your savior, you silly child, I am here to open the Gates between worlds to let a wave of my children wash over it like a plague."

"What?" was all that Sibylla remembered saying in reply. Barely a squeak.

Chapter 30

Heartbeat.

Sprinting as fast she could down the main street, far too slow, her powers gone.

Heartbeat.

Running down the main street, trying to remember where she had parked the car, hoping she could make it there before she was caught and torn to pieces like Mr. Darrow.

Heartbeat.

Risking a glance back, expecting to see the outstretched claws of a werewolf, ready to snatch her back to be fed into the monster's jaws.

Heartbeat.

The Infected stood poised right where she had left them in a circle around the Gate, pulling forward like a dog on a leash.

Heartbeat.

"Goodbye, Sibylla!" Yadder called after her. "We will see you again!"

Heartbeat.

Driving recklessly down the road once again trying to make it home to outrun her panic. In no time at all she was tearing herself out of the car without bothering to put it in park, the car moving too fast for her to find her footing. She tumbled to the ground rolling through the gravel several times while the car continued, plowing through the fence and into the shed next to the house. The shock of pain brought her brain to a grinding halt, the pain and terror, and grief tumbling together like rocks in a dryer.

Swaying where she sat, she barely noticed Aubri rushing to her side, asking her something that she couldn't understand. Dumbly she stared at Aubri, the tumbling rocks preventing comprehension.

"What?" she asked. Her voice sounded strange in her ears, too distant and soft to be her own.

"What happened?" Aubri asked again slowly but firmly, her blue eyes locked on Sibylla's.

"Mr. Darrow is dead," Sibylla said simply. "And Yadder has the three mantles and Savage is their boyfriend and they want to unleash their horde of werewolf love children on the world."

Aubri blinked in surprise. "What?"

"Yeah," Sibylla nodded, getting up on her feet unsteadily. "And I did it. I did all of it."

A terrible emptiness opened up in her stomach, spreading to her chest and up her neck to her mind. She wasn't sad anymore, there wasn't anything left. In one day her entire world had collapsed around her, and she was the one who had done it.

"It was me," she said, letting Aubri lead her up the stairs and into the living room. "All me."

Aubri didn't say anything as she sat Sibylla down on the couch and went back into the kitchen, rummaging around for something that Sibylla couldn't see. She didn't care enough to see what Aubri was trying to find. Fatigue settled on her like a wet blanket. Too tired to think, she let her mind go dark. Too tired to move, she didn't even reach for the glass of water that Aubri tried to hand her. Everything felt too heavy to resist, so she didn't even bother to try. Even the darkness within fell silent.

"Hey," Aubri said gently, sitting on the couch next to Sibylla. "Hey."

Tenderly, Aubri hooked a finger under Sibylla's chin and pulled her attention from the floor to her face. Immediately a crack formed in the shell around her emotions at the sight of Aubri's sad smile.

"It is okay," Aubri whispered.

Tears filled Sibylla's eyes, her lip trembling, the motion traveling down to the rest of her body.

"It is okay," Aubri whispered again, tears filling her own eyes.

Sibylla surged forward and wrapped her arms around Aubri, who immediately returned the gesture. They sat there for some time, crying into each other's shoulders. Sibylla knew that Aubri hadn't known Mr. Darrow for long, but he had been her whole world before she had met

Sibylla and her family. He had taken care of her since she first passed through the Gate, had supported her, and had trusted her.

"I miss him," Sibylla said, tears coming forward again.

"Me too," Aubri agreed.

They stayed that way a moment longer, then released each other. Wiping away her tears with the heel of her hand, Aubri chuckled with embarrassment. Sibylla got the feeling she didn't cry often.

"What happened?" she asked.

"It was me," Sibylla said, guilt washing over her again, threatening a new wave of tears.

"You killed him?" Aubri asked, eyebrows furrowing in confusion.

"No," Sibylla shook her head, "but I didn't stop them. I sat there and did nothing. Nothing at all!"

She stood up, her heart hurting too much to stay seated on the couch. It felt too weird to be having the conversation a second time, too close to what she had said to Yadder. The last thing she wanted was to relive anything that had happened with the old Keeper.

"Red," Aubri said, still sitting on the couch, "tell me what happened."

So Sibylla did. Taking a deep, shuddering breath, she told Aubri everything. She told her about the fight with Chad, the text from Mr. Darrow, watching Mr. Darrow die, and being tricked into giving up her mantle as Ranger to Yadder, giving the faun total control over the Gate and the ability to leave it for the first time in hundreds of years. Aubri listened without asking a question or making a noise, only nodding occasionally.

With every passing minute, Sibylla was sure that Aubri was beginning to see how terrible she was. How could someone like her still want to stay with Sibylla? The last twenty-four hours had been a string of missteps, mistakes, and heartache. Anyone with half a brain would leave the house running without looking back, sure to be better on their own over being stuck with someone like Sibylla.

Though she thought she would understand when Aubri did walk away, Siyblla knew it would also break her heart. Sibylla had already lost so much, but she couldn't bring herself to lie or hold anything back. What did she have to offer anymore anyway? Without the mantle that made her special, what did she have to offer? Still, she had grown attached to Aubri over the past few months, and not just because she had saved Sibylla's life so many times since they met.

Sibylla had grown to truly care about her, and knowing that she would be gone soon because of her mistakes only added to the terrible squeezing sensation on her heart.

By the time she finished her story her eyes were firmly fixed on her feet, too afraid to meet Aubri's eye. For a long moment, neither of them spoke, the room descending into an uncomfortable silence. When Aubri didn't immediately leave, Sibylla risked a look, finding Aubri deep in thought, her blue eyes glowing and unfocused.

Probably thinking of her exit strategy, Sibylla thought sadly, feeling the knot tighten in her chest.

"So," Aubri said, eyes focusing on Sibylla. "What is the plan?"

"What's the plan?" Sibylla choked out, confused. "What plan? Without the mantle, I'm not strong or fast enough to face even the worst werewolf. Without Mr. Darrow, I don't even know how to fix any of this. I have nothing to offer here, to you or anyone."

Aubri stepped forward and took Sibylla's face in her hands, the action so sudden and gentle that Sibylla froze. She became keenly aware of how soft and warm Aubri's hands were.

"Listen to me," Aubri said, her eyes searching Sibylla's. "The only mistake you have made is thinking that you ever had control over any of this."

She paused to brush away a tear from Sibylla's cheek, the action so soft that Sibylla felt her cheeks heat. She fought off the sensation, trying to focus on what Aubri was trying to tell her.

"In the first week, I first arrived here, when he first took me in, I found a poem in Mr. Darrow's classroom, do you know it?" Aubri asked.

Sibylla didn't have to think hard about the poem that she was talking about. She had read it dozens of times when she was waiting for the bell to end, and Mr. Darrow had a habit of referring to it often.

"Invictus," she replied with a sad smile, "by Henley."

"Mr. Darrow was the master of his fate, Red," Aubri said. "As are we all. He chose the time and place his fate would end, and did it to give you the chance you needed to survive. That was not your fault, and to say that would be doing your mentor a disservice."

Another tear rolled down Sibylla's cheek and once again Aubri wiped it away. "You are and have always been more than what the mantle offered you."

Aubri slowly pulled closer while she spoke, creating a nervous excitement in Sibylla.

"When I first met you I noted your ferocity as a fighter. Being with you, I have realized that you believed and valued beauty. When you rushed into that barn to save your brothers I knew you were a protector. I have never seen you give up before, and I will be damned if I let you do it now."

Their faces were only inches away, Sibylla's face turned down to look deeply into Aubri's glowing eyes, flecks of gold and silver light swimming in the blue. Aubri was close enough that Sibylla could smell her scent again. She had noticed it before many times, a sweet, earthy, piney smell, like the forest in the rain.

"And I will not allow you to face this alone. You will always have me, Red, for as long as you will have me." Aubri's voice was barely above a whisper, as if to speak louder would shatter the silence that descended around them like a veil.

The world around them froze, and for a split second Sibylla wasn't sure what to do, her heart beating like an excited drum. For months her feelings for Aubri had grown, no one could deny that, and she certainly wasn't going to try. For months they had spent hours training together, hours talking and learning about each other. Sibylla had found little nuggets of joy in everything that Aubri did. From how gracefully she moved to how she took care of Sir Moo to how patient she was with Nate and Hunter. Gracefully, seamlessly, she had woven herself into Sibylla's life like she belonged there.

And Sibylla realized that she wanted her to stay. She never wanted her to leave. Aubri had seen the worst part of who she was and still wanted her. Still wanted to help her and stay with her. Kane had never been able to offer that to her, had never even tried.

Yet, as much as she wanted to close that small space between them, there was a part of Sibylla that couldn't do it. Mr. Darrow had died hours earlier and she had made the biggest mistake of her life by giving up her mantle soon after. She had surrendered everything that had given her the ability to fight back in a moment of weakness. Was kissing Aubri another moment of weakness? 'Wrecked' didn't even begin to describe how she felt at that moment. Was she just using Aubri as a way to feel better?

No, she decided.

Before the weakness and the pain, there was lightning between them, even when the world seemed to be going right. She could feel that lightning now, crackling between their eyes, surging between their lips. She had been robbed of enough, she wouldn't let another good thing slip through her fingers.

Without another thought she wrapped her arms around Aubri's waist and drew her in the last few inches, pressing their bodies and their lips together. Lightning danced through her, from the top of her head to the tip of her toes, warming her all over with a passionate heat that she never wanted to leave.

For the briefest of moments, the world not only froze but fell away, leaving them alone to just be with each other. Sibylla pulled Aubri even tighter to herself, their kiss deepening and becoming more magnetic. She never wanted it to end.

After what felt like too short a time they pulled apart, still holding each other, bodies pressed together. Electricity and heat broke over her in waves, her fingers and toes curling with each pass of the sensation. Smiling drunkenly, she looked deeply into Aubri's eyes.

"Wow," she breathed deeply.

"Wow is right," Aubri said back, grinning from ear to ear. "I've been waiting for that for months."

Sibylla blinked in surprise. "We've only known each other for months."

For the first time since they'd met, Aubri managed to blush, surprising Sibylla. She hadn't thought that Aubri was capable of feeling embarrassment or shame.

"In Laternum we experience something like a natural bond, created by our gods so that we know who we are fated to be with for eternity," Aubri explained sheepishly. "The moment I saw you in that gym I knew that we had been destined to be together."

"Really?" Aubri said, surprised. "You never said anything."

"I have never heard of bonds crossing the bridge between two worlds before," Aubri said, "and you were with that boy Kane. I knew our worlds were different, I wanted to respect that."

It was surprising to think about, but Sibylla couldn't deny it. Since the beginning, she had felt a pull towards Aubri, and she still felt electricity when they touched.

Sibylla smiled. "Well, okay. I'd say that we're officially bonded then."

"Finally," Aubri replied, eyes flashing a brilliant blue. Then they flashed with a realization and she chuckled awkwardly. She broke the hug, much to Sibylla's disappointment, though she took Sibylla's hands and held them tightly. "I nearly forgot, there's been a bit of a change in your brother's situation."

A shot of panic ran through Sibylla and she immediately started looking frantically around the room, realizing for the first time that neither Nate nor Hunter were in the room.

"Where are they?" she asked frantically.

Aubri squeezed her hands tightly, bringing Sibylla's focus back to her. "Red, your brothers have experienced… a slight change."

Sibylla frowned, panic beginning to rise. "What are you talking about? What change? Where are they?"

Aubri took a deep breath before answering, pursing her lips. "Nate and Hunter are werewolves."

Chapter 31

Sibylla didn't waste time waiting for an explanation. Exploding out of the house, she paused for one frantic moment, realizing that she didn't know where they were. If Nate and Hunter were werewolves, they could be anywhere at all. Werewolves could cover a significant area. Searching her memory, she wondered if they had been at the Gate, under Savage and Yadder's control.

Hands clenched into fists at the thought, she turned to face Aubri. She was standing in the door, face devoid of any expression.

"The barn," was all she said, pointing past the wrecked shed to the lone structure that stood in the darkness. Light spilled from the door as it swung lazily on its hinges.

Sibylla vaulted the railing of the back porch and took off, cursing her sluggish pace. It took an eternity to reach the barn. When she finally arrived, she slowed to a stop, horrified at the realization that she couldn't hear anything at all. Not a single growl or whimper could be heard coming from inside. Heart sinking, she heard the crunch of dried grass behind her. Typically Aubri never made a noise that Sibylla could hear, even when she did have the Mantle.

"Did you…" she said, unable to finish the question.

Aubri remained silent behind her, either unable to answer or unwilling, and Sibylla's heart sank further. Just when she thought there could be something good out of the day, the person she was bonded to killed her brothers. Some numb part of her knew that it was better that way. If they were truly werewolves then she would have had to have done it, and there wasn't a world she could think of where that would have been possible.

Before Aubri could answer Sibylla threw the door open, stepping into the blinding light of the barn. What greeted her brought her up short, blinking rapidly to clear the dark spots that swam in her vision and to try to make sense of what she was looking at.

Two concrete pillars stood at either side of the barn, thick silver chains bolted to them. The chains were coiled on the floor like giant snakes, ending at the silver collars that were attached to two werewolves who lay limp on the floor. They were both covered in thick red fur, arms splayed out to the side, tongues sticking out of their mouths like dead animals in a cartoon.

"They are fine," Aubri said.

"Come on!" one of them grumbled, sounding like Hunter's voice processed through gravel.

Sibylla blinked again, trying to sort through the fear and anger, and confusion that clashed in her brain. Two werewolves were sitting in the middle of the room, calmly talking to her in the voices of her brothers.

"This is… I don't…" she stammered.

"She has had a hard day today," Aubri said sternly, "drop the act."

"What is going on?!" Sibylla demanded, anger conquering the other emotions.

"Well," Nate said, one of the werewolves gesturing between the two of them. "We're werewolves."

"Obviously," Hunter added.

"And Aubri was supposed to play along," Nate continued, looking meaningfully at Aubri, "but insisted on ruining the joke."

Sibylla turned to look at Aubri, who stood behind her rubbing her eyes tiredly. Then Sibylla looked back at her brothers, trying to decipher whether or not she was having the strangest fever dream of her life.

Her brothers were werewolves.

It couldn't be. They looked nothing like the Infected she had been hunting for months. She thought back to Chad's appearance, covered in sores and puss, no matter how closely he looked like a Pure, how much like a more refined version of the Infected he looked. Nate and Hunter looked nothing like him.

She thought about how Savage looked and determined immediately that they looked nothing like him either. He looked like a massive wolf, the size of a horse and full of teeth and claws. Her brothers looked more like a perfect hybrid of the two, like something out of a horror movie. They stood on their two legs, towering over Sibylla, covered in muscle and exuding power and strength.

"How did this happen?" she asked, still not believing what she was looking at.

"That is an excellent question," Hunter replied.

"With an excellent answer," Nate said.

"An excellent theory at least," Hunter said. "Though, before we dive into that, would it be possible for either of you to unlock us and then turn around for a minute or bring us clothes? The change kind of destroys everything and the silver isn't super comfy."

He gestured to the pile of ripped shirts and pants behind them.

Sibylla crossed her arms, irritation joining with her disbelief. Too much had happened that day for her to be truly angry with the last family she potentially had left on Earth. Instead of being angry, she decided she would at least try to mess with them back. No need to let their little attempt at a joke go unpunished. They could learn to have a little patience.

"As much as I would love to wait to know how my brothers have hidden being bitten and Infected from me and everyone else, I would rather hear it now," she declared. "So spill it."

"What?" they both said simultaneously.

"Tick tock," Sibylla said, arching an eyebrow.

"Well, how does anyone become a werewolf?" Hunter said, chuckling nervously.

"Yeah," Nate added. "We found out one day that we had something called Umbra Lupus and were confused, since, you know, we've never been bit by a Pure."

"You haven't been bit?" Sibylla asked, surprised. "Scratched? Sneezed on?"

"Not once," Hunter confirmed.

"So we did some digging and realized that there was only one way it could be the case," Nate continued. "And that's by birth from two Pures."

"Super rare," Hunter added, "there aren't many actual documented cases of a female werewolf, no more than a handful over the past few hundred years. Not to mention there hasn't been a documented case of two Pures knocking boots here on Earth."

They paused and looked at her, probably hoping that she had had enough information to allow them to change back, or at the very least take off the silver collars. Sibylla wasn't ready to do that, however. With the shock and relief wearing off, she had become keenly aware that her brothers, as much as she loved them, were absolutely without question werewolves. As much as she wanted to believe that they were okay, she wasn't sure if she was quite there yet.

"Go on," Sibylla said, voice even.

"That would mean that Dad and Mom were both Pures, or that Mom was a Pure and had gotten jiggy with it with the Red Falls Pure," Nate explained.

"Not possible," Sibylla cut in. "Mom never would have cheated on Dad, even if she was a Pure."

"Not only that," Hunter agreed, "but we would have changed years ago when we hit puberty. And the Infected don't look nearly as good as we do."

"Obviously that didn't happen," Nate said. "So we had to find an alternate theory."

"What did you come up with?" Sibylla demanded, seeing small tendrils of smoke rising from where the silver had burned through their fur.

"Best guess is that either Mom or Dad is the Pure, and the mantle they had was somehow passed down to us in some kind of genetic hybrid that's never been seen before," Nate replied. "That's Hunter's theory, anyway."

"What's yours?" Sibylla asked

"I concur with him completely," Nate said, clasping his massive hands behind his back like some kind of canine scholar.

"So…" Hunter said, holding up the silver chains.

Sibylla hesitated. They were talking so clearly, so evenly. Not even a hint of irritation or anger or bloodlust. Were they truly okay? Was she willing to take that chance?

"They are safe," Aubri said, seeming to read her mind. "Honestly, I would have freed them hours ago if they would have let me."

"You?" Sibylla said, shocked.

She noticed then that Aubri wasn't holding any weapons. Her rifle was gone, and there weren't any knives hanging at her belt. She wasn't even wearing body armor. Sibylla couldn't think of a single time that she had seen Aubri without even a knife close at hand.

"But you told me that all werewolves were monsters, that the most humane thing I could do was to put them down," she said, hating saying it in front of her brothers.

"I know," Aubri said, smiling. "And I was tempted to follow my own advice and training."

"Why didn't you?" Sibylla asked.

"Part of it was how… harmless they looked," Aubri said, looking past Sibylla. "They reminded me of some of the puppies I saw around town."

"Offensive!" Nate said.

"But, mostly it was because they are your brothers," Aubri continued, ignoring their interruption. "I could not bring myself to destroy something so important to you, not if there was even the hint of a chance of saving them."

Relief flooded Sibylla, pouring cold water over the heat of her anger. She had lost so much in one day, even if her brothers were twisted, vicious killers. To lose them would have been the end of everything for her.

"It is another example," Aubri continued, "of something that you cannot control. Your brothers have Changed despite all of our best efforts. Yet they are fine, better than fine. They are werewolves without a Pure, perfect hybrids capable of free thought. They are still your brothers, even with the beast evident within them."

Aubri put a heavy key in Sibylla's hand. Sibylla stared at it for a moment longer, wondering what would happen when she unlocked the collars. Would Aubri's faith be misplaced, both of them being torn to pieces in an instant? Or would they prove the rules of nature wrong?

There's only one way to know, she thought.

Without any more hesitation, Sibylla crossed the room and unlocked first Nate's, then Hunter's collar, letting them fall to the floor with the key. All the while she considered what it meant to be werewolves without a Pure guiding them. Would that mean that killing the Pure would set the others free? Or was it too late for the Infected? Were her brother's examples of a cure, or were they a fluke?

All signs pointed to the latter over the former, but still, there could be a chance for the others. If nothing else, then maybe they could do what Mr. Darrow had hinted at before he died, challenge Savage and take his pack away. Maybe it was the Pure who made the Infected twisted, not the infection itself.

Her train of thought was derailed when she felt first one set of strong furry arms wrap around her, then another. It took a second for her mind to overtake her training to realize that they were hugging her. She did her best to return the hug but found it a little difficult.

"You guys okay?" she asked. It was a question she had asked them hundreds of times, and it was the only question she asked that they took seriously.

"Yeah," Hunter said quietly.

"A little scared maybe," Nate added. "Thanks for not killing us Red."

"Never," Sibylla said, burying her face in their fur. "I love you guys, and I promised Dad I would take care of you. I don't care what you look like, you are still my brothers."

A fat drop of water landed on her shoulder and it took a second for Sibylla to realize that it was a tear. Hugging them tighter, she couldn't help but lose a tear herself, surprising since she didn't think that she had any left to give.

After a few minutes, a thought occurred to her.

"Does this mean I'm a werewolf too?" she asked, looking over her shoulder at Aubri. "Since they have it genetically, so should I, right?"

"I am not sure," Aubri shrugged.

Sibylla wasn't sure how she felt about the idea. Being okay with her brothers being werewolves was one thing, but finding out she was one too was a little too much for her to handle. How would it affect her bond with Aubri? Would she want to be connected to the monster that she had sworn to fight? Maybe she wouldn't try to kill Sibylla, but she certainly wouldn't want to stay with her.

As if reading her mind, Aubri walked forward and pried Sibylla loose from her brother's arms.

"Listen," she said, "I knew that it was a possibility the moment I saw your brothers tonight. And I would be lying if I said that all of this made sense, or that none of it made me nervous. Yet, of all the things that I know for sure, I know that you are no monster."

Face burning, Sibylla smiled. For the first time in a long time, the world didn't feel like it was falling apart.

"What do we do now?" Hunter asked, plopping down on the floor.

"Do we know who the Pure is?" Nate asked, sitting down next to Hunter.

"We do," Sibylla said bitterly, "it's Savage."

Nate and Hunter exchanged a knowing glance.

"That makes sense," Hunter said.

"Prick," Nate added.

"It gets much, much worse," Sibylla began, then paused. It would be the third time in a few hours that she would have to detail the death of Mr. Darrow and the second time she would have to describe how she had unwittingly given unparalleled power to a traitor. She wasn't sure if she could do it.

"Yadder, the Keeper, is a traitor who now possesses all three mantles," Aubri said, thankfully stepping in for her. "And Savage killed Mr. Darrow. We are all that stands between your world and an onslaught of evil."

Nate and Hunter blinked at the stark description of their situation. Thankful that she didn't have to say it herself, Sibylla reached out and took Aubri's hand, pulling her close. Whether or not she would have to give details or explain she didn't know, but she had a feeling that her brothers would prefer action.

"Okay," Hunter said, turning his burning eyes on Sibylla. "So what's the plan?"

Chapter 32

"That's your plan?!" Kane exclaimed, sneering at Sibylla. "You brought me out here and tell me all this bullshit and then throw out…" he waved at the butcher paper that covered the kitchen table, "this as a legitimate plan to deal with all of the bullshit you just told me?!"

Kane, Kayla, Aubri, Nate, Hunter, and Sibylla were seated around the table. It had only been a few hours, so admittedly the plan they had come up with wasn't necessarily perfect, though Sibylla thought it could work. Unfortunately, it necessitated bringing in some extra people for it to even have the smallest chance of working, so Sibylla had agreed with her brothers and Aubri that they needed to bring in Kane and Kayla.

Sibylla hadn't had the chance to explain the nature of her breakup with Kane, which had only happened the day before. The amount of time it took to convince him to even show up in the first place was probably a good enough indicator of what was going on between them. In the end, she had been forced to call him multiple times to even get him to pick up, and the admission that Mr. Darrow was dead after several minutes of arguing to get him to her house.

Conversely, Kayla had barely heard Sibylla say a word before she was out the door, jumping into her car.

"Whatever it is, I'll be there in fifteen," Kayla said, the sound of keys jingling in the background.

"Kay, we're thirty minutes away and I haven't even told you what's going on," Sibylla said, surprised.

"It's in your voice Red," Kayla said, "that's all I need. Plus speed limits are more of a challenge anyway. See you in fifteen."

It had taken her twenty, but Sibylla was impressed that Kayla arrived so quickly without being tailed by the cops on the way in. It had taken Kane much longer to arrive, eventually showing up just as Sibylla was convinced he wouldn't come. After that, he may as well have been a statue, staying icey toward everyone, even Kayla as Sibylla detailed the plan and their part in it.

"That's freaking dangerous Red," Kayla said when Kane had stopped. "I want to help and all, but that's freaking dangerous."

"I know," Sibylla admitted.

The plan as it was was split into three parts. The first part was separating Savage and Yadder. Both were dangerous on their own, but Sibylla couldn't imagine trying to take the two of them together. She and Aubri would take Yadder and Nate and Hunter would take Savage. If they could separate them, there was a very, very small chance that they could at least beat one before the other.

That being said, it was the part of the plan that Sibylla liked the least. She had no idea what abilities she may have as a werewolf and was hesitant to even let the beast out in the first place. As much as she wanted to accept it as a part of who she was, it felt too dark and dangerous to trust. Aubri would be by her side the whole time, but the last thing Sibylla wanted was to lose control and force Aubri to have to face both her and Yadder at the same time.

The other part was that her brothers were also untested. Once they joined the fray there would be nothing Sibylla could do to keep them safe while they battled a Pure that was hundreds of years old and who had faced down thousands of threats in his lifetime. It was hard to swallow, but she knew that she couldn't do it alone and that their abilities at least gave them a fighting chance. It didn't feel like enough, but it was all they had to work with.

The second part of the plan involved destroying the Gate itself. That part was essential, no matter what else happened. Through their research, Nate and Hunter had discovered that the Gate had been constructed on something called a 'ley line,' part of a spider web-like network of energy and magic that crisscrossed the planet. It was what powered the Gate and made it possible to access Laternum. If they could destroy it down to its foundation, then the Gate wouldn't be able to open. Possibly it could also separate Yadder from their powers, leaving them vulnerable.

"On that note," Hunter said, "we found a brief description of the binding ritual that trapped Yadder in the Gate in the first place."

"Nasty business," Nate said.

"Truly," Hunter confirmed. "It says it needs an unwilling sacrifice. But, more importantly, it requires the skull of the sacrifice to be placed somewhere in the Gate to physically bind their spirit to it. If we break that, it sets Yadder's spirit free."

"Free?" Sibylla asked. It didn't sound that bad, considering that Yadder had been forced to reside in the Gate for eternity against their will. It made sense that they were so angry.

"Eh," Hunter said, flattening his hand and waggling it in a 'kind of' gesture. "The description is pretty vague there, more on the theoretical side. No one has ever broken a Gate before or gotten rid of the trapped Keeper if there is one."

"Are there Keepers who aren't trapped in the Gate?" Aubri asked.

"Oh yeah, it's not a requirement," Hunter confirmed.

"Yadder must have royally pissed off whoever it was that trapped them in there," Nate said.

"So what will happen then?" Sibylla asked, unsure of whether or not she liked the uncertainty of the situation. Yadder may have double crossed her, but in light of the fact that everyone involved seemed to be a victim of some bigger game she didn't know yet, it was hard to be angry at them.

Hunter shrugged. "Their spirit could be released and be at rest, or it could wander the Earth as a vengeful ghost."

"A coin toss," Nate said.

"So you're saying that, on top of the werewolves, a murderous ghost could be lurking in Red Falls forever?" Kane asked.

Nate and Hunter shrugged in reply. Kane made a scoffing noise and sat back in his seat, hands shoved into his pockets.

The problem, of course, was how do they destroy a magical Gate that was bound by magic and built to withstand battles with mythic monsters? Sibylla couldn't even begin to think of a viable option. The Gate looked strong enough to withstand a wrecking ball, not that there was one even available in the town. To her surprise, her brothers didn't share her appreciation of the problem.

"That's easy!" Nate said.

Before anyone could ask him why he was so confident, he slapped down a brick on the table. When he moved his hand, everyone could read the C4 printed on the label. They all took an involuntary step back, except for Nate and Hunter, and Aubri, who probably didn't know what it was in the first place.

"Where the hell did you get that?!" Kayla demanded. She had stood up so quickly that her chair had tipped over and almost tripped her as she tried to get away from the table.

"Mr. D!" Nate said cheerfully. "He's been stockpiling the stuff for a while now. He has a bunch in the safe house."

"Dad too, as it turns out," Hunter added.

"Where the hell did they get it?!" Kane demanded. "This whole family is freaking messed up man."

"Hey," Nate said, pointing a warning finger at Kane. After a moment he dropped it and shrugged. "We got some issues I guess."

"He's not wrong," Hunter agreed. "But I don't think even the magic of the Gate could stand up to what we got stashed away."

Nate gave a wicked, excited grin. "We definitely have enough."

Kane and Kayla looked at each other uncertainly. Sibylla didn't blame them, she didn't know how much Roger and Mr. Darrow had stashed away and had frankly been too nervous to ask. She made a mental note to double check how much they would use to make sure it wasn't excessive. Not that she would know what 'enough' really looked like in the first place.

"What is it?" Aubri asked, confused.

"Boom bricks!" Nate and Hunter said together.

"You got a magical Gate?" Hunter asked.

"We have a way to make it disappear!" Nate added.

"I'll explain later," Sibylla said.

"There's no freaking way this is your plan," Kane muttered, running his hand over his face tiredly.

"So," Kayla quickly cut in, "we have explosives, how are we supposed to get it to the Gate? Didn't you say there were a bunch of werewolves over there?"

That part of the plan was two-fold because there were so many Infected. The last thing Sibylla wanted was to kill someone who had no control over their condition. So the plan was that she, Aubri, Nate, and Hunter drove in like a bat out of hell in Sibylla's car, catching everyone by surprise. Then Aubri and her brothers would ditch from the car and Sibylla would steer it into the Gate before jumping out herself at the very last minute. There it would sit until it was time to detonate, for which there were two devices. One was a clicker like what someone used to unlock a car, and the other was a timer.

If, for some reason, Sibylla and the rest were killed before they had a chance to detonate it remotely, she wanted a backup. The timer would guarantee that the bombs would go off no matter what, hopefully with enough time for the Infected to get out of range.

The second part of the plan involved Kane and Kayla rolling up in their cars and antagonizing the Infected into following them while the others kept Savage and Yadder distracted. According to the book, once the Pure was killed the Infected would lose focus and their coherence, which would ensure Kane and Kayla's safety.

What happened after that was anyone's guess. Sibylla hoped that she would be around long enough to help them however she could, even if that meant setting up her house as an Infected quarantine for them to live out the rest of their days. It wasn't a great plan, but she figured the best thing to do was to focus on just getting the Gate destroyed. At least that way Red Falls would be safe from invasion, even if they did have to deal with the leftovers.

"There's no freaking way this is the plan," Kane muttered again.

Sibylla rolled her eyes, irritated with his constant stream of negativity. He had known about the werewolves long enough now to come to terms with it, as far as she was concerned. All he needed to do was drive after all.

How hard can that be? She thought.

"Well it is the plan," Aubri said flatly. She looked at him with such an aggressively neutral expression that he was forced to look away, pretending to look over the rough diagram of Old Town.

"Here's the deal," Sibylla said, getting their attention back. "This is going to be dangerous for all of us, so I can't force anyone to do this. But I can't do this alone. I need all of you to help me. If we can't do this, and that Gate remains intact, I don't think Yadder and Pure are going to wait long before letting loose a wave of Infected over our town, maybe even the country or the world. So what do you say? Will you help me?"

Nate and Hunter nodded immediately.

"We have some C4 about to expire," Nate said. "And today is the 'best by' date."

Aubri slid her hand over Sibylla's, intertwining their fingers together. "I will always be by your side."

Sibylla smiled at her gratefully, then turned to Kane and Kayla. "What do y'all say?"

Chewing her lip nervously, Kayla hesitated. Kane just stared at Sibylla and Aubri's hands.

"I can do it," Kayla said finally, nodding her head resolutely. "Can't let the world go to the dogs."

Kane waited a long moment longer, tapping his fingers on the table in an anxious rhythm. Sibylla felt a little guilty about involving him, considering she hadn't told him that Savage was the Pure. She told herself it was because he had struggled so much with the existence of werewolves in the first place, finding out his father figure, the man who had taken him in every time his parents kicked him out, the man who had helped him through their divorce when Sibylla hadn't even known it was happening, was the Pure at the root of all the town's problems.

If she thought about it, however, she may have been able to bring herself to admit that she was afraid he wouldn't help if he knew the truth. How could she ask him to help her destroy Savage and expect him to be okay with it? The best option was to keep him in the dark, at least for the moment. They could handle that once the dust had settled and the Gate had been destroyed.

"Fine," he said and left it at that.

"Okay," Sibylla said, clapping her hands together. "Let's meet back here at around five and get the plan in motion. We need to move quickly, and there's a lot to get ready."

As everyone moved away from the table Nate and Hunter held back. Sibylla knew what was on their minds before she asked, "Thinking about Dad?"

Hunter nodded. "With Yadder being able to open and close the Gate now, what if they took him over to the other side?"

"As fun as it would be to blow this thing sky high, what if it means never having the chance to get him back?" Nate added.

Sibylla had thought about it the moment she knew she needed to destroy the Gates. As much as she wanted to think that Roger was still somewhere in Red Falls, some part of her knew that Yadder had most likely moved him over to Laternum. Even after several hours of planning and wondering and thinking, she wasn't sure if she was ready to literally close the door on the opportunity to save their dad.

"This is a big ask," she admitted. "I don't know if he's over there or over here. We could be destroying our only opportunity to get him back."

Nate and Hunter stayed silent for a moment, both of them staring at the outline of the plan. Knowing what was going on in their minds would have been impossible to guess, even on a good day. But she could see the anguish roiling between them. And, despite her history with Roger, she could feel it too. They would all be putting the fate of Red Falls over the fate of their own family, and it didn't sit right with any of them.

"The book does mention that there are most likely other Gates in the world," Hunter reasoned.

"Nothing for sure," Nate grumbled.

They both looked miserably at each other and then to Sibylla. Without having to speak, she knew that they would follow her lead.

"There's a lot that could happen," she admitted. "There could be other Gates, there could be a way to stop Yadder and Savage without breaking the Gate completely, anything. But, if we don't stop them here…"

She trailed off and they nodded, understanding what she was saying. Deep down she hated herself for even saying it. He had been caught helping them escape and had spent decades of his life keeping them safe. It didn't feel right to leave him in a lurch, cut off from any hope of rescuing. They needed a trump card, something to even the odds.

"I need your help with something," she said, feeling her nerves tighten.

Chapter 33

Kane and Kayla left Sibylla's house together at Kayla's request, claiming that she was so anxious that she didn't want to drive home alone. They drove in silence, neither eager to be the first to speak. It wasn't until they were out of sight of the house that Kane pulled the car off the road and parked on the shoulder, deep in thought. Kayla remained quiet, eyes glued on the horizon.

Even though she knew what he was going to ask she knew better than to rush him. They had clashed enough times that she had a pretty good idea where his buttons were, and the biggest, easiest one to push was rushing him. It infringed upon his perceived importance.

Delusions of grandeur, she thought, careful to keep from rolling her eyes.

"What do you think?" he asked finally, stroking his chin in thought.

"I think we should tell them," Kayla said immediately.

He grunted, then shook his head. "No, I don't think we should."

"What?" Kayla said sharply.

"Savage is old news Kay," he said resolutely, "and Yadder? She's been trapped in that Gate for so damn long she's lost the plot."

"They," Kayla corrected.

"I don't care," Kane snapped, flashing her a warning glance. "They, she, it, whatever. That damned faun is so focused on revenge that it can't lead effectively."

"What, and you're not, lover boy?" Kayla asked.

Kane rolled his eyes. "Please, you know that I didn't give two shits about her. I prefer someone a little..." he ran his hand over her thigh, "someone a little tougher. Someone who likes it rough."

Kayla rolled her eyes again but didn't knock his hand away. It had been painful enough to pretend there was nothing between them when he was 'dating' Sibylla. Plus, somehow, the lies made it way hotter.

"We did our jobs," Kane continued. "I dated her and kept tabs on her, you made sure her idiot brothers recovered from those wolfsbane bombs they gassed themselves with. What's he going to use us for now? Especially now that he has his 'love.'" He sneered at the word.

Kayla knew that he was right. They were the most successful Infected so far, the closest to Pure that Savage had managed to get. Yet, now that Yadder was out of the Gate, they had become essentially worthless. That being said, Savage was still their Pure, and if he survived and discovered they knew anything about the plan in the first place he would rip the flesh from their bones while the Pack watched.

"We should still tell him," Kayla persisted. "If he finds out…"

Kane turned toward her, putting his around her shoulders, and ran his hand higher up her thigh. A shiver ran over her while she locked eyes with him, her breathing increasing with her heart rate.

"Come now," he said softly, inching closer. "You trust me, don't you?"

Not trusting herself to speak, she nodded slowly, biting her lip.

"Then we don't tell them a thing," he said, his lips brushing hers. "And when the dust settles, we kill them all, and the pack is ours. We can be in charge, just the two of us, right?"

Breathing heavily, heart racing, Kayla nodded again.

"Good girl," he said, lingering for a moment longer before pulling away from her, pulling the car back onto the road.

Damn him, she thought, licking her lips, still tingling from his touch.

There was nothing for it, Savage was an old fool and Yadder was out of touch. If they wanted to survive, then they had to take what they could when they could, everyone else be damned.

Chapter 34

"I'm not entirely sure how to do this," Sibylla said hesitantly.

Since a big part of the plan hinged on everyone being able to hold their own against monsters, she needed to make sure that she could call on her inner monster when the time demanded it. More importantly, she hoped she would also be able to force it back down when that time was over. Still, standing in the middle of the barn, a big silver collar weighing heavily on her shoulder, she felt more than a little embarrassed.

"Just let it happen," Nate called down from his position in the loft. Hunter was sitting next to him, the pair looking like they were there to watch a show more so than offering moral support as they claimed.

"It's like breathing," Hunter added. "It's all natural."

It doesn't feel natural, Sibylla thought nervously.

Though, fundamentally, it did. There had always been some part of Sibylla that had lived beneath the surface. It scared her, certainly. It had an energy to it that felt like a tsunami, threatening to sweep her away if she wasn't careful. What if it got out of hand? What if it shoved her aside and took over completely? "Of all the things that I know for sure, I know that you are no monster." The words Aubri had spoken to her that morning rang in her ears.

"Remember," Aubri said, stepping forward to adjust the collar. "You are strong, stronger than the thing that resides within you. Force it to submit, be the Pure."

Hunter stepped forward. "It's not a monster in you, or a sickness, it's just… you."

"Right," she said, feeling the pressure of the moment beginning to weigh on her.

Aubri gave her a big smile and then leaned in to kiss Sibylla, a fairly awkward maneuver with the silver collar playing interference. The moment Aubri's surprisingly soft lips made contact with her confidence surged through Sibylla like wildfire. Aubri pulled back, stroking Sibylla's face with her thumb, brushing away a stray hair.

"You can do this," Aubri said softly, "we are all here for you."

Sibylla nodded quickly, pursing her lips, not wanting the feeling to fade away.

"Ooooooooooooh," Nate and Hunter said together.

"Shut up," Sibylla said, not fighting the smile that came to her face.

"Young love," Nate said, ignoring her.

"Inspiring," Hunter agreed.

Sibylla shook her head and focused. Shaking out her hands, and rolling her neck, she wasn't sure what she was supposed to do to make it all happen. So she tried to relax, searching herself for the inner beast, the part of her subconscious that she had been fighting for years and years. When did she feel it most?

That's easy, she thought, when I'm angry.

So she thought about anything that made her angry. She thought about Kane being the absolute worst boyfriend. She thought about how he had not only thought that she was disgusting for being bi, but that he had told the whole football team about it. Every little nitpicking word he'd said, every time he had made her feel small and insignificant.

Immediately a fire lit inside of her, burning hotter than anything she had felt before. To fuel it she thought about how Yadder had pretended to be an ally, someone that Sibylla could trust. She thought about how Yadder had taken Sibylla's gifts and turned them on her like she was nothing more than a means to an end, a joke.

The fire increased in intensity, and Sibylla could feel her body shifting, shaping, stretching, and breaking. She thought about how her dad was taken away from her, and how she had been forced to once again be the adult in the family. About how she had never fully been able to live life as a real teenager, even now, at the beginning of the end of humanity. About how she had given up everything because she was weak because she was small and insignificant.

The heat grew more intense but the words felt wrong. Fire was burning who she was away, too much of herself was being lost. Panic seized her as she realized that she couldn't control the flame as it tried to force its way through her, filling her bones with a fever that was reducing her soul to ashes.

Her hand shot up and shoved the collar against her neck, the silver barbs pricking through her skin. A searing pain shot through her, boiling water against the inferno. Collapsing to her knees, she shoved the collar again, screaming in pain, something wet trickling down her arm. It was the worst pain she had ever felt in her life, without question. But it was killing the fire, pushing it away and deep back into herself.

Breathing heavily, she crawled forward blindly, unable to open her eyes. The tension and strain in her limbs were receding, returning her to her normal state. After a long while she felt a cooling hand on the bare skin of her back. She didn't need to look up to see that it was Aubri.

"I couldn't do it," Sibylla panted, voice sounding misshapen in her ears.

"It's okay," Aubri said, kissing the back of Sibylla's head.

"Do you think we still have a chance without it?" Nate asked, sounding unsure.

Sibylla looked up and saw that he and Hunter were standing further back, uncertain of the situation. She knew what it had felt like to her, but she couldn't imagine what it had looked like to them. Aubri unlocked the collar and started working out the barbs from the skin of Sibylla's neck.

"There's only one way to know," Sibylla winced. "We don't have much of a choice."

Chapter 35

Over two thousand years. Yadder had been trapped in that cursed Gate for over two thousand years. From the days of Rome, watching the legionnaires struggle to fight back against the Pures who had broken through the portal, to watching that pathetic girl crumble from the smallest pressure. Over two thousand years.

Yadder took a deep breath, welcoming the sting of winter into their lungs. They hadn't experienced true winters in two thousand years and found Earth winters to be far more refreshing than anything they had experienced in their time in Laternum. Even two thousand years later they could still remember how magical and full of potential that new planet was, eyes as wide and naive as a faunling. It hadn't taken long for them to learn just how cruel the new world could be, being betrayed and trapped in a cage for the 'greater good,' as Felix, the Gate's first Sentinel, had put it.

After two thousand years and hundreds of new Sentinels and Rangers, Yadder couldn't have cared less about Earth's 'greater good.' Now they finally had a chance to give someone else a chance at enjoying the bounty that Earth provided. Turning toward the Gate, a giddy giggle escaped their lips, drawing the loving eyes of their mate, Savage.

Yadder didn't much care for that century's new name for the Pure, but he seemed to like it fine, and they could admit that at least it was fitting. They had met him before being trapped when he was disguised as a legionnaire among the Roman army in Gaul when the portal between the worlds had opened. Since that time he had stayed close by as the Gate languished in obscurity in France, even tracking the Gate down when that fool Baft had moved it. Yadder admired the Pure's loyalty and had grown to love him as dearly as their own life, bonded by eternity.

"What is it, my love?" Savage asked, a smile spreading across his face. He was speaking his native Latin, sounding like bells ringing in springtime to Yadder's ears.

"I am happy," they replied, "for the first time in over a millennium, I have hope."

Savage took their hand in his and squeezed.

"All thanks to that useless girl," he said.

"All thanks to you," Yadder corrected him.

Though they could put some small amount of credit in Sibylla's hands. Her whole family. The girl hadn't been trained properly, and couldn't fully appreciate the sacrifice she was making by giving the last mantle to Yadder. The failure of Roger to properly train his daughter in the life that he should have known she would be taking over made that possible. And then there was Delphine. Precious, arrogant Delphine. None of it would have been possible if she hadn't done what she had all those years ago.

A low growl snapped Yadder out of their thoughts. Savage's grip tightened on theirs, and it didn't take Yadder long to know why. The sound of an engine, of multiple engines, carried over to their ears despite the distance. Three cars were racing down Main Street, headed straight for the Gate.

"Cute," Yadder said, "she's going to try and break the Gate with three cars."

Focusing, Yadder saw that Sibylla wasn't in any of the cars. Which made sense, considering she was now essentially useless in a fight against even the weakest Infected. Still, Yadder had hoped that she would show up anyway. The lead car was being driven by a girl who was obviously from Laternum, and they could remember when she first came through the Gate. Some Sacred Legionnaire called Aubri. The other two cars were being driven by none other than Savage's lieutenants, Kane and Kayla.

"Your pack does not seem to be invested in loyalty," Yadder quipped.

"I will break them," Savage growled, releasing Yadder's hand.

Barking orders, he walked to the edge of the lawn that separated the Gate from the buildings that occupied the fringes of the shabby town. A group of Infected had been loitering nearby, watching everything with obvious boredom, and they jumped up at the opportunity to finally have some action.

The pack was larger than what Yadder had seen in some time, being fifteen strong with Savage. But they could remember the ancient packs in Laternum, made up of dozens, hundreds of werewolves. Earth would know that power soon enough. For now, a handful broke away and charged at the cars, their bones popping with disgusting volume. Those Infected were truly hideous and twisted, and Yadder hated each of them.

The Infected had barely changed when they were knocked off their feet by two orange blurs. Quick as they moved, Yadder was surprised to see two werewolves of a type they had never seen before, standing tall and hitting hard. It didn't take them long to take care of the weaker Infected, and the cars continued to charge forward.

"Who are they?" Yadder demanded.

"Sibylla's twin brothers," Savage said in disbelief.

"They were not to be touched!" Yadder said, annoyed.

"We didn't infect them," Savaged snapped, turning away to bark more orders.

"*Sine imperio*," Yadder muttered. Werewolves without masters. Savage would fix that soon enough.

More of the Infected surged forward, nearly all of them changed at that point. Sighing, Yadder turned to the Gate and extended their hands to it. The ceremony would have been easier on a full moon or even at night, but the night was close enough. Opening the Gate would be simple enough, but it could always be closed again. Yadder would break it, and keep the portal open permanently. It would be tricky, the hardest part is locating where in the Gate their skull was located. It was the only real thing linking them to the Gate, more than that it was the only thing linking them to the mortal plane at all. If it broke, Yadder would cease to exist.

A gunshot rang out, dragging Yadder's attention back from the Gate. Another shot rang out, the flash revealing that Sibylla was sitting on one of the decrepit roofs, a rifle in her hands, firing quick, barely aimed shots at the Infected. Yadder guessed the bullets were silver, but they didn't seem to be hitting even remotely close to the Infected. It would seem that they would have their chance to deal with Sibylla after all.

The three cars continued forward, unmolested by even one of the Infected, who were now so distracted by the sheer number of factors that they were barely able to mount a remotely coherent offense. Two of the cars peeled off, driving in two opposite directions. Only the car with Aubri was still driving their way, headed toward the Gate like a ballistic missile. Yadder could easily see the grim determination in her eyes and shook their head.

Fools, she thought, disappointed.

"Deal with them," they demanded, turning back to the Gate. "Now. This magic is hard enough without distractions."

"Go after Kane and Kayla, bring me their skulls and flesh," Savage growled to his pack. "I can handle these on my own."

ψ

Sibylla watched the plan unfold without a hitch with no small amount of surprise. Considering they had created the plan in a few hours and had had only a couple of hours to prepare it, things were going well. Squeezing off a few more rounds in the general direction of the Infected to further distract them, she wondered how long it would take for Savage to take the bait and send them after Kane and Kayla.

It was the weakest part of the plan in her mind, a close second to having to fight Yadder and Savage. Would two cars peeling off be enough to entice him to send his pack after them? She couldn't see how it could. Best case scenario they would pull away a handful of the Infected, and they would just need to adjust the plan as necessary. Hopefully, they wouldn't need to kill any of them, but she had known that it was a possibility.

To her complete surprise, every single one of the Infected split off and raced after the retreating cars, leaving just Savage and Yadder to contend with, and Yadder seemed distracted by something they were doing at the Gate. That meant that, maybe, if only briefly, they could be handling Savage four on one, and those odds looked much better than even her brightest hopes.

Far be it from me to look a gift horse in the mouth, she decided.

Sibylla didn't need the enhanced optics of the scoped rifle for her to see Savage square up on the rapidly approaching Aubri. Sibylla had never seen what a car and a Pure could do to each other, but even if he knocked the car off its course a little, it could ruin the whole plan. Focusing the scope on his chest, she noticed that he hadn't fully Changed. Like Chad, he had grown in height and had taken on the features of his werewolf form, but had stopped the transformation short.

He must be wearing one of those vests, she thought, heart sinking.

Maybe, like Chad, the silver bullet could at least knock him off his feet. If only for a second, it could be enough. A flash from the Gate drew Sibylla's attention to it, and she saw that whatever Yadder was doing was beginning to gain momentum. She didn't know if silver had the same effect on fauns as it did on werewolves, but whatever they were doing looked like it could mean trouble.

Gritting her teeth Sibylla swung the reticle over to Yadder and squeezed off two shots before she had a chance to change her mind. Immediately the flashing lights vanished, and Yadder cried out in pain and crumpled to the ground. A roar from Savage told Sibylla that she should have also considered the fact that she had just placed two bullets in the back of the only person that Savage truly cared about.

That works just fine, she thought with satisfaction, turning just in time to see him get tossed to the side like a ragdoll by Aubri.

For the first time since she had met Aubri, Sibylla got a true sense of what she was capable of. Graceful, cat-like, moving with a fluidity like water, Aubri jumped out of the car at the last second, rolling to her feet without even breaking her stride, completely ignoring the car crashing into the Gate. Sibylla's pistols in her hands, she was unloading both of them on Yadder, who had, incredibly, already recovered.

Roaring again, Savage leapt to his feat, so enraged that he tore off his silver proof vest and finished the Change, growing to his impressive height, blood, and murder clear in his eyes. No sooner had he taken a step than Nate and Hunter were on him. Even Sibylla couldn't keep track of who was who, the three of them turning into a mass of fur and teeth and claws.

Swiveling back to Aubri, Sibylla saw that she was locked in hand to hand combat with Yadder, the two of them moving so rapidly that there wasn't a prayer that Sibylla could contribute from where she was. Dropping the rifle she slid down the roof's shingles, landing heavily on the ground. Racing forward, she wondered what good at all she could do in that moment. Heart pounding in her chest, she reached out once more to that subconscious presence, that part of her that, earlier that day, had almost burned her up.

Drawing nearer, she realized that anger and rage and guilt would not be the answer. Powerful as they were, leaning into them meant losing herself, and that wasn't something she could come back from. They just gave the beast within too much power over her, let it take too much from her. She couldn't risk losing herself like that, even if it meant that it gave them a fighting chance.

The distance between her and Yadder was rapidly closing, and Sibylla was still distressingly human. Slowing down was out of the question, so she pumped her arms harder. What would be better than all of the anger and rage and guilt?

Damn it, I don't have time for this! She thought.

Gritting her teeth, she reached deep down, easily finding that other presence within her, the thing that she had always thought was nothing more than her subconscious and impulsiveness. It was both familiar and terrifying, comforting and anxiety inducing. As much as she didn't want to admit it, that beast within her was part of her, and she needed to finally join it together with herself. Not with hate or anger, but with just accepting that it was a part of her.

We need each other, she thought, still running, only a few yards away now. Aubri was on her feet again, both of them so intent on killing each other that neither of them seemed to notice she was getting nearer. That's the only way this works. So work with me damn it!

She leapt into the air, noticeably feeling herself going higher than she ever could before she had taken on the mantle. As she sailed through the air, she felt it rising within her, and she embraced it, letting it intertwine with her mind and body, feeling herself stretch and grow and shift painlessly. It had been so long that Sibylla could hardly remember a time when she had felt so at peace with herself.

Yadder looked up, eyes widening in surprise.

Good, Sibylla thought, grinning eagerly while her clawed hand came down hard on Yadder's face, sending them spinning backward into the Gate's tower. Aubri, breathing heavily, looked Sibylla up and down approvingly. Unfortunately, she didn't have time to comment on the change, as Yadder was rising to their feet, four gashes across their face already binding back together.

"Well well," they said, smiling eagerly. "I didn't think I could be surprised after so many years. First your brothers and now you. Perhaps this will be an engaging fight after all."

Not waiting for an invitation, Sibylla and Aubri surged forward, roaring and screaming, intent on tearing Yadder to shreds.

Yadder did a spinning kick that knocked Aubri heavily onto her back. Red flashed before Sibylla's eyes, and she growled with an intensity that snapped Yadder's shocked gaze toward her. Hitting harder than she ever had before, Sibylla tore Yadder to the ground, jaws snapping hungrily for their neck. Moving faster than smoke on the wind, Yadder dodged the bite, shoving their stiff fingers up under Sibylla's jaw, their other hand jabbing into the soft flesh where her arm met her body.

Snarling, Sibylla was vaguely aware of the fact that her arm had gone completely numb and the stars that exploded in front of her eyes. She didn't care, no one, no one, sent Aubri to the ground. Despite Sibylla's rage, Yadder was able to land several more strikes that forced Sibylla to step back, arms and legs tingling or numb.

"This is interesting," Yadder said, back on their feet in a flash. Tilting their head to the side, they didn't even look winded. "No one warned me about this. Truly, of all the things that could be said about your family, boring would not be one of them."

Aubri stepped up next to Sibylla, breathing heavily but with steady hands, both of which held long knives.

"Well," Yadder said, adopting a stance Sibylla had never seen before. "Let's not waste any more of my time. I have a portal to open and a plague to unleash."

Sibylla had spent hundreds of hours over the previous months training with Aubri, learning new techniques around taking down monsters that were bigger and stronger than her. They had learned to fight together, as a team. Aubri had saved Sibylla's life; they had hunted together. At that moment, they were at their peak with their teamwork, fighting around each other, supporting each other, launching attacks, and defending each other against Yadder.

It was quickly apparent that it wasn't enough.

Repeatedly, effortlessly, Yadder threw back their attacks, not even bothering to attack them directly. Again and again, Sibylla and Aubri were thrown to the ground, taking longer and longer to get back on their feet. Sparing a glance at her brothers, hoping in vain that maybe they were faring better, she saw that they were barely standing anymore, launching sloppy attacks and swaying on their feet. Whatever anger Savage had been experiencing earlier, it seemed to have evaporated in the face of their feeble assaults.

Finally, Sibylla hit the ground hard and lay there, limbs heavy and numb, chest heaving as she fought for breath. Aubri, noticing her plight, stood between Sibylla and Yadder. Sibylla could tell that Aubri wasn't doing much better than she was. Her knives were gone, pulled from her hands early on in the fight. She was covered in bruises and cuts, her limbs visibly quivering from the effort.

If they had landed any strikes on Yadder at all, Sibylla couldn't see them. The three mantles alone would have taken care of that, even without whatever faun-ish healing abilities Yadder may have had. To her frustration, they looked bored with the fight.

"It's obvious that neither of you have ever fought a faun, much less one that has lived for over two millennia," they said. "Even with all of your little surprises, you have failed to more than slow my plans by a few minutes. You two are no match for me, even if your brothers weren't being battered by the oldest Pure that lives on this miserable rock."

Body aching, Sibylla craned her head painfully to see that both of her brothers were on the ground, Savage standing over them, almost completely Changed back into his human form. They weren't enough of a threat for him to stay Changed.

They're far enough away, she thought.

Gingerly, wincing from the pain, she nudged Aubri's foot, eliciting the smallest of nods from her.

"I can't even say you've earned my ire," Yadder continued, "I am too disappointed to be angry. You are all nothing but wasted potential, barely worth attempting to work up a sweat against."

They start walking toward the car, and Sibylla's eyes flick over to Aubri, whose hand was in her pocket, trying to pull something out.

Push the button, Sibylla wants to scream. They wouldn't be getting another chance if they failed.

Horror flashes over Aubri's face, her hand pulling out the shattered remains of the detonator.

It must have been broken in the fight, Sibylla realized in a flash of understanding.

ψ

Yadder was so disappointed that they almost were angry. For the briefest of moments, it looked as though they would get the fight they wanted. They had to hand it to Sibylla, there had been more than one surprise, none of them minor. It never would have occurred to them that the three siblings would be hybrid Pures, nothing like it had been seen before. Maybe they would be able to study the Lavigne children, pull them apart and see if they could come back together.

Reaching the car, they reached down to grab it by the bumper and yank it away. More than anything it was just another way to rub salt in the wound, to show them just how futile every facet of their plan truly was. The Gate could come down with it where it was, the portal would not be hindered by it.

Just when they were about to yank it away, Yadder noticed a strange noise coming from the trunk, some kind of beeping. Overwhelmed by curiosity, they tore away the trunk and saw a pile of bricks wrapped in yellow paper, C4 printed on them, all wired together. In the middle of the stack, knocked askew by the impact, was a timer. Counting down in bright red numbers, it read *3:45*.

It took a moment for the meaning of the object to sink in.

3:44.

Were they so foolish to think that human explosives could undo the deep magic that flowed through the Earth, connecting it to Laternum?

3:43.

Sighing deeply, disappointment growing, Yadder reached down to rip the timer out.

3:42.

In an instant, the world changed. The force of the blast knocked Aubri to the ground, tumbling back several feet. Heavy smoke and ash filled the air, filling her lungs as Aubri tried desperately to take a breath. Chunks of dirt and debris rained down like deadly hail all around her.

Drawing herself to her hands and knees, Aubri blinked against the smoke, tears rolling down her cheeks from the irritation. The smoke was clearing gradually, but it was immediately obvious that the Gate was no longer in quite the same condition that it had been in the moment before.

The tower had collapsed completely and the doors were gone, disintegrated by the blast. The stone arch the doors had once inhabited was still, remarkably, in one piece, leaning back at a dangerous angle, chunks of rock and mortar crumbling away. A crater was all that was left of the car. Nate and Hunter had promised that there would be enough of the explosives to do the job, but Aubri never could have imagined that this was what they meant by that.

Staggering to her feet she immediately collapsed to her knees. The fight with Yadder had been a humbling experience, and even her advanced healing was struggling to keep up with the damage they had caused. Coughing, blood dripping from her lips and splattering bright red against the dust and dirt, she looked up to see if she could find Sibylla. It didn't take long. She was still lying prone where she had fallen after the fight, unmoving. Attempting to crawl forward, a sharp pain in her arm sent her sprawling to the ground again.

"Damn it," she muttered, urging her healing to catch up already.

An enraged howl pierced the air like a fog horn. Searching for the source, Aubri's heart dropped when she saw that Yadder was standing at the edge of the crater, screaming like a wild animal at the night sky. Seeing them standing there, Aubri's body seemed to lose all hope, refusing to respond to her commands.

One of their hands was gone up to the elbow, slashes and lacerations and burns covering the entirety of their body. The side of their face that Aubri could see was missing the ear and the eye socket was empty, the shattered bone visible. Their appearance of calm serenity and radiant beauty had been shattered completely.

How were they supposed to beat someone like that? Anything that could survive that kind of utter devastation couldn't possibly be mortal.

Even with the damage, Aubri could also see that it was already beginning to repair itself, debris and shrapnel being forced from Yadder's muscles and bones.

"You wanted my attention?" Yadder snarled, stalking forward on unsteady legs toward the still unconscious Sibylla. "You have it!"

Aubri forced herself to her feet, realizing that Sibylla was in very real danger. She collapsed to the ground again, her legs screaming in protest.

Just move! She willed herself.

If she couldn't walk then she would crawl, the sharp pain duller, less noticeable as she tried to scramble forward.

Not fast enough, she realized, Yadder healing significantly faster, moving much easier, their longer stride carrying them further with each step.

"No!" Aubri screamed, scrabbling at the Earth for something to throw.

A flash of light pulsed from the Gate and Yadder screamed in agony, collapsing to the ground in a writhing mound. The Gate was failing, Aubri realized, and it was the source of the mantles that were keeping Yadder alive outside of it. There wasn't anything she could do to speed up its destruction, so she tried to capitalize on the reprieve it gave her.

Again she tried to get to her feet, again she collapsed to the ground.

"Come on!" she screamed at her own body, looking down at her useless legs.

There was a piece of metal protruding from her shin she realized, and her body wasn't as capable of pushing it out as Yadder's was.

Frenzied, she reached and ripped it out without thinking, the sudden wave of pain and nausea was nearly enough to knock her unconscious. Fighting against it she threw the piece of metal away. Looking up she saw that Yadder was already back on her feet and worse, they were standing over the still unconscious Sibylla.

"Wake up!" she screamed. She grabbed a rock and threw it as hard as she could.

The piece of stone ricocheted off of Yadder's head, barely leaving a scratch on the almost perfect skin. Their body was almost healed, except for the missing hand. Aubri was still yards away, the short distance feeling like miles.

"Is this yours?" Yadder asked, sneering as they gestured at Sibylla.

Aubri didn't bother to answer, still trying to scramble forward, legs still not working well enough for her to get on her feet. She couldn't let Yadder do anything to hurt Sibylla, she wouldn't let them.

Scoffing in disgust, Yadder reached down with their good hand and grabbed a fistful of Sibylla's fur. Without another look, they started dragging Sibylla toward the Gate. Horrified realization hit Aubri then. Yadder was going to do something worse than killing Sibylla, they were going to take her to Laternum.

"No!" she screamed again, forcing her legs under her.

The pain was sharp and horrible, but she pushed it away. Scooping up another rock she staggered forward until she was close enough to leap onto Yadder's back.

"You... can't... take... her!" Aubri screamed, punctuating each word with a heavy strike to Yadder's head and neck.

Yadder shrugged her off easily, but Aubri wasn't ready to give up. Side arming the rock toward Yadder's face, Aubri grabbed another and launched her attack again. Dodging both easily, Yadder dropped Sibylla to lash out, her vice-like grip wrapping around Aubri's throat, holding her a foot off the ground.

Growling and snarling like a feral animal, Aubri struck out with her hands and feet. She wasn't trying to break Yadder's grip. Every fiber of her being was intent on destroying them, gouging out their remaining eye and ripping off their fingers, of ending their existence for even thinking that they could take Sibylla away from her. In response, Yadder swung Aubri high in the air and slammed her into the ground. Aubri gasped, the air driven from her body.

"Pathetic," Yadder hissed.

With that Yadder picked her up and drove her back down, again and again until Aubri could scarcely breathe. Releasing her, Yadder reached back and grabbed Sibylla by the scruff of her neck, dragging her unconscious body over Aubri toward the Gate. Feebly, fingers numb and useless, Aubri tried to grip Sibylla's red fur.

Yadder dropped Sibylla unceremoniously, snatching Aubri's hand and yanking her into the air. Whimpering, Aubri batted at Yadder's wrist feebly.

"Fool," Yadder sneered, "There is not a world that exists, this side of the Gate or the other, where you could keep me from taking her. You are not enough, and never will be."

The words and the truth behind them cut through Aubri like a knife. They were right. She wasn't even a full-blooded member of the Sacred Legion. What chance could she have against something as powerful as Yadder? A flash of light broke through the stones of the Gate and Yadder cried out, dropping Aubri to the ground in a heap.

"Wake up," Aubri gasped at Sibylla, barely audible.

She tried to roll over, to get to her feet, to get to the only person she had truly bonded with to save them. The healing was going too slow, her body's natural ability to heal itself overloaded.

You are not enough and never will be.

Too many things were broken.

You are not enough and never will be.

With one hand she pulled herself forward, her eyes fixed helplessly on Sibylla's unconscious form. If only she could reach a gun, or a knife, or anything at all that could slow Yadder down, then she could try to stop them again. All she needed was another chance.

Just one more, she thought, gritting her teeth against the pain. Please.

Then she saw it. Sticking up out of the dirt and rubble, only a few feet away, was a small twisted horn, white as paper. It had to be Yadder's skull, the only thing tying her to existence. If Aubri could destroy that, then Yadder would be gone forever. Willing her broken body to move, Aubri dragged herself forward, the few feet feeling like miles. Her thoughts were a jumbled mess of pain and terror, screaming at her to stop and give up, there was nothing more that she could do to help Sibylla. Gritting her teeth against the agony of her shattered body dragging itself over the broken rocks, she gave one final heave. Her hand closed around the horn and she pulled with everything left.

The skull came free of the dirt more easily than she expected, something she was eternally grateful for.

"Yadder!" she roared, holding the oversized skull in the air in triumph.

Yadder turned, their eyes growing comically wide at the sight of the only thing in existence that tied them to the mortal plane. Aubri could see the calculations going on behind their eyes as they considered their chances of crossing the distance between them. Not trusting herself to stay conscious long enough for her to do what needed to be done, Aubri struggled to her knees, keeping the skull high in the air.

"Wha-" Yadder began, seeming to think that they could bargain with Aubri.

But Aubri was done with them. They were without honor, untrustworthy. They had pulled the strings on other people's lives long enough. So without warning she slammed the skull down on a jagged chunk of stone in front of her. As light as it was, it was surprisingly sturdy, only cracking with the first strike.

"Stop!" Yadder screeched, cracks and fissures opening across their body as though their skin, so tough and ungiving before, was now made of glass.

Aubri brought it up again and slammed it against the stone, begging her body for more strength. The cracks on the skull widened and spread across its smooth, perfect surface. Yadder roared with pain and collapsed to their knees.

One more, Aubri told herself. Just one more.

Locking her glare on Yadder's broken face, she raised the skull again. It was her moment of triumph, her final test. Yadder was the great evil her instructors and family always warned her about. The great evil that she had been trained to fight and destroy. Better still, she was going to save Sibylla, the girl she had bonded so strongly with and who had become essential for Aubri's life.

As she brought the skull down, Yadder did something that Aubri didn't expect. Snarling, face covered in lacerations and cracks, they grabbed Sibylla with their remaining arm. Time slowed as Aubri watched with greater understanding and horror. She couldn't stop her momentum if she'd wanted to, the skull was on an unstoppable trajectory to destruction. Helplessly she watched Yadder lift Sibylla off the ground and heave her unconscious body through the Gate.

When the skull connected with the ground it shattered into a thousand pieces, doing its best to replicate what was happening inside Aubri. Before her eyes Yadder imploded into a cloud of shrieking smoke and flashes of light, their mortal form destroyed and their spirit released from the Gate.

The Gate crumbled, releasing a crackle of magic that danced across the ground, crumbling stone and extinguishing fires. It skittered across her skin, feeling like the paws of mice as it passed over her. A flash of blinding light and a searing heat washed over her, taking her breath away and forcing her flat against the ground.

Then it was gone.

Aubri could feel the emptiness it left behind like a heavy cloud. The portal was closed, and the Gate was destroyed, just like they wanted. Of course, they would never have thought that they would be separated.

"You killed them," a rough growl said, breaking through the fog.

Savage was on his knees, back in his human form. Covered in dirt and grime and sweat and blood, his arms pinioned behind him by the still Changed Nate and Hunter. All three of them had the same shocked expression of disbelief that Aubri had. Swaying heavily, legs feeling like jelly, Aubri staggered to her feet. Taking a few drunken steps forward she collapsed again, but never took her eyes off Savage. A flash of silver drew her attention to the ground in front of her, where one of her silver knives had been discarded.

Grabbing it with a heavy hand she got to her feet again, pleased that, finally, her body was healing some of the worst damage.

"Are there other Gates?" she demanded, brandishing the knife as she stumbled closer.

There had to be. The Gate in her city couldn't be the only connection to earth.

"I waited centuries," Savage said, disbelief thick in his voice. "Centuries of killing, murdering, bleeding, hiding, scheming, and you just… killed them?"

Grip tightening on the knife, Aubri wasn't in the mood to wait for him to process his feelings. "Are there other Gates?" she asked again.

"You killed them!" Savage said, angry.

Aubri pulled back and slapped him across his face as hard as she could. His head whipped back, nearly knocking him to the ground. Nate and Hunter barely kept their balance, caught off guard by the reaction. From what she could see, they were still in shock.

"Where are the other Gates?" she demanded.

"Fuck you and your Gates," Savage snarled, eyes darkening. "This was my last chance to go home and be with the one to whom I was mated. I would sooner crush the bones of my brothers than do anything that could help you."

You are not enough and never will be. Aubri shook her head.

"This is your last chance, Pure," Aubri snarled back. "How can I get over to Laternum?"

In reply he let out a furious roar, wrestling easily out of Nate and Hunter's grasp. Before he had a chance to even grow a whisker Aubri lashed out, the silver blade slashing easily through his throat. A gush of warm blood, hissing from contact with the silver, poured out, turning the snow at his knees a dark red. The Change halted by the wound, he reached out with surprising speed and violence, fingers closing on empty space.

Aubri had taken a single step back, allowing the swing to hit the empty air and pull him off balance. He landed hard in the puddle of his blood, and there he lay, twitching and gurgling at the feet of an indifferent Aubri until he finally succumbed to the injuries. Aubri didn't look away until he breathed his last. Only then did she drop the knife.

"Come on," she said to Nate and Hunter. "We have work to do."

Chapter 36

Standing at the large window, Aubri watched the dozens of trucks and smaller cars zipping around the tarmac. She was alone, a stranger in a strange land, surrounded by strange people. Back in Laternum, she had lived in what she had considered a fairly large settlement, home to a few thousand people. Over the past week since the Gate's collapse, she had come to realize just small her home was.

It had been a temporary distraction, seeing what Nate and Hunter had called 'skyscrapers,' weaving in and out of heavy traffic, surrounded by what seemed like a limitless supply of cars. As intoxicating as it was, she could never pull her attention away from their situation.

Events had proven to be more serious than they could have imagined. When they had made it back to Sibylla's home Kane and Kayla hadn't been there. There wasn't any evidence at all that they had even made it back to the house at all. After some careful searching over several days, when they hadn't found their wrecked cars or mangled bodies, it had become apparent that Sibylla's friends were more than they had appeared to be.

"Those bastards," Nate had said when they had finished searching Kane's house. All they had found were the corpses of his parents, long dead and decaying in the shed behind the house. "Kane killed his parents."

It hadn't taken long for them to find that Kayla had done the same to her family.

"It's the Severing," Aubri had explained. "For true initiates, those who willingly take on the Infection, it's their proof to the Pure of their commitment. They cut all ties."

It wasn't overly common, since most Infected, no matter the Pure, find it impossible to kill their own families. Which made sense, in its own way, considering that being a werewolf required intense loyalty to a pack. For most, cutting ties with family was enough. Others, like Kane and Kayla, who wanted to be important in the pack or wanted to ingratiate themselves with the Pure, would go the extra mile and do away with their families completely.

Aubri shuddered to think how many other homes around Red Falls had the remains of families who had been sacrificed in the name of loyalty to the Pure.

Regardless, it quickly became obvious that Kane and Kayla had taken over the Pack and had left Red Falls. That was why Aubri was at the airport alone. Nate and Hunter had decided that they would search for the Pack on their own, to make sure it wasn't wreaking havoc somewhere else. That left Aubri to investigate their new lead.

In the chaotic aftermath of the Gate's explosion, after they had confirmed that Kane and Kayla were gone, Sibylla's brothers had been scouring the book to see if there was any hint as to where another Gate could be. After cross referencing notes and research they had found in Mr. Darrow's and their parent's safehouse, they had finally found a clue. The Gate was called Porta Sanguinis, located, hopefully, at Aubri's final destination.

"Flight AF313 to Romania, now boarding," a voice said over the intercom.

With a final glance out the window, Aubri shouldered her bag, making sure she hadn't accidentally dropped the passport that Mr. Darrow had made for her. Part of a larger identity package that also included a driver's license and a decent amount of cash, it had successfully gotten her through several layovers around the world.

You are not enough and never will be.

Aubri gritted her teeth at the words, wishing that she could ignore the truth that rang in them.

"I'm coming Red," she whispered, taking her place in line. "I promise I'll find you."

ψ

Sibylla groaned as she rolled over, feeling like she had been hit by a semi truck. Her whole body ached terribly like it had been pulled apart and put back together without a manual.

What happened? She thought. For the life of her, she couldn't remember a single thing.

Rising unsteadily, it was quickly apparent that she was in a hospital room of some kind, the pure white walls hurting her eyes and making her head throb. Squeezing her eyes closed, she rubbed her temples, trying to remember what had happened. The last thing that she could remember was kissing Aubri, which, while certainly not the worst thing to remember, didn't explain what she was doing in a hospital room. She considered standing, but the thought of moving sent an excruciating wave of pain across her body.

"Look who's finally awake," a pleasant voice said.

Sibylla opened her eyes to see a nurse sitting in a chair that she hadn't noticed. Though 'nurse' may not have been entirely accurate. It was a faun, shorter than Yadder and far less beautiful. Dressed in a pale green tunic, their goatish eyes were fixed on Sibylla, their smile revealing sharp white teeth.

"Who are you?" Sibylla asked uneasily. Were all fauns like Yadder? Broken and exhausted was not the condition she wanted to be in to find out.

"I am Yikkish," the faun replied with a small nod in greeting. "Your caretaker."

"Where am I?" Sibylla asked.

"You, dear child," a voice said from the doorway, "are in Laternum, the City of Light."

Sibylla's head snapped up, recognizing the voice immediately. The action almost sent her tumbling from her bed, but strong hands gripped her arms and held her steady. Sibylla stared up into the steady blue eyes of the last person she ever thought she would see again.

"Mom?"

www.ingramcontent.com/pod-product-compliance
Lightning Source LLC
Chambersburg PA
CBHW020150310726

48970CB00006B/2077